Praise for

Firebrandt's Legacy

"Commodore John Grimes move over. Captain Ellison Firebrandt is coming at ftl to take away your claim to best space opera. *Firebrandt's Legacy* by David Lee Summers combines explosive space battles with political intrigue, conniving alien races and the human need to love and belong and serve. The Firebrandt universe is complex and wrapped up in astronomy with careful thought about human expansion and out of this world cosmic science. Join the privateer and his crew on their journey of adventure." Robert E. Vardeman, author of *The Klingon Gambit* and *Darklight Pirates*.

"'A privateer can be a force for good if he's not too tempted to be a pirate.' Meet Captain Ellison Firebrandt a privateer who walks that fine line – targeting enemy ships, rescuing damsels and protecting priceless relics. Swashbuckling adventures await all who come aboard *Legacy*." Carol Hightshoe, author of The Chaos Reigns Saga.

Other Books by David Lee Summers

The Solar Sea
The Astronomer's Crypt

The Space Pirates' Legacy Series
Firebrandt's Legacy
The Pirates of Sufiro
Children of the Old Stars
Heirs of the New Earth

The Clockwork Legion Series
Owl Dance
Lightning Wolves
The Brazen Shark
Owl Riders

The Scarlet Order Vampires Series
Dragon's Fall: Rise of the Scarlet Order
Vampires of the Scarlet Order

Firebrandt's Legacy

David Lee Summers

Hadrosaur Productions, Mesilla Park, NM

Firebrandt's Legacy
Hadrosaur Productions
First Edition, first printing, continuous printing on demand

First date of publication: February 2019
Copyright © 2019 David Lee Summers
Cover Art Copyright © 2019 Laura Givens

ISBN-10: 1-885093-85-3
ISBN-13: 978-1-885093-85-1

This is a work of fiction. Names, characters, places, and incidents are
either the product of the author's imagination or are used fictitiously,
and any resemblance to any person or persons, living or dead, events
or locales is entirely coincidental.

Acknowledgments

Firebrandt's Legacy is a book over ten years in the making. It got its start when David Boop asked me if I'd be interested in editing an anthology of space pirate stories for Flying Pen Press. He suggested that I contribute a story to the collection as well. I thought about it and decided to revisit characters from my novel *The Pirates of Sufiro*, which tells the story of a pirate captain, his lover, and his first mate who are stranded on an alien world. I thought it would be fun to explore the pirate captain's career before he was marooned. In a nutshell, that's the genesis of the first story in this collection, "For a Job Well Done." First and foremost, I owe a debt of gratitude to David Boop and Flying Pen's publisher, David Rozansky, for sending me down this path, and casting editorial eyes on that very first story.

That first anthology, *Space Pirates*, turned into a series of six anthologies known collectively as Full-Throttle Space Tales. Stories featuring my space pirates appeared in four of those volumes and were selected and developed with the help of such talented editors as Carol Hightshoe, Bryan Thomas Schmidt, and Jennifer Brozek. I also owe a debt of gratitude to editors J Alan Erwine, Steve B. Howell, and Dayton Ward, who either selected stories for other anthologies or gave me additional feedback on these stories.

This book was also created with the generous support of my Patreon supporters. Among them are Robert E. Vardeman, John D. Payne, and the Creative Play and Podcast Network. A special shout out goes to Anthony D. Cardno who served as a beta reader on the finished collection.

Finally, this book would not have happened without the support of my family who read and commented on the book over the years as it was compiled and written. Many thanks to my wife, Kumie Wise, and my daughters, Autumn and Verity Summers.

To Robert E. Vardeman
Swashbuckler Extraordinaire.
One of the first to sign aboard my space pirates anthology.
One of the first patrons for this project.
Comrade in penmanship.

Firebrandt's Legacy

Chapter One
For a Job Well Done

On the whole, our galaxy revolves like a disk and the stars move little relative to one another. A closer look reveals a more complex story. Each star orbits the galactic center in a different plane and at a slightly different speed than its neighbors. The scales involved are so vast that maps depicting the relative positions of more than two stars change little in a human lifetime, but the motion affects gravity and energy density in the interstellar medium almost constantly. This means the points star vessels use to jump from system to system at super-light velocity are always on the move.

The star system G.S.C. 575303 was of little significance except that it contained two such jump points. One led to the powerful, human-inhabited world of Alpha Coma Berenices 3 and the other led to the resource-rich world known as Prospero, putting it on the trade routes for many freighters traveling between the worlds. Although it took several days for ships to move from one jump point to the other, it required less fuel than making multiple jumps. The only problem was the risk of pirates.

The privateer *Legacy* hid in a cloud of ionized dust, watching for cargo-laden ships to make the crossing between the two jump points. *Legacy's* captain, Ellison Firebrandt, had a letter of marque—a privateer's license—from Earth and was under orders to raid ships bound for Alpha Coma and bring the earnings home.

On the *Legacy's* command deck, Firebrandt and his first lieutenant, Carter Roberts, stood before the holographic tank at the bow and watched a ship emerge from Prospero's jump point. Tall and wiry, Firebrandt wore a mane of red hair and a matching beard. He smiled as he considered the potential prey. Stocky and bald, Roberts scowled as he typed a command into his handcomp. A course projection appeared in the holo tank. "They're taking a parabolic course to the jump point for Alpha

Coma, well away from our position. Do you think they suspect we're here?"

Firebrandt shook his head as he retrieved a pipe from his trousers' pocket and slowly packed it with tobacco. "We haven't been operating in the area long enough." He raised the pipe to his mouth and lit it. "More likely, they suspect law enforcement of some kind." He turned and looked at a pale, almost emaciated man sitting at a nearby console. "Computer, scan that ship."

The man known as Computer activated the ship's sensors via chips implanted in his brain. He stood and glided toward the hologram like a wraith. The view shifted to a close-up of the ship from Prospero. "It appears to be a freighter with a cargo capacity of 100 metric tons. However, it carries no markings and its locator beacon is only transmitting the minimum required information—no name, no corporate or government registry, just the destination: Alpha Coma Berenices."

"That's quite interesting," mused Firebrandt around the pipe stem. "I wonder if they're hauling something they don't want certain authorities to know about."

"If that's true," said Roberts, "and we fenced the cargo in the right market, it could prove a valuable haul for Earth … and us."

Firebrandt nodded. "Is that virus you've been working on ready to try?"

Roberts grinned, resembling the skull from a Jolly Roger flag. "It is. I'll piggyback the file onto their uploads from the galactic mapping net. It should confuse their computer systems, effectively clouding their sensors and keeping them from firing any weapons they might have."

"Very good. Let's give it a try." The captain turned and faced Kheir el-Din, the tall, muscular navigator at the wheel console with beads woven into his beard. "Plot an intercept course for that freighter."

The navigator gave a curt nod and set to work.

☠

As hoped, Roberts' computer virus locked up the freighter's systems and the *Legacy* made the two-day crossing from the ion cloud to the other ship unchallenged. *Legacy* matched velocity and docked. In many cases, Firebrandt would order knockout gas pumped into a freighter once they locked on. This ship's cargo still proved a mystery and he didn't want to risk damage by exposing it to the gas. Instead, he decided to lead a frontal assault with hepler pistols and swords.

The *Legacy's* outer door opened, revealing the freighter's airlock. Roberts stood to the side, typing on his handcomp. When ready, he nodded to the captain. Firebrandt held his own sword high, then lowered it. At the signal, Roberts entered a command and the airlock opened. Several men knelt inside the freighter and fired hepler pistols into the *Legacy*. Firebrandt and his men deflected the high-energy beams with their swords and rushed in, firing their own hepler pistols.

The captain struck out at one of the defenders. A gush of blood followed as his sword connected with the man's neck. Splattered with blood, the ship's defenders fell back. Firebrandt and his crew followed—killing where necessary, but simply disabling where they could. If captured and tried, it went easier on pirate and privateer crews who didn't kill at every opportunity.

It soon became apparent the freighter wasn't heavily manned and most of the defenders fled to the relative safety of their cabins. Firebrandt and Roberts strode forward to the ship's command deck. There, Firebrandt pointed his hepler pistol at the captain and mate, who both raised their hands. Three of Firebrandt's crew rushed in behind and took up strategic positions around the bridge.

"Well well well," said Firebrandt as he approached the ship's computer console. "It would appear that some kind of virus has disabled this vessel. I think we can help with that." He winked at Roberts, who placed a data chip into the appropriate slot. The anti-virus program executed and they examined the ship's manifest. It said they were hauling toilet paper.

Just then, Firebrandt's communicator beeped. He tapped the device on his belt. "Go ahead."

"This is Lowry down in the hold," came the disembodied voice of the *Legacy's* boatswain. "I think you should get down here."

"I take it you found more than toilet paper." The captain had already turned to leave the command deck trusting his crew to guard the freighter's officers. Roberts followed close behind.

"There are indeed several palettes of toilet paper," reported Nicole Lowry. "It's what's tucked in the middle of the tubes that I think you'll find interesting. Pollens, seeds and other plant materials along with a whole pharmacy worth of chemicals."

"Ah, the poppies of Prospero are galaxy-famous." Firebrandt shut off the communicator and looked at Roberts. "I think we've found ourselves quite a haul."

"Sounds like we should load up our holds with toilet paper and go visit our friend, Chris, on Epsilon Indi 2," said Roberts.

"Yes, I've heard they have a shortage of toilet paper in the Epsilon Indi system," quipped the captain.

"Bad thing to be without," said Roberts as they entered the hold.

Firebrandt nodded to Lowry and then approached a palette containing several rolls of toilet paper. He grabbed a roll and drew out a brown leaf. "I do believe this is tobacco." Firebrandt's smile widened. "It would seem they're growing a good deal more than poppies on Prospero these days." The captain glanced around at the cargo hold, then turned to Roberts and Lowry. "Okay, I want a systematic scan of the cargo. Then organize a crew to take the most valuable items to *Legacy*. I think we'll be able to leave the captain of this ship with just enough to make a profit. It might be sufficient to keep any of his friends from hunting us down."

"Very good, Captain," said Roberts as Firebrandt grabbed a roll of toilet paper loaded with tobacco and returned to the *Legacy*.

☠

One of the first planets colonized by humans, Epsilon Indi 2 had been inhabited for several hundred years. There were farms and ranches in remote parts of the planet, but most inhabitants lived in the large cities and worked in factories owned by Earth-based corporations. Those factories paid low wages and many city residents lived in discarded cargo pods on the city's outskirts. In spite of that, Epsilon Indi was only one jump away from Earth and proved a popular weekend destination. People could visit Epsilon Indi's largest city, Palomar, and buy cheap trinkets, alcohol and other entertainments not readily available on Earth. This led to a flourishing drug trade in Palomar and all around Epsilon Indi.

Before he became *Legacy's* captain, Ellison Firebrandt had been introduced to Chris Bowman—a simple trader according to the record books, yet one of the richest men in Palomar. As the *Legacy* approached Epsilon Indi, Firebrandt contacted Bowman and explained he had a cargo that might be of interest. Bowman told the captain he would have a hover car waiting at the spaceport when they arrived.

The next day, Firebrandt took a launch from the *Legacy* to the planet. Two young men, dressed in soft, black leather decorated with chains, met the captain. One drove him through Palomar's bustling streets while the other sat in silence beside him. They passed the plaza, where people in rags begged for cash next to ragtag booths where people who were slightly better off sold trinkets. The hover car continued into a tourist district with tidy shops and inviting restaurants. From there, the driver turned into a neighborhood of veritable mansions. They pulled up to a gate in a wall surrounding a beautiful garden with a large house in the center. The hover car's driver waved to the man in the guard tower next to the gate. The gate opened and Firebrandt noticed that the car waited until the dashboard computer indicated a force field had also been lowered.

The hover car continued up the driveway and the driver stopped at the bottom of the steps leading up to the house. Firebrandt stepped from the car and climbed up to the front door where Chris Bowman met him. The captain caught the sound of music and voices from within the house. "How nice of you to come," said Bowman. "You have something for me?"

Firebrandt passed a handcomp to Bowman and then looked around, noting several cars parked on the grounds near the one that delivered him. Bowman whistled as he scanned the information on the handcomp. "That's quite a load of ... toilet paper," he said with a smile.

"I thought it would be safer here than at Alpha Coma." The captain nodded toward the house. "Did I interrupt a party?"

"Just a small gathering of friends." Bowman clenched the handcomp and beamed at the captain. "I am very impressed. I think there's someone here you should meet." With that,

Bowman escorted Firebrandt into the house.

The loud music inside wasn't piped in from speakers, but rather came from a live band playing on a stage. People in colorful and expensive clothes stood around, sipping cocktails from fine crystal glasses. Firebrandt realized that any one of those glasses was likely worth a week's income to the vendors he had seen on the plaza. He grew conscious of people staring at him in his black trousers and long, black coat, which seemed out of place at the gathering.

Bowman grasped the elbow of a tall, but slightly plump, man with silvery hair and an elegant, silvery suit to match. "Ellison Firebrandt, I'd like you to meet Friedrich Baum. Mr. Baum is the senator for Epsilon Indi."

The captain bowed slightly, then held out his hand. "It's a pleasure to meet you, Senator Baum."

The senator briefly touched the captain's hand, while evaluating the man who stood in front of him. Bowman handed the senator the handcomp. "This is what the captain has brought us."

The senator scanned the list and then scowled at the captain. "What is your asking price?"

Firebrandt stepped around and typed a number into the handcomp.

Baum nodded approval. "That seems quite reasonable."

"Quite reasonable, indeed," echoed Bowman. "In fact, I think the captain deserves a bit of a bonus and I think he may just enjoy helping with the matter we were discussing before he arrived."

Firebrandt's eyebrows came together. "What matter is that? What kind of bonus?"

Baum's eyes traveled over Firebrandt again and fell to the captain's scabbard. He ignored the captain's questions and asked one of his own. "Why do you carry a sword, Captain Firebrandt?"

Firebrandt licked his lips and looked around at the people in the room. "It seemed it would help me blend in better at a social event of this caliber."

Baum's lips turned upward ever so slightly. "I've heard that certain space farers use swords when dealing with merchant ships." The senator's eyes narrowed. "The sight of a little blood can go a long way to making a merchant crew more amenable to ... bargaining."

"I've heard that, too," said the captain.

Baum looked to Bowman. "I think you're right; the captain might be interested in helping us out. If the bonus is to his taste, perhaps there would be other work for him and his crew."

"To my taste?" asked the captain.

"You'll understand tomorrow," said Bowman. "I'll have my boys meet you at the spaceport, if you would be so kind as to return around noon. In the meantime, I'll give you the coordinates where you can deliver the cargo and receive payment."

"So, what exactly is this 'bonus' and why do I have to pick it up personally?" Firebrandt narrowed his gaze. "Is it a cash payment? That would certainly be to my taste."

Bowman led the captain to a table and handed him a glass. "It's more of an ... entertainment ... for a job well done."

Firebrandt scanned the room and noted the hospitality Bowman showed his guests. He nodded and lifted the glass. "Very well," said the captain. "I look forward to it."

Bowman also took a glass and the two drank together.

The next day, Firebrandt returned to the spaceport at the appointed time and the same two men met him. They drove by the plaza as they had before, but this time, instead of continuing into the district with the shops and restaurants, they turned and followed a road that passed several blank-faced factory buildings. They continued past the factories into a district filled with warehouses. At last, they stopped in front of a particularly dilapidated building. The guard who served as escort indicated they'd reached their destination.

The captain's eyebrows came together as he eyed the warehouse. "This doesn't seem like the kind of place I'd expect to be entertained."

The driver and guard looked at each other, confused. "This is quite a privilege," said the guard. "Mr. Bowman only lets his most honored guests spend time with the girls."

"The girls?" asked Firebrandt.

"Yes," said the guard, "real girls."

Not certain he understood, and more concerned about an ambush, Firebrandt allowed them to lead him inside the warehouse. His mind whirled, trying to comprehend what was happening. An ambush made little sense. After all, Bowman had been true to his word and had transferred payment as promised. There were far easier double-crosses than attacking the captain planetside. Besides, the guard had not disarmed Firebrandt.

By the same token, Firebrandt didn't really understand what they meant about real girls. There were plenty of real women and girls in the human colonies—even Epsilon Indi. The captain had seen many at the party the day before.

The guard opened a door and ushered the captain into a dark room, then turned on the lights. The driver remained outside. Sitting naked in a chair, but bound and gagged was a young woman. She shivered, even though the sterile room with bare walls and a stained concrete floor was quite warm. The captain also shivered when he recognized the stains as dried blood.

"What's going on here?" asked Firebrandt.

"She's all yours," said the guard. "You can do with her what you want. She isn't a good girl at all. You can use your sword or your hepler. You can even have—" he caught his breath "—sex with her."

Ellison Firebrandt stood a little straighter. Sexual activity was a very real taboo among human populations throughout the galaxy. Sexually transmitted diseases had evolved in frightening ways over the centuries and the medical establishment had argued that controlled, laboratory breeding was the best way to counter those diseases as well as the propagation of genetic defects. Ultimately, the politics of marriage, sex, and birth had simply become more complicated than people wanted to deal with. Even so, the captain took in the sight of the young woman and long-suppressed instincts came to the surface. He could imagine running his fingers through her long, black hair. He wanted to touch her soft, velvety skin. Firebrandt took a step toward the woman. The young man used the word "sex" but the captain realized that wasn't the word he meant. He meant a far uglier word: rape.

"Yes, please go on," said the guard. "Mr. Bowman wants you to enjoy yourself. If you do, there will be more money and even better jobs for you."

Firebrandt drew his sword. The guard's breath grew fast and heavy in anticipation. With that, the captain whirled around and ran his sword through the guard's belly. As he screamed out, the captain drew his hepler, set to full power. The door opened and the driver's head evaporated the moment the captain's pulsed beam struck it.

The captain turned on his heel and went to the young woman. He knelt down beside her chair. "Your captors are dead. I want to untie you and remove your gag. If you don't scream, I'll do my best to get you to safety. Do you understand?"

The woman nodded and Firebrandt undid her gag first, then undid her blindfold. She looked over at the bodies on the ground and gasped as the captain worked on the ropes binding her wrists. "What's happening? What's going on? Who are you?" came the stream of questions.

Captain Ellison Firebrandt removed his coat, then helped her to her feet. She gratefully donned the coat and buttoned it as he introduced himself.

"Suki Mori," she said to the captain.

He took another look around the room, then cursed under his breath as he noticed a camera he hadn't seen before. "Hurry. We need to get out of here." He pointed to the dead guard, blood pooling around his still-twitching body. "It would appear that he wasn't the only one who liked to watch."

The two stepped over the bodies and made their way through the corridors until they were outside, next to the hover car. "I fear I need something from my coat pocket." He reached toward her and she shrank back, her eyes wide. He frowned. "There's a dataprobe in the left pocket and a ... button about so big."

She reached into the pocket and handed him the probe, then dug for the other thing. "That's a scrambler drive, isn't it?"

He nodded, a little impressed and a little worried that she recognized the device for what it was. Opening the car's door, he climbed under the dashboard and examined it with the probe. Finally, he selected a place and pushed the button-like scrambler drive onto the underside of the dash, then climbed out.

"Let's get going," he said. "Bowman's men will be here before long."

"Thank you for rescuing me," said Suki as she climbed in, on the passenger side. "But I have to ask, what are you doing here?"

"I'm a … businessman … working with Bowman," Firebrandt activated the hover's controls. He smiled when it ascended, satisfied that he had disabled the keycodes and passwords. "He was very pleased with a shipment I brought him. Apparently he thought I'd enjoy the opportunity to … spend time with you."

She examined him, her eyes lingering on the sword at his waist. "Given Bowman's point of view, I can see how he might have made the assumption. I'm glad he was wrong in your case." Suki frowned deeply. "Women are being abducted all around the planet. When they're found, it's in mass graves, either in remote locations or near businesses or homes of people who oppose Mr. Bowman or that joke of a senator, Baum."

Firebrandt took a deep breath and let it out slowly as his fingers played across the hover car's computer console. He called up a map of the city and set a course back to the spaceport. "Why women?"

"Bowman is into power—power in all possible forms. He wants power over Epsilon Indi. He's one of those throwbacks who believes men should have power over women." Suki shuddered and pulled the coat tight around herself. "When the authorities find the women's bodies, they often find evidence that they've been raped, but the genetic material never matches men who live on Epsilon Indi. If the men involved are spacers, that explains why."

"So, why were you abducted?"

"Probably because I belonged to the party that opposed Senator Baum. I've been volunteering for a candidate who could seriously challenge him in the next election." She turned her head and looked out at the plaza. "Where are we going?"

"Back to the spaceport," explained Firebrandt, "so we can

get back to my ship as fast as we can, before Bowman and his men hunt us down."

"I'd like to go home," said Suki.

"I understand." Firebrandt sighed. "However, I think that will cost us time and put both of us in danger ... as well as your family."

"I don't have any family on Epsilon Indi," explained Suki. "My mother and father are mineralogists working in the asteroid belt back in the home system. I came here to teach at one of the computer schools."

"If you stay, I don't think Bowman will want you around. It would be very dangerous."

"Where would I go?" asked Suki. Silence fell between them as they approached the spaceport.

A moment later, Firebrandt's communicator beeped. He tapped the device on his belt. "This is the captain, go ahead."

"This is Roberts, sir. A Gaean Alliance battlecruiser has just jumped into the system and is approaching the planet. Orders?"

The captain cursed under his breath. He worked for the Gaean Alliance, but the battlecruiser's captain wouldn't know that. They could easily delay *Legacy's* departure from the system by demanding a search and then sorting out licenses and permits. "I'm returning to the ship. In the meantime, try to stay out of sight. We'll be out of here as soon as we can." The captain turned off the communicator.

"Stop the car!" called Suki.

The captain stomped his foot on the brake. A hover behind them applied thrusters and shot over their heads, honking its horn.

Suki pointed to a nondescript man standing idly near the port's entrance. "That's one of the men that abducted me."

"Damn!" growled the captain. "Are you certain?"

Suki nodded. "Positive."

Firebrandt gritted his teeth. Whether Suki was correct or not, Bowman probably had men stationed at the space port. That would explain the lack of pursuit. "I'll bet Bowman's men are guarding my launch." Firebrandt grabbed the controls, dropped altitude and turned back the way they'd come.

Suki fought to catch her breath. "Where are we going now?"

Firebrandt typed on the hover's computer keypad again. "We can't get off planet using my launch, so we have to find someone who has a private ship or a yacht we can use—something that's docked at their compound or nearby."

"The only people with that kind of money would be Bowman and Baum," said Suki.

"Exactly."

"But trying to steal Bowman's yacht would be suicide."

"Which is why we're heading for the senator's compound," said Firebrandt.

Suki narrowed her gaze. "Baum's compound is also guarded."

"I imagine so, but, as you said, Baum is Bowman's puppet. He won't have as many guards." Firebrandt considered the sudden appearance of the battlecruiser and smacked the steering wheel. "Bowman must have ordered Baum to call in that Gaean battlecruiser to give my ship trouble." He grinned as another thought occurred to him. "Even if I'm wrong, he has the authority to order it away."

"Why would a Gaean battlecruiser give a cargo ship trouble?" asked Suki.

"Depends on the cargo, my dear." Firebrandt winked. "Thing is, we're on the same side, but battlecruisers don't always stop to ask about our letter of marque before they open fire."

"Ah," said Suki. "You're a privateer."

Firebrandt inclined his head and grinned. "That I am."

Continuing to follow the computer's directions, they soon found themselves in front of a compound, similar to but smaller than Bowman's. A guard approached from the booth next to the gate. Without waiting for him to speak, Firebrandt drew his hepler and shot him in the chest. He slammed back into the wall, then slumped to the ground.

Suki gasped. Ignoring her, Firebrandt leapt from the hover and entered the guard booth. Retrieving his dataprobe, he scanned the controls and soon opened the gate and lowered the force field. Returning to the hover, they sped to the house itself. Two guards ran across the porch, then crouched in front of the double doors and fired at the hover.

"Keep your head down," called the captain as he lowered his own head below the dashboard. He accelerated and sped between the two guards, then ran the hover car right through the mansion's front doors in a tremendous crash. The hover dropped to the marble floor and skidded to a stop in a shower of glass and wood splinters.

Once debris stopped pelting the car, he pushed the door open and rolled to the ground, drawing his own hepler pistol. As the guards ran around the corner, he cut them both down, then rose to his feet. Spinning around, he caught sight of Baum at the top of the stairs.

With a little shriek, the senator turned and started down the hall. Firebrandt jumped over debris and sprinted to the stairway. Once there, he ascended, taking the steps two at a time. At the top of the stairs, he quickly caught up to the senator and pushed his hepler to the man's head. "Did you order the Gaean ship into this system?"

"Only because Bowman ordered me to." The senator trembled.

"I want you to order it away and then direct me to your private yacht."

"If I do, Bowman will kill me," squeaked Baum.

A bit wobbly, Suki appeared at the top of the stairs.

"I'm the one holding the gun to your head," said Firebrandt.

The senator's eyes grew moist. "I'd rather you shoot me dead than face what Bowman will do to me if he finds out I helped you."

"He has a point," said Suki. "I think you'd be doing him a kindness just to kill him."

"If you promise to call off the battlecruiser and help me get off the planet, I'll find a way to keep you alive." Firebrandt lowered the hepler pistol a little.

The senator took a shuddering breath. "It can't look like I helped you willingly. Otherwise Bowman's syndicate will hunt me down."

"I'll do my best and I'll get you safely to Earth," said the captain. "After that, you'll be on your own."

The senator nodded. "This way." He led the captain and Suki down the hall and opened a door. Inside, a pair of technicians stood up from a console. With the hepler pistol, Firebrandt motioned them back into their seats while the senator told them the message he wanted sent to the Gaean battlecruiser.

"Is that wise?" asked one of the technicians. "What will the boss say?"

The senator rose up to his full height. "Who is the boss here?"

Firebrandt nodded approvingly as he aimed his hepler pistol.

The technician swallowed and sent the message, saying that the request for a battlecruiser had been an unfortunate mistake. "We thought we'd seen a pirate ship," explained the tech. "It turns out they were a legitimate trading vessel."

"Earth central isn't going to be happy about this," complained the battlecruiser's comm officer. "You need to be more careful next time."

"We will." The technician turned around and Firebrandt yanked him to his feet and knocked him cold. Suki put her hand to her mouth as the other technician leapt on Firebrandt. The captain grabbed the man's arm and pulled him over his shoulder, where he landed on the floor with a thud.

Firebrandt turned to the senator. "Which way to your yacht?"

The senator gave directions and Firebrandt raised his fists.

"Must you?" asked the senator.

Firebrandt pointed to a camera in the corner of the room. Undoubtedly it was one of the senator's own security cameras, but the captain knew all too well Bowman could retrieve the data. Instead of striking the senator, Firebrandt turned to Suki. "There's a jet injector in the pocket."

She handed it over. Before the senator could say anything, Firebrandt stepped forward and applied it to his arm. A moment later, the senator crumpled to the floor.

The captain looked down at the senator, then up at Suki. "See if you can find an anti-graviton cart or something. I don't relish carrying this guy all the way to the yacht."

"So that's it?" Suki planted her hands on her hips. "We're just going to run away. What about the other women in this city? Bowman's going to be very angry. Who knows what he'll do after this."

Firebrandt blinked a few times. "We're only two people." He started to say more, but the withering look she shot him cut him short. Then he turned and looked at the console and smiled. "There should be a data chip in my coat pocket."

She reached in and held it out. "This?"

The captain nodded and took it from her.

"What are you doing?" asked Suki.

"This chip contains a computer virus. It will take a few minutes to propagate through the planetary network, but I can set it up to disable all their systems. It'll take several days, perhaps weeks for them to get rid of it. In the meantime, Bowman will have his hands full just trying to run things while the power grid and security systems are malfunctioning." He winked at her. "We're only two people. It may not stop Bowman completely, but it will slow him down. The resulting chaos may even give some of the people a fighting chance to do something. Now go, find something that will help carry the senator. He'll do more good back on Earth than here."

Suki gave the captain an appreciative nod and darted from the room. The captain set about his task. A few minutes later, Suki returned with a small hover sled. "Will this do?"

"That'll do nicely." Firebrandt touched a button on the console. A few minutes later, as they lifted the senator onto the sled, all the lights went out. "Right on schedule. You should find a flashlight in the coat pocket." She found it and turned it on while he activated the hover sled. Suki and Firebrandt followed the senator's directions and made their way down a back set of stairs and followed a hallway until they came to a back door. Outside, they found the senator's yacht waiting on a launch pad.

Stepping out into the light, the captain turned to Suki. "You have a choice," he said. "You can come with me or you can stay here and fight against the injustice." She started to say something and he held up his finger. "I'll warn you, Bowman will be very angry. He won't hesitate to kill you if he finds you."

"I know." Suki released the hover sled, letting it float on its own and stepped over to the captain. "But it seems you're pretty good at fighting injustice in your way. A privateer can be a force for good if he's not too tempted to be a pirate."

"Some would say that's a very fine line you're drawing there, lass," said Firebrandt.

"Perhaps," conceded Suki. "But the line is real nonetheless and I think I would like to get to know you better, Captain Ellison Firebrandt." She kissed him lightly on the cheek, then returned to the sled.

Firebrandt smiled and then opened the door to the yacht. They pushed the senator inside and secured him in one of the seats. Firebrandt sat down at the controls with Suki next to him. Once she strapped in, he activated the controls and they lifted off, bound for the *Legacy*.

Chapter Two
Hijacking the *Legacy*

Suki Mori stood before a door not marked on any plan of the privateer vessel *Legacy* she'd found on the computer. At a casual glance, one might think the space was an extra fuel cell or a backup oxygen supply. However, only standard utility power lines and ventilation shafts fed the space—and there was a door.

A little over a month ago, the ship's captain, Ellison Firebrandt, rescued her from the clutches of Chris Bowman, a drug lord on the planet Epsilon Indi 2. From there, they traveled to Earth, dropped off the senator from Epsilon Indi 2 who they persuaded to help, and picked up a load of cargo from one of Firebrandt's contacts. They now traversed the galaxy and there was little to do aboard the ship other than read and study the contents of the ship's computer. While studying the ship's plans, she came across the mysterious room. She also discovered several databases that contained codes and passwords—encrypted, but she was very good with puzzles and was pretty sure she had broken the encryption.

She pulled a paper from her pocket that contained several codes, her first choice circled. Typing it in, she smiled when the door slid aside. "Lights," she said as she cautiously stepped inside. Low-level lights came on and Suki looked around at a room full of shipping containers—not very exciting for a secret room. As she moved farther in, she caught sight of a glow from behind one of the containers. A few more steps and she noticed several transparent stasis boxes, like the ones museums and universities used for transporting fragile items in a controlled atmosphere. Suspended in the boxes were paintings—very good paintings.

Suki's parents were scientists and she had been raised on the asteroid Ceres in the home system. She didn't know much about art, but she had seen holograms of many of Earth's great masterworks. As she looked around, she thought she recognized a painting by Van Gogh and another by Rembrandt. The signatures on the paintings confirmed her suspicions. Continuing along the row of paintings she came across one that caused her to gasp. She put her hand to her chest and felt her heart pound. The serene face and the hint of a smile were unmistakable, even to someone who knew little about art. It was the Mona Lisa.

"Ah, now there's a compelling siren," came a voice from behind her. "What songs she would have sung if she hadn't been frozen in time."

Suki whirled around and nearly fell back into the stasis boxes. She found herself looking into Ellison Firebrandt's gray eyes. His head was cocked to the side and his fists were on his hips. His lopsided smile conveyed a mixture of admiration and annoyance. "I thought Roberts and Computer were the only ones who could decrypt the code for this room," said the captain referring to his first mate and drone-like computer specialist.

"Is that … is that really…?" Suki couldn't quite find the words, but she pointed at the Mona Lisa.

"It is." Firebrandt took her hand and led her from the room. "She, along with many of these other works, were on a transport going to Nouveau Paris on Alpha Coma Berenices." He sighed and shook his head. "They were created on Earth and that's where they belong, not out among the colonies."

"But the Louvre was destroyed almost four centuries ago in the Lunar Uprising." Her brow furrowed. "That meteor they threw at Paris…"

"It destroyed the museum, but most of the artworks had been moved before the meteor hit." He shrugged. "It played better in the press to make people think the works had been destroyed, when in fact they were secreted away. The Earth government 'uncovers' a few from time to time and sells them to museums off world."

Suki chewed her lower lip. It seemed plausible. "But we were just on Earth," she said. "Why didn't you leave the paintings then?"

Firebrandt commanded the lights off, closed the door, and entered a new code. "It's not that simple," explained the captain. "If I gave them back to the original owners, they would just ship them back to the museum they originally sold the paintings to. Most of the other contacts I have are … shall we say a bit unsavory. They would take the paintings, but again, there's no guarantee they would stay on Earth, nor that they would be available for public viewing. I have to give them to the right person."

Suki looked at the door. "Still, it doesn't seem right for them to be shut up in your hold like that. No one but you gets to see them."

"And you see that as a problem?" He smiled and winked. When she didn't return his smile, he looked away. "I know I need to find them a good home, but it needs to be the right home."

She didn't like the answer, but she didn't have a good argument, either. "So, what do we do now?"

"Now?" The captain freed his long red hair from the ponytail he normally kept it in while on duty. "Now, it's time for dinner. I just prepared two lovely roast quail that I acquired with our earnings on Earth and I thought you might like to join me."

"That sounds delightful," said Suki in a forced monotone, even though her stomach growled. As they walked away from the hold, she looked back at the closed door and pondered the paintings on the other side. Turning her attention forward, she followed the captain through the other holds and up a ladder to the deck above.

A few minutes later they reached the captain's cabin. Inside, candles on the table bathed the room in a soft, flickering glow. Ellison Firebrandt had paneled his cabin in wood, an expensive luxury, but it gave the room a home-like feeling—or like it belonged aboard a ship at sea rather than aboard a space vessel. She sat at the table and watched Firebrandt as he scurried about the cabin, removing the quail from his small oven, setting them on plates, and spooning a cherry sauce over them.

Captain Ellison Firebrandt compelled her. He was handsome and, in many ways, very sensitive. She looked up at his letter of marque, hanging in a frame on the wall. He saw himself as a soldier fighting for Earth and yet it was clearly illegal, even by Earth laws, for him to possess the paintings she had found in the hold.

Just as the captain placed a plate in front of her, the intercom chimed. Placing the other plate at his own place, he answered the call. "This is the captain. Go ahead."

"This is Roberts," came the voice of the first officer from the command deck. "We came out of jump and found ourselves right on top of a freighter bound for New Earth. We've jammed their signals. Shall we pursue?"

"Yes," answered Firebrandt. "How long until she's in range?"

"About thirty minutes," said Roberts.

"I'll be up shortly." The captain sat down and indicated Suki should eat. He tore into his own quail like a man famished. About halfway through, he remembered to pour some wine for Suki. He didn't partake, preferring to sip water.

"What happens when we catch the freighter?" Suki asked the question almost certain she knew the answer.

"A lot depends on what they're carrying, but New Earth has not been on the best of terms with the home world lately. We're under orders to take any ships we come across."

"I understand." Suki took small bites, attempting to savor the quail but having a difficult time really appreciating the fine job the captain had done.

After a few minutes, Firebrandt stood and placed his plate in the sanitizer. He turned on the harsh overhead lights, blew out the candles, and looked at Suki. "I'm sorry about the timing," he said. "Stay here. You'll be safest in this cabin." With that, he strode through the door.

Suki sighed and pushed the plate away.

Raised on an asteroid and having lived on a planet for the previous three years, Suki wasn't sure what to expect from a space battle. She cleared away her plate with the half-eaten quail and moved the candles to shelves and secured them. She activated the holographic display at the center of the table and brought up the scene being displayed in the primary holo tank on the command deck.

She could just make out the black, Erdonium hull of the New Earth freighter, illuminated by the gentle blue glow of the Erdon-Quinn engine at the ship's stern. As time passed, Suki could tell they were getting closer to the freighter. About a half-hour after the captain left, high-energy pulses flew from the *Legacy* toward the other ship. They struck the freighter's engine which flared a bright blue for a moment then went black. From numbers displayed in the hologram, Suki could tell the ship continued forward. It still had momentum, but could no longer change its course or speed.

It took another two hours for *Legacy* to catch up with the freighter and lock on after the engines had been disabled. During that time, Suki browsed the captain's library and wondered what he was doing up on the command deck. She imagined he must be plotting strategy and keeping an eye on the ship's functions. Still, it was nothing like the action she had seen in pirate holograms she'd watched as a little girl. There, a pirate ship would catch and dock with another ship in a matter of minutes if not less. She barely felt the gentle bump indicating *Legacy* had docked with its prey.

After another hour, the silence in the cabin grew truly oppressive. In spite of the captain's admonition to remain in the cabin until he returned, Suki decided to see what was happening. She found the door locked. "What? Doesn't he trust me?" she growled.

Suki stormed back to the holographic display and called up databases containing passwords and door codes throughout the ship. After a few minutes, she found the code for the captain's door. Applying the encryption algorithm she'd developed, she stepped to the door and punched in the code. The door slid aside.

Suki peered around the door frame. With no sign of fighting, she crept down the corridor toward the ship's bow. The eerie quiet unsettled her. She could just make out the soft whooshing noises of water pumps and the air circulation system. Three of *Legacy's* crewmembers stepped past, pushing anti-gravity sleds. The last one in line nodded to her and smiled. She continued until she reached the airlock. The door was open and she could look into the other ship. Two people lay on the deck, one in a pool of blood, his head at an odd angle—almost severed from his neck. Next to the man was a woman with a gaping, black hole in her chest. Further along the corridor, more bodies were scattered, some with bloody sword wounds, others with cauterized holes blasted through them. One was completely missing a head; another's intestines lay exposed and glistening. Suki fell to her hands and knees and vomited the lovely quail dinner onto the deck.

Legacy's boatswain, Nicole Lowry, stepped around the corner and helped Suki to her feet. "Easy there," said Lowry. "What are you doing out and about, wandering the decks? This isn't a good place for passengers."

Suki looked at Lowry, her eyes wide, and wondered what part the woman had played in the carnage around them.

Lowry sighed and helped Suki find a place to sit away from the airlock. Then, she activated her wrist comm and contacted the captain. "Sir, I think we have a problem."

Ellison Firebrandt appeared a few minutes later. "Quite a haul," he said as he escorted Suki back toward her cabin. "They were carrying weapons for a ground invasion. It seems Earth was right. New Earth planned to invade some other colonies. It's all the same nonsense that destroyed the Louvre, caused all those paintings to be squirreled away."

Suki heard the words, but didn't completely register what the captain said. In the past four weeks, Suki had been abducted by a drug cartel, rescued by a privateer who carried valuable paintings in his hold, and was now overwhelmed by the sight of the bodies she had seen on the ship from New Earth. It was all too much.

"I'll be back to check on you later," said Firebrandt as he opened the door to her cabin.

Suki nodded, thinking it was time to make a change in the way her life was going.

Firebrandt did return a few hours later, expressing pleasure at the haul but also concern for Suki. "We are a privateer vessel," he said gently. "We fight for Earth like any other soldiers. We do our best to minimize losses on our side ... and theirs."

"I know all that. It's just that the difference between knowing and experiencing is more than I'd imagined." She turned and took his hands in hers. "I'd like to go home. I'd like to go back to my parents and spend a little time rethinking my life—maybe with the credits I earned on Epsilon Indi 2, I could make a new start on Mars or even Earth."

Firebrandt breathed out a long sigh. He looked down and then sniffed. Frustrated? Irritated? Honest regret? She couldn't tell. "You should have said something when we were at Earth. Now, we're a long ways from the home solar system and the asteroid where your parents are," he said. "We have to push on and deliver the cargo we're carrying. We can take you back when we return."

"So, does that make me a prisoner?" Suki narrowed her gaze. "You did lock me in your cabin during the battle."

Firebrandt rubbed the bridge of his nose. "I locked others out. The battle could have gone badly. I knew you could get out any time you wanted." The last sentence sounded like an afterthought to Suki.

"I want to go home now," she said through clenched teeth.

"I'm sorry." The captain's regret sounded genuine. "We can't just yet." He closed his eyes and then opened them again. "Soon." He stepped forward, took her chin gently in his hand, and looked into her eyes. "I'll see you tomorrow. We can talk more then." He bent down and kissed her tenderly on the forehead, then turned and left the cabin.

Suki fell back on the bed, unhappy. If the course were carefully planned, *Legacy* could be back at Earth in just a few jumps. It wouldn't take long and the captain could refuel with the money he earned from the arms he just captured. She didn't understand why he felt he had to press on, unless she was also a spoil of war.

She began thinking about *Legacy's* schematics. The ship had many automated functions, which would allow a single person to fly it, if needed. She lay on the bed for a little while and tried to go to sleep. Still awake an hour later, she sat up, stepped over to the holographic console, and checked the location of the ship's compliment. As she suspected, most were in their cabins after the raid. Only the man known as Computer occupied the command deck as they moved away from the sacked freighter.

She spent an hour poring over charts and found a way back to Earth. It required *Legacy* turn back on its original course and make for a jump point to Prospero. Two more jumps after that and they would arrive in Earth's solar system, near the asteroid belt. *Legacy* would be low on fuel but Ceres should have plenty and Firebrandt would be back on his way in no time.

Continuing her search of the ship's database, Suki found the codes to the chips implanted in Computer's brain. She sat back and took stock of her plan. For a moment, she thought it would be better to forget the whole thing and just go back to bed. Surely Firebrandt and Roberts would stop her before she made it very far. Despite that, she thought Firebrandt's fondness for her might cause him to relent and take her home once he saw her determination. With that thought in mind, she wrote a short program that would command the ship to travel the course she had plotted. Then, she activated the code that locked all crewmembers into their cabins.

"See how you like that, Captain Firebrandt," she said to herself with a sneer.

Finally, Suki sent a short, sharp burst of information through the chips in Computer's brain. With that, she went forward to the command deck. Carefully peering around the door frame, she saw the pale, thin man slumped over his station. She entered and checked Computer's pulse. Satisfied he was just unconscious, she grabbed him under the armpits and yanked him unceremoniously out of his chair. From there, she dragged him to a storage room just outside the command deck.

Returning to the command deck, Suki closed and locked the door behind her and then stepped up to the ship's wheel console and activated the program that would take her home. The holographic tank at the front of the command deck displayed the ship's new course. Thrusters fired and the ship vibrated as it turned back toward the jump point for Prospero. She found a chair and sat down, monitoring the information in the holographic tank and stealing glances back toward the command deck's main door. She hoped the ship would make its first jump before Firebrandt retook the bridge. By then, she hoped they'd be committed to the course and the captain would have no choice but to take her home.

She wasn't that lucky.

About thirty minutes from the jump point, the door to the

command deck flew open. Firebrandt and Roberts strode in with hepler pistols drawn. They scanned the deck and the captain's shoulders sank. A moment later, Suki found herself looking down the barrel of Roberts' pistol.

"Drop your weapon," ordered the captain.

"But, sir," protested Roberts, "she hijacked the ship. That's mutiny."

"I know," said Firebrandt, his voice catching. He looked around at the men and women behind him. "Assume your stations. Find out where we are and get us back on course." He reached out and took Suki's arm. "Now I need to figure out what to do with you."

"Captain," called Lowry from the forward sensor station. "We have a problem."

"This is the Cruiser *New New Jersey*," boomed a voice from the intercom. "You will stand down and prepare to be boarded."

Roberts spat a string of curses and turned around to face Firebrandt and Suki. "It's a New Earth Cruiser responding to the distress signal from the ship we attacked." He put his hand on his hepler pistol and Suki could see the muscle in his jaw tensing and untensing, as though the first mate would like nothing better than to shoot her on the spot. Looking up at Firebrandt's scowl, she could tell he was tempted to allow Roberts to do so.

"Analysis," ordered the captain.

"They outgun us twenty to one," said Roberts. "There's no way we can fight."

"And they're right on top of us," said Lowry. "We have nowhere to run."

Suki looked down at her feet. She had been overwhelmed by the reality that Firebrandt was a privateer, that he killed people in the line of duty. However, the last thing she wanted was for him to be captured. She felt a lump in her throat and knew she was responsible. Looking up at the hologram, she saw the New Earth ship almost on them. Turning to Firebrandt she whispered, "I got us into this. I'll get us out … somehow."

☠

When the boarding party from *New New Jersey* stormed the

Legacy's command deck, they found Firebrandt holding Suki's arm and Roberts' weapon drawn. They had no doubt she was their prisoner. The marines escorted the *Legacy's* crew to *New New Jersey's* brig and took Suki to the bridge. One of the marines escorting her saluted the man sitting in the command seat.

The commander, sporting a blond crewcut and wearing a crisp tan uniform, stood. "I am Captain William R. Stewart." He looked her up and down with a smirk. "You're a prisoner of the pirates?" he asked.

"I just want to go home." She hated the way her weariness leant a mousy quality to her voice, but none of it was affectation.

"And where would home be, little lady?" asked the captain.

"My mother's the chief mineralogist on Ceres," explained Suki. "My dad's a chemist."

"Well, New Earth isn't on the best of terms with the home world," Captain Stewart said as though trying to couch complex politics in terms a child could understand. "We'll take you back to New Earth and from there we can let the diplomats work things out. In the meantime, we'll put you in guest quarters." He nodded to the marines. As they escorted Suki off the bridge, she heard the helmsman report they were approaching the stranded freighter.

The marines led Suki down one deck. She scanned the name plates as she walked and noted the guest cabin was next door to the captain's quarters.

The guest cabin proved small and tidy with a desk, a bunk, and a small private restroom. There was also a door in the wall between her cabin and the captain's. Made some sense, since most "guests" on a military vessel would be VIPs the captain needed to entertain or senior officers he might consult.

She dropped into the chair, tempted to let this ship take her where it would, away from pirates, guns, and paintings that shouldn't be. She sat for a moment, her eyes closed. She couldn't shake the image of Captain Firebrandt and the shock and hurt he'd shown when he found her on the *Legacy's* command deck.

She stood and pushed the button next to the door not

expecting anything to happen. Apparently in the excitement of capturing *Legacy*, no one thought to lock it. She entered Captain William R. Stewart's cabin and looked around.

Unlike Firebrandt, he owned no books, just a few holos about military history. A photo on the captain's desk showed a bleach-blonde with an ample bosom in a bikini. It was signed, "To Billy Bob with Love."

"Give me a break," Suki muttered as she found the controls to the captain's command console. Apparently, Captain "Billy Bob" Stewart wasn't *completely* stupid and didn't leave her access to everything, but she could view sensor telemetry and monitor communications. She followed *New New Jersey's* progress as they approached the freighter and deployed a rescue party.

After watching the start of the rescue operations, Suki returned to her cabin and peeked out into the corridor. Even though she was a "guest," one of the marine escorts stood guard. He gave a curt nod. She smiled, ducked back inside, and returned to the captain's command console where she called up the ship's schematics. *New New Jersey* was about twice the size of *Legacy* and came equipped with shuttles that could carry marines down to a planet for an attack. Better yet, the shuttles had sufficient capacity to return the crew of *Legacy* to their own ship.

Suki started looking through the captain's desk drawers. She found a data pad and grinned as she turned it on. The captain, afraid he would forget his passwords, had saved them. He really should have ordered the door between the cabins locked.

It didn't take long for Suki to find her way into *New New Jersey's* secure files. A search of the crew manifest told her much of the technical crew had gone aboard the freighter, helping repair the damage done by *Legacy*. Captain Stewart and his command crew were on the bridge. One guard was stationed outside of the guest quarters and three more were stationed outside the brig.

Continuing her perusal of the ship's computer, she found the captain's audio logs. A plan began to form and it didn't take long for Suki to construct three audio files that would serve her purpose. Knowing she didn't have much time, she went into action.

First, she enabled the security protocols that locked down the bridge and disabled communications and weapons. She then piped three audio snippets from Captain Stewart through the rest of the ship: "This is the captain." "We have a situation in the airlock." "All security forces report on the double."

With that, she chanced a peek outside the cabin. Her guard retreated down the corridor. Suki grabbed the captain's data pad and ran the other direction, toward the brig. There she noticed the guards had left their posts, trusting shields and automated defenses to keep the prisoners secure until they returned. She entered the brig where she was met by the scowling faces of *Legacy's* crew.

She stepped up to the cell that held Firebrandt and looked him in the eye. "You rescued me from the drug cartel on Epsilon Indi," she said. "Now it's my turn to return the favor." She typed in a code and opened Firebrandt's cell.

"You'll go to prison for helping us," said Firebrandt, stepping out.

"We wouldn't be here if it wasn't for her," growled Roberts from the adjoining cell.

"I know." Suki turned around and entered the code, opening his cell. "It's your choice. Take me with you or leave me here. I'm willing to face my fate whatever you choose."

"Very well," said Firebrandt. "Release the rest of the crew and lead us to the shuttles."

Two days later, *Legacy* had successfully outrun *New New Jersey* and jumped to the next star system on its original course. Suki found herself in the ship's mess facing Firebrandt, Roberts, Lowry, Computer and the rest of the crew.

"Ms. Suki Mori," Firebrandt began, "you stand accused of hijacking *Legacy* and of mutiny against her captain." Suki could hear the strain in Firebrandt's voice. Anger tightened his neck muscles while red-rimmed eyes betrayed sadness. "Because this vessel is a duly appointed privateer, the crew must vote on the charges against you. Do you understand?"

Suki nodded, her shoulders squared.

Firebrandt stood and moved around the desk so he faced

the crew. "Does anyone dispute the facts in this case?"

Heads shook in unison.

"Does anyone wish to speak on behalf of Ms. Mori?"

Suki tried to find words to speak for herself, but couldn't. She saw Nicole Lowry open her mouth and then close it again. Finally, the first mate, Carter Roberts stood. "I'm not happy about being locked in my cabin or in the brig of a New Earth vessel, but Suki Mori showed us what a damn good pirate she was by hijacking this ship out from under us. I think she's learned her lesson and she has skills we can use." He rubbed his hand over his bald head and then turned to face the crew. "What say you all?"

Members of the crew looked from one to the other. Finally, Nicole Lowry raised her thumb. Computer and Roberts followed. Soon, the rest of the crew gave a thumbs-up.

Firebrandt nodded. "Very well," he said, his voice tight. Suki couldn't tell if he was happy because she was to be spared or disappointed because she wouldn't be punished for betraying him. He turned and looked her in the eye. "Suki, you are a siren who has captivated this crew, myself included. I just hope you won't lead us to disaster."

"I'll do everything I can to earn your trust back, Captain Firebrandt," said Suki solemnly. "All I wanted to do was go home. Maybe I can make one here, instead."

Chapter Three
Hot Pursuit

Carter Roberts entered the bar of Space Station Xiūxí qū sān. The dank hole of dark metal held only two tables and smelled of vomit and cheap booze. The bartender wore a stained, white apron and leaned on the dented counter, eyes half closed. A video screen above the bar displayed the names of drinks along with images of people enjoying them on some faraway resort planet.

Roberts stepped up to the counter. "Rum."

The bartender dropped a plastic cup on the counter and filled it half full from an unmarked bottle. The *Legacy's* first mate suspected the same bottle was used no matter what was ordered. The bartender swung a greasy payment pad around and Roberts swiped a card loaded with credits carefully routed from several bank accounts, none of which actually belonged to him.

He grabbed his cup and moved toward the table farthest from the door. Something slimy and unidentifiable covered one of the seats. Roberts opted to sit at the other table. He lifted the plastic cup and the contents smelled like rocket fuel. He ventured a taste anyway. Not only did he suspect the bartender only sold one type of booze, he thought it might be equally good at cleaning out toilets as intoxicating the drinker.

A man in a suspiciously good suit stepped into the bar. He evaluated the counter and the unshaven man behind it, then turned to Roberts without ordering anything. "Are you Mr. Wong?" he asked.

"Depends on who's asking?" Roberts took a sip of the "rum" and tried not to grimace.

The man sat down and retrieved a cigarette from a case. He offered one to Roberts, who declined. He decided the cheap booze would make him ill enough. He didn't need to add the buzz from whatever weed the man was smoking. "I'm Mr. Wright." He turned his head and lit the cigarette. "I'm told Mr.

Wong has an heirloom for me."

"More of a legacy, actually."

Mr. Wright scowled. Roberts knew he wasn't being as co-vert as this guy wanted, but he didn't care. They would be long gone before anyone figured out he'd spoken the name of his ship and that Mr. Wright was arranging transportation.

Roberts sat back and folded his arms. "If you're ready, we could go take a look and see if it's satisfactory."

"I'm sure it will be. We need to retrieve my ... charge on the way. Do you want to finish your drink?"

"I'd rather not." Roberts stood.

The man who called himself Wright dropped the cigarette to the deck and crushed it under his shoe, then led the way out of the bar through a series of pipe-lined tunnels to a bank of storage lockers. He dug through his pockets for a key, opened one of the lockers and retrieved a large duffel bag. Presumably it contained the item he was responsible for—his charge.

With the first mate in the lead, they wound their way back through the maze of corridors. As they turned the corner into the station's reception area, they were greeted by four men and two women in gray uniforms without insignia. A blond haired man stepped forward. "We need to see your passports."

Roberts shook his head. "You don't look like station per-sonnel to me. Your uniforms are much too new." He wondered how strangers to the station could find them so quickly. Per-haps he should have been more careful about his word choice at the bar.

"Can we see some identification?" asked Mr. Wright smoothly.

The uniformed agents drew hepler pistols. "I believe you're carrying contraband in your luggage, sir. We need to inspect it."

"You don't look like customs officials, either," said Roberts. "I suggest you let us pass."

"We're the ones with the guns," said the blond man.

High-energy pulses tore through the uniformed man and woman who stood at each end of the line blocking Roberts and Wright. The first mate smiled. The strangers in gray whirled to face Captain Firebrandt of the *Legacy*. Nicole Lowry stood next to him, hepler at the ready. Alarm klaxons sounded as sensors detected the weapons' fire. Station police would be there soon.

The four remaining agents formed a circle. Wright crouched low and drew a pistol from inside his jacket as Roberts ducked back into the corridor for cover. The blond man fired, burning a hole through Wright's chest.

Lowry and Firebrandt took out two of the agents. Roberts pulled his own hepler and took aim from his position of cover. He fired at the blond man who dove out of the way.

The remaining woman stood, holding up her hands. The blond agent let out a cry of rage and aimed at her. As he did so, both Firebrandt and Lowry fired at him. One pulse went through his chest, the other through his head.

Roberts heard footsteps from behind. He rushed into the reception area and grabbed Wright's duffel bag. He almost toppled over as he tried to lift it. It was much heavier than it looked. He hefted it and tottered toward the airlock. Seeing his difficulty, Lowry ran out and gave him a hand.

Just then, station police appeared in the corridor. Firebrandt lay down covering fire as Roberts and Lowry carried the load past him. Once they entered the ship, Firebrandt darted back through the airlock, closed the door, and rushed forward, along the corridor. Roberts and Lowry left the parcel against the wall and followed on his heels.

"Detach from the station and find me the nearest jump point away from here," called Firebrandt as he reached the command deck.

"Aye, aye, sir," said the helmsman, Kheir el-Din, from the wheel console at center of the deck.

"Scanning jump point catalog." Computer scanned the galactic network using the neural net strung through his brain.

Roberts proceeded forward to his station near the holographic tank that filled the command deck's bow. He activated his console and monitored both Computer's search and el-Din's maneuvers.

The *Legacy* gracefully rolled away from the space station as a series of tiny spheres materialized in the holographic tank showing the positions of jump points. One of them began flashing green.

"Nearest jump point leads to Kepler-17, an active G2 star

with no inhabited planets." Computer spoke before Roberts could scan the search results.

"Make for that." The captain pointed at the holographic display. "Hopefully it'll give us time to figure out what that courier had and what to do with it."

As the captain spoke, a course projection appeared in the holographic tank and a warning light flashed on Roberts' console. He looked up. "Two ships have just disengaged from the station. I'm guessing they have an interest in Mr. Wright's package."

"Stay on course to the jump point," said the captain.

"They'll just follow us through," protested the helmsman.

Firebrandt nodded. "Sure, but if we get there ahead of them, we might find someplace to hide before they get there, or maybe another jump point." He retrieved a pipe and a pouch of tobacco from his pocket. "Computer, what can you tell me about Kepler-17?"

The view in the holographic tank dissolved into a schematic of the star system. A planet orbited so close to the star, it nearly touched the surface. "Kepler-17 is an extremely active star with an intense magnetic field."

Firebrandt considered the schematic as he packed the pipe. He returned the tobacco pouch to his pocket and pointed at the hologram with the pipe stem. "What can you tell me about the planet close to the star?"

"It's a Jovian planet known as Kepler-17b with a period of approximately 1.5 days."

Nicole Lowry let out a long, low whistle. "Sounds a bit torrid for my taste."

Roberts scowled as he checked his monitor. "Those ships that disengaged from the station are definitely on an intercept course. They've nearly matched our speed and they're accelerating."

Firebrandt's brow furrowed. "Who are these people? Will they catch us before we make it through the jump point?"

Roberts shook his head. "Not unless they're magicians who can exceed the speed of light in normal space."

The captain placed the pipe in his mouth and lit it as he considered the schematic. "Once we jump, can we reach that planet near the star before those cruisers catch us?"

The first mate considered the numbers on his screens. "Depends a bit on who they are and whether they want to recapture whatever's in that bag. They'd have a hard time disabling us before we got in near the planet, but if they don't care about being subtle, they could throw enough heavy fire our direction to blow us out of the sky."

Firebrandt looked up at the chronometer and Roberts followed his gaze. They were nearly at the jump point. "After we come out of jump, take Lowry and look in that duffel. I want to know our options. Should we just give it back to them or is it something we want to hang on to?"

"Aye, aye, sir," said Roberts as Lowry nodded.

"We're at the jump point for Kepler-17," reported Computer.

"Head for that planet—17b—as soon as we're on the other side. Best speed."

☠

Suki Mori had been reading in her cabin aboard the *Legacy* while Roberts met with the courier. The captain had been avoiding her after her attempted hijacking of the ship. Although the crew forgave her, they still kept their distance.

She assumed Roberts or Lowry would give her a job when they had something they needed doing, but she wasn't sure what she could do to benefit the crew. She taught computer classes back on Epsion Indi, which seemed the farthest thing she could imagine from being a swashbuckling space pirate—whatever that meant.

Every now and then a member of the crew asked for her help moving cargo, or making a repair. Otherwise, she just stayed out of the way. When she heard the *Legacy* would pick up a mysterious package and courier at Space Station Xiūxí qū sān, she figured she should remain in her cabin until they were underway.

When the ship disengaged from the station's airlock and the engines began to whine, she checked the ship's computer and followed their progress. A few minutes later, the jump warning sounded. She'd secured her tablet and strapped herself in. After a moment, all sense of direction was lost as the ship leapt beyond normal three-dimensional space into a realm where left, right, up, down and the march of time held no meaning—or more precisely, they were no longer the limits of meaning.

A short time later, reality snapped back into focus as the jump completed. Suki figured it was safe to find out what was going on. She unbuckled her harness and left the cabin. Walking along the corridor, she noticed a duffel bag abandoned against the wall.

Curious, she opened it and found a metallic device that looked like three spheres welded end-to-end. She rolled it over and revealed several sockets that looked like power feeds and data connections. Rolling it a little further, she found an input screen. She pushed a black button next to the screen and a menu appeared. "Huh…" she said as she considered the options presented to her.

Footsteps clanked down the corridor and she looked up. Roberts and Lowry approached. "What are you doing, Miss Suki?" asked Lowry.

"Sorry, I just saw this in the corridor and was trying to figure out where it belonged."

"Have you learned anything?" Roberts' question held a note of danger mixed with genuine curiosity.

Suki stood up. "Is this thing even real? According to the diagnostic screens, the device generates nodal points to go beyond space." She shook her head. "Could it be a gravity wave sensor like those they use on mapping vessels?"

Lowry had a blank expression and shrugged. Roberts knelt down by the device and began scrolling through the menus. "My God, I think you may be right about this. It does look like some kind of nodal point generator." He looked up. "We better inform the captain."

They turned toward the command deck. Lowry shook her head. "I still don't get it, what do you mean by a 'nodal point generator'?"

"How well do you understand jumps?" asked Suki.

"You can imagine space as a surface like a piece of paper and we're a flat object confined to the surface that can't perceive up or down." The boatswain held her hand palm-up and traced a path with the index finger of her other hand. Then she cupped her hand. "However, gravity bends space. We can use that fact to jump the gap, moving quickly from one point to another." She moved her finger in the cupped hollow of her palm.

"That's basically it." Suki nodded. "Jump points are those places where we can easily go beyond the three physical dimensions we know." She looked over her shoulder. "I think that device can be used to generate a jump point anywhere, not just a place where gravitational fields converge."

Lowry's eyebrows came together. "You've gotta be kidding me."

Suki shrugged.

With that, the three entered the *Legacy's* command deck. Suki's mouth fell open as she saw the view in the holographic tank.

They approached a turbulent, yellow star with numerous spots darkening its surface. A prominence formed a hellish arch thousands of kilometers above the star's surface. Beyond that and impossibly close to the star sat a banded planet, like Jupiter—although if she believed the numbers floating in the holographic tank, the planet was bigger around than Jupiter with over twice its mass. Material poured off the star and swirled around the planet in a great whirlpool.

"Where are we?" asked Suki.

"Welcome to Kepler-17b." Roberts held out his hand as he stepped past the two women on his way to his station.

"Looks more like a vision of Hell," muttered Suki.

"The pursuing ships are now in weapons' range," reported Computer.

A moment later, the ship rocked as a high-energy pulse from one of the ships hit it.

"Whatever it is we have," said Firebrandt around the pipe stem, "they would rather destroy it than let it fall into someone else's hands."

"They must have another," said Roberts.

"You know what it is, then?" The captain narrowed his gaze.

"We have an idea, but it's pretty hard to believe."

The ship shuddered again. At that point, the image in the holographic tank began to break up. Enough of the image remained that Suki could tell they sped toward the material flowing from the star to the planet.

"We're encountering sensory interference. I won't be able to keep the display in the holographic tank," reported Computer. A moment later, the image dissolved and faded away like a clearing fog.

Roberts peered at his console. "It's hard to get a reading on the pursuing ships, but it looks like they've slowed. They're not going to follow us."

"That's good, and if we can't see them, they can't see us." Firebrandt nodded. "How long can we stay here?"

Roberts shook his head. "Not long. Hull temperature is already climbing to dangerous levels. I'm guessing we have four or five hours at max."

"So, what exactly did you learn about our cargo?" asked Firebrandt.

Roberts explained what they found. "It looks like it's designed to connect into a star vessel's engine and generate a jump point on the spot."

Firebrandt's bushy red eyebrows lifted. "Do you think we could make it work with our engines?"

Roberts sat back and folded his arms. "Balancing the power would be the real challenge. Too little and it won't do anything. Too much and it'll scatter our molecules throughout the cosmos." He took a deep breath, then blew it out again. "I could probably manage it with time, but it's not the way out of our current dilemma."

Suki stepped between Firebrandt and Roberts. "I think I could make it work in two or three hours."

Firebrandt took the pipe from his mouth and Roberts sat forward.

She shrugged. "The interface looked pretty straightforward."

They continued to stare at her.

She planted her fists on her hips. "Look, I taught hyperspatial programming to engineering students on Epsion Indi. I can do this, especially if Mr. Roberts and the mechanics give me a hand."

Firebrandt nodded slowly and placed the pipe back in his mouth. "Can you leave my engines intact so we can get out of here in a hurry if we need to?

Suki thought about that for a minute. "At most, we'd need them down for fifteen minutes while we hook up power couplings."

"Let me know before you disable anything. If it won't work, leave well enough alone. I like the possibilities this gadget presents, but I'm not going to count on it."

Suki swallowed and nodded. "Understood." She looked back at Roberts who surprised her with a heartening grin.

"Let's get going. The clock's ticking," said the first mate as he stepped past her on the way back down the corridor. She hurried after him.

☠

Two hours later, Captain Firebrandt stood on the command deck staring at a holographic representation of the Kepler-17 system. The *Legacy* was between the spotted star and the gas giant in the flow of material between the two bodies. The ship sat in the Lagrange point, traveling around the star every hour and a half with the planet. With no external sensors, the two pursuing ships were not visible. The deck dropped out from under the captain's feet for a moment as the walls shuddered and a deep rumbling caused the hairs on the back of the captain's neck to stand up. Firebrandt took the pipe from his mouth. "What the hell was that?"

"By the magnitude of the disturbance, I'd say a high energy discharge," reported Computer.

"From the star?" asked the captain.

"More likely a discharge from an external source. We felt it because of the density of the material around us."

"Damn! They're taking pot shots at us, hoping to get lucky." He stepped over to Roberts' console and checked the diagnostics screen. They would burn up soon. What's more, the hot hull covered in charged particles meant they would glow in nearly every wavelength when they emerged from hiding.

Another rumble passed through the ship, weaker than the first.

"Captain," said Roberts from the intercom.

"Go ahead." The captain set his pipe down on the console.

"Suki and I have programs ready to load into our engine controllers and we're ready to hook in the nodal-point generator."

"Warning!" Computer's voice rang out. "The power consumption for our shields and cooling is dangerously high. We only have battery reserves for ten minutes. We cannot disengage main power longer or we'll lose our ability to maintain position."

"Did you hear that?" asked the captain.

"Five minutes should do it," said Roberts.

The ship shuddered again, sending Firebrandt's pipe clattering to the deck. He blinked at the glowing embers surrounding the spilled pipe, then smiled.

Firebrandt leaned close to the intercom. "I think I have a way out of here that won't need the generator. I'm not sure we should risk it."

"Captain," interrupted Suki. "I was conservative allocating power to the device. In the worst case, this thing just won't work. Installing it won't prevent the engines' normal operation."

"She's got a point," said Roberts. "Better to go into the next match holding as many cards as possible."

"All right. Five minutes, no more."

As Firebrandt reached over to pick up the pipe and stamp out the glowing ash, the emergency lights replaced main lighting and the holographic display of Kepler-17 winked out. The mechanics had cut main power. The captain rotated in the seat to face Computer. "Let me know if any systems approach critical."

"Yes, sir." Computer's eyes slowly scanned back and forth as he monitored ship's systems.

Firebrandt stood and loaded more tobacco into his pipe. He lit it as he paced toward the command deck's stern hatch. Nicole Lowry sat at the engineering console, monitoring Roberts' and Suki's progress.

"Stand by at the starboard gunner's rig," ordered the captain. "Get Martinez up here to take port. As soon as main power's back on, bring the weapons on line and stand by."

Lowry nodded and called Cesar Martinez to the command deck. Firebrandt turned and paced back toward the inactive holographic display, only briefly losing his footing when another jolt hit the ship. He loosened the top two buttons of his jacket and wiped sweat from his brow.

"Battery reserves down to one minute," stated Computer.

As Firebrandt turned toward Roberts' console, Martinez entered the command deck. He and Lowry stood by to power up the ship's weapons. The captain sat down and activated the intercom. "We're running out of time."

Instead of responding, the lights came back up to full power.

"Main power is back on line," reported Computer.

Firebrandt nodded, then looked at the intercom. "Status report."

"It looks good," said Roberts. "We'll be up in a minute."

Firebrandt stood and noted both the satisfying rumble of the main engines and the whine of the weapons coming on line.

Roberts and Suki appeared on the command deck a few minutes later.

"So, what do you have for me? Can we jump out of here?" asked the captain.

Suki shook her head. "We're too close to the bottom of the system's gravitational well. We're going to need some distance before we can try."

"What's more," added Roberts, "we won't be able to jump to a different system. The device only lets us make a brief jump. A timer controls our reentry into normal space. I'm guessing our maximum range using the device is a few hundred million kilometers."

Firebrandt nodded. "That might be useful. If it fails, can we switch back to main engines?"

Suki gave a curt nod.

The captain removed the pipe from his mouth. He had smoked through the tobacco. He placed the pipe in his pocket and cleared his throat. "All right, here's the plan. We're going to spin around, firing bursts with the main pulse cannon and the turret guns. Those ships, whoever they are, are looking for something hot to come out of here. We'll give them something hot! Once we've finished our spin, we'll blast out of here and begin scanning as soon as we can." He looked toward Computer. "Do we have a jump point to a safe harbor?"

"There is one. I have approximate position on record. I'll fine tune the position as soon as sensors are on line again."

"That's good enough. Send that position to el-Din." The captain smiled. "Get to your stations. This is sure to be a hell of a ride."

Firebrandt grabbed the railing near the holographic tank. Roberts crossed to his station and Suki strapped herself into the seat Nicole Lowry had vacated earlier. She brought up the command system for the nodal-point generator.

"Let's make this happen." With that, the captain tightened his grip on the wooden rail running along the front of the command deck. In the holographic tank, the ship pirouetted between the planet and the star. Thundering bursts sounded as the main pulse gun fired, punctuated by the staccato of the turret guns. In the holographic tank, hot spots flared out in all directions. Most fell rapidly into Kepler-17, but all they needed was a little time with the warships distracted. The captain pointed to el-Din. "Punch it!"

The helmsman activated the controls and the ship shot from its hiding place. The captain ground his teeth as he waited for the sensors to come back on line, giving him a real picture.

The computer model soon dissolved into the real view in front of the ship. Something glimmered in their path. "Computer, enhance! What's that?"

The view in the holographic tank snapped into a close-up view of one of their pursuers. It fired thrusters to bring its main gun to bear.

"Crap!" He turned around and pointed at Suki. "Let's hope this nodal point generator works!"

The enemy ship's forward gun began glowing as she typed. A cone showing the ship's estimated firing vector appeared in the hologram. "They're in range," declared Roberts.

"Ready," called Suki.

"Jump!" ordered the captain.

At first, nothing happened.

Suki spun around, her eyes scanning the displays. Without a word, she began typing.

"What's going on?" asked Firebrandt.

"We have a slight imbalance," said Suki. "I'm adjusting."

"Enemy ship has fired main pulse gun," reported Computer.

Firebrandt pointed to el-Din, "Evasive..."

"Jumping," said Suki.

The deck dropped out beneath the captain's feet. He slammed his eyes shut against the strange sounds the engine made and, without thinking, he slammed his hands over his ears to shut out the sight of his ship swirling just beyond the reach of normal space. A moment later, reality came back into focus and Firebrandt found himself sprawled on the deck, his shoulder screaming in pain.

The unmistakable slosh and splatter of someone emptying their stomach sounded from astern.

Firebrandt sat up. "Get this holo live again!"

An image appeared in the holographic tank. An empty star field lay ahead.

"Pan around the ship," ordered the captain. "Where are we, exactly?"

As the view shifted, they saw they had jumped just beyond one of the two warships. A set of letters appeared along with an arrow. The second ship had just appeared and was moving into position to help its companion. The first ship's thrusters fired.

"They just figured out where we got to," said the captain. "Turret guns, fire into their engines, buy us some time!"

Nicole Lowry fired several bursts. One burst knocked out the pursuing ship's thrusters. Another took out their main EQ engine. The explosion sent the ship hurtling toward Kepler-17.

"Jump point in one minute," announced Kheir el-Din.

"Number two vessel has stopped pursuit and is moving in to assist its companion," reported Computer.

"Excellent," said Firebrandt. "Everyone, prepare for jump. This place is getting too hot for me."

That evening, Firebrandt invited Suki and Roberts to his quarters for dinner. The ship's cook, Juan de Largo, outdid himself preparing Suki's favorite meal, Yakitori. The captain lifted a glass of South African wine. "To our newest crew-member. Long may she keep our fat out of the fire."

Roberts held up his glass. Suki blushed, but held up her glass as well.

After taking a drink, Suki set her glass down. "So, what do we do now?"

"We fried a few systems sitting between that star and planet, then attaching an untested new device into our engine." Roberts folded his arms. "I think we need to sit tight for a little while and make repairs."

"I agree," said the captain. "Besides, we could do with a break before we figure out our next move."

Suki blinked. "What about the nodal point generator? Clearly the agent you met was stealing it to take it back to Earth."

"But which agency? Did they even know we were involved?" Firebrandt shrugged. "Quite honestly, I think that device is worth more to me right where it is than any payment we'd get from Earth."

"But what if they notice you have it and come looking?" Suki's eyebrows came together.

Roberts sat back. "Secrets like this are pretty fleeting and I suspect we don't have the only prototype in existence, but she has a point. Someone may decide the easiest way to get one of these units is to try and take ours."

Firebrandt picked up his chopsticks and began rubbing them together. "Miss Suki, you need a job aboard this ship, and I think I have the perfect one for you." He snatched a piece of chicken and savored it.

Suki leaned forward. "What did you have in mind?"

"Your job is to learn everything you can about the generator so we can keep it running." He picked up another piece of chicken. "One of the best ways to learn is to build me a second one."

Roberts grinned. "That way if someone comes looking, we'll have one to give them."

She smiled, pleased to finally have a job on the ship, and an interesting one at that. "I can't wait to begin."

Chapter Four
Locator Beacons

The Privateer *Legacy* settled near a jump point frequented by freighters from the human colony at Alpha Coma Berenices. Upon arrival, *Legacy* vented a cloud of good, old-fashioned coal dust obtained from Earth. Visually, the coal dust obscured the black hull of the privateer vessel. Sensors scanning the region would detect a cloud of carbon particles, not uncommon in that part of the galaxy. In the time it would take to make a deeper scan, the ship could pounce. However, several days passed and the *Legacy's* supply of coal dust ran low.

Captain Ellison Firebrandt sat on the couch in his quarters with Suki Mori snuggled against his side. Intimacy like that was strange, forbidden, and yet it felt natural. It pleased the captain that Suki seemed to take such comfort in his presence, even if his occupation troubled her. "How is it that such a gentle, considerate man can be a thief and take lives so easily?"

The captain frowned. "It's hardly easy." He was silent for a long moment. Finally, he sighed. "My dad's a miner. My mother was a transport captain."

Suki sat up and Firebrandt found himself reading a question in her brown eyes.

"She used to shuttle dad and his crew from our home in South Africa out to the asteroid belt for their six-week shifts. Sometimes I would go along with her on the runs to the belt. Other times, I would stay home with one of my aunts."

The captain took a deep breath before continuing. "One day, she left. I thought she was going to retrieve dad and his crew. However, a week went by and they never arrived. Finally dad came home—alone. I later found out that my mother had met a pilot from Alpha Coma Berenices. She left us for him. Two months later, Alpha Coma seceded from the Earth Alliance."

"You're happy to kill people because your mother left you and your dad for Alpha Coma?" Suki's brow furrowed.

Firebrandt snorted. "These things are never that simple, but..." He let the sentence trail off.

"That's where the anger started." Suki finished the thought.

The captain nodded. "A victim has two choices. He can cower away and hide, hoping not to be a victim again, or he can strike back."

"And the treasures you have in your hold? My God! You have the Mona Lisa aboard this ship."

"Only until I find a good home for them. They need to be in a museum on Earth."

"How's your search for new owners going?"

The intercom signal sounded before Firebrandt could answer. He stood, straightened his shirt and strode to the intercom. "This is the captain, go ahead."

"Computer has detected a chronoton signature from the jump point." The voice belonged to the first mate. "Looks like a ship will be coming through any minute."

"I'll be right up." He turned off the intercom. "Want to come along? I could use your help."

"The work I've been doing on the jump engine doesn't take all my time, I could help you look for a new home for those paintings." She stood, holding his gaze.

"I'm not entertaining you enough during your off hours?"

She stood on her tiptoes and brushed his cheek with her lips. "That's the thing, I think I'm beginning to like you enough to keep you around. I don't want you losing your ship and becoming some kind of space vagabond."

Ellison Firebrandt strode onto the command deck followed by Suki. Kheir el-Din stood at the helm console. Off to the side of the command deck sat Computer, his brain permanently jacked into the ship's computer and sensors. His eyes flitted from side to side as the sensors scanned the region of space around the ship. At the front of the command deck, Roberts rubbed his bald head as he stared at the jump point, indicated by a small, floating sphere in the holographic tank.

Suki took a seat at the station next to Computer.

As the captain stepped up to Roberts, the jump point flared.

"It's a freighter," announced Computer. "The registry

beacon says Alpha Coma."

Ellison Firebrandt scowled. "Plot an intercept. I want us to jump immediately to her stern, so we can take out her engines before she sees us."

"Intrasystem jump engine on line," reported Suki.

"Intercept plotted," said Computer.

The captain moved over to the wooden railing at the side of the command deck and grabbed hold. He looked to el-Din who nodded.

Firebrandt turned to Nicole Lowry, at the gunner's rig. "Ready your weapons."

"Charged and awaiting your order." Lowry patted the gunner's rig, proud of her babies. She was the boatswain, in charge of the ship's equipment. Serving as occasional gunner was one way she kept that equipment safe.

Firebrandt gave el-Din a sharp nod. The helmsman turned to Suki. "On your mark, Miss Mori."

"Intrasystem jump calculations complete and loaded on your screen," she said.

The helmsman read the data and pursed his lips. "Jump in thirty seconds." He sounded the warning, then grabbed the rail on the side of the wheel console with one hand. The thumb of his other hand hovered over the activation button. "Jump in three ... two ... one." Kheir el-Din pressed the button and reality collapsed.

The captain watched as the gray wall of the command deck seemed to dissolve into an orange and yellow miasma. He refused to unclench his hand, even though he could no longer feel the railing he held or the deck he stood upon. His senses tried to tell him he was falling through a world of light and sound, even though his brain knew nothing had changed. The ship had simply jumped into a dimension his senses could no longer comprehend—a dimension that allowed faster-than-light travel. A moment later, Firebrandt fought back nausea as the sense of free fall suddenly ended and he found his feet firmly on the deck and his white-knuckled hands gripping the familiar wooden rail.

He looked toward the holographic tank at the front of the command deck. The freighter's Erdon-Quinn engine glowed an eerie shade of blue. "Shut it down!"

Lowry fired the *Legacy's* high-energy pulse guns. There was a silent, blinding flash. The captain blinked a few times, then nodded, satisfied as the engines faded from a soft blue to black.

Firebrandt turned to el-Din. "Lock on to that ship." He reached into the pocket of his trousers and retrieved a pipe and tobacco. "Roberts, prepare a boarding party."

"Aye aye, sir." Pale as he was after the jump, Roberts' head looked unsettlingly skull-like. He nodded, then swallowed and straightened his jacket. As the turned to leave, he paused, then pointed at the holographic viewer. "They're opening one of the launch bays."

The captain continued tamping tobacco into his pipe as he watched. A sizable yacht dropped from the wounded ship's bay. Lifting the pipe to his lips, the captain lit it. The yacht made its way to the jump point and vanished with a flash.

"I guess they didn't have the stomach for a fight," observed Roberts.

The captain sucked in smoke from the pipe, then blew it out through his nose. "No, I suppose not." He turned to his first mate. "Be careful all the same, and look lively. I suspect we'll be joined by a warship before the day is out."

"Aye aye, Captain." Appearing more collected than he had immediately after the jump, Roberts turned and strode from the command deck.

☠

Within the hour, *Legacy* had docked with the freighter and Roberts stood at the airlock. He swallowed hard as the door opened with a hiss. Across the way stood a decidedly non-threatening, brightly lit corridor. Holding his hepler pistol at the ready, he led his men across to the freighter. Roberts' eyes scanned the corridor, looking for any sign of a trap. When he reached the main corridor that ran the length of the ship, he decided to lead the crew to the bridge before going to the cargo hold.

The boarding party's footsteps echoed as they walked down the corridor. The only sound the ship made was the soft whisper of air blowing through the ventilation system. Arriving at the bridge, they found it empty and pristine. There wasn't even a coffee cup or a pen lying on a console. "Looks like they were preparing for a short flight," mused Roberts.

Stepping up to the ship's command station, he activated the holographic flight recorder. In the holo tank, the crew of the freighter jolted as the *Legacy* attacked.

Several voices spoke at once. "Damn!" "They just came out of nowhere!" "What the..."

A woman with a beak-like nose and stringy hair—the computer officer—looked at the captain. "The enemy has no transponder signal."

"Pirates, just as we thought," said the freighter's captain. "All hands to the yacht. Abandon ship."

As though rehearsed, the freighter's crew shut down their stations with cool efficiency and filed neatly out of the bridge.

Roberts called the *Legacy*. "It looks like they were expecting us."

"Us specifically?" Firebrandt raised his bushy eyebrows.

Roberts shook his head. "I don't think so. Just fishing for pirates."

Firebrandt grunted. "Anything of value over there?"

Roberts checked the cargo manifest. "If this is accurate, they're hauling military supplies."

"Munitions?" asked the captain.

Again, the first mate shook his head. "No. Looks like uniforms ... tools and hardware ... toilet paper."

"Lovely."

Roberts smiled. He could picture the captain rolling his eyes. He continued scrolling through the manifest. "Looks like about a dozen lifepods in inventory."

"Hmmm..." The captain sounded interested. "We might be able to sell those and even some of the tools on Sigma Draconis. At the very least we might be able to break even. Meet me in the cargo hold and we'll take a look."

"Aye aye, sir." With that, the first mate signed out and left the bridge with the rest of the boarding party following close behind. They made their way through the corridors, still wary for potential traps.

Reaching the cargo hold, they fanned out and began

making an inventory of what could be useful and what they should leave behind. A moment later, Ellison Firebrandt entered the hold and looked around, eyeing the contents with keen interest. He stepped up to Roberts.

"Could be better," grumbled the first mate.

"Still not bad." Firebrandt made his way over to one of the lifepods and ran his hand over its smooth surface. "They've extended the life support capacity on these pods. The demand for them is growing since they don't take up as much space as full-sized..."

A sneeze from a nearby cargo container interrupted the captain. He and Roberts drew their sidearms and cautiously approached. The captain nodded to his first mate, who stepped over to the controls. Firebrandt aimed his gun as Roberts opened the container.

Inside was a man in baggy coveralls with several days' growth of beard on his chin. He blinked in the sudden light, then slowly held up his hands when he saw Firebrandt's weapon.

"Well, well. What do we have here?" asked the captain.

"Don't shoot," said the man. "My name's Spencer Conklin. I'm ... I was just looking ... I just wanted transport back to Epsilon Indi."

"It looks like this freighter had a stowaway." Roberts grinned.

The captain inclined his head. "Epsilon Indi's no treasure. What do you want there?"

Conklin ventured a step out of the container. "I was going to rejoin my family."

"Why were you on Alpha Coma?" asked Roberts.

"I was looking for work." Conklin shrugged.

"Work? Or a handout?" asked the captain.

Conklin frowned. "Whatever will help feed my kids."

Firebrandt scowled and holstered his weapon. He looked toward Roberts. "I have no use for space tramps. Shove him out the airlock, then get this stuff aboard the *Legacy*."

"Wait," called Conklin. "They were planning a trap for you."

The captain's gaze narrowed. "What makes you say that?"

"They planted locator beacons in a number of these storage containers and in the lifepods." Conklin stepped over and opened up the pod Firebrandt had run his hand over. From within, he retrieved a small disk-shaped object. "I saw the freighter crew install them." The stowaway swallowed hard, then licked his lips. "If you spare me and drop me at your next port, I'll show you where they are."

"His story's consistent with the flight recorder footage we saw on the bridge, Captain," said Roberts. "The Alpha Comans were planning a trap of some kind. If he can show us the beacons, and we can leave them behind, we might still make use of this cargo."

The captain looked from Roberts to Conklin. Finally he nodded. "Very well, but make it quick. I want everything aboard the *Legacy* within two hours."

"Yes, sir." The first mate gave a curt nod.

Back aboard the *Legacy,* Ellison Firebrandt stepped onto the command deck with his hands behind his back and his brow furrowed. The only other crewmember present was Computer, who sat silent, eyes roving the room. The captain grinned, remembering when the officer came aboard. Without introduction, he had walked up to the captain. "I hear you're looking for an Information Interface officer. Admiral Luke Williams of the Alliance Fleet recommended your ship. I've long been fascinated by privateers." His eyes had flitted to the computer station in the way a hungry man might eye a table full of food. "My references should have already been transmitted."

Firebrandt had looked at Roberts who nodded. "He's right, there's a reference here from the admiral. There are also references from half a dozen other high ranking Earth officers."

The captain had nodded. "What do we call you?"

"If you pay me, assure I'm fed and tended, you may call me Computer."

Good officers were rare. To have one recommended by top brass had been overwhelming. In the three years he'd been aboard, Computer had been as good as his word. Firebrandt often wondered what went on in Computer's brain. How did he see the world? Was it like a simulation or a game? He never complained about his treatment. He rarely left the command deck. He seemed content, sitting in one place, only leaving for rare breaks to eat or relieve himself.

The captain sighed and sat down at one of the empty stations. "Computer, can you check the census records for Epsilon Indi 2? Is there anyone named Spencer Conklin?"

Computer's eyes snapped straight ahead for a few seconds and then began roving the room again. "There are four-hundred thirty-three people named Spencer Conklin on Epsilon Indi 2 according to the last census."

"Any of them listed as off-world or missing? Anything like that?"

"Forty-two are off world on travel visas. Three are listed as wanted criminals, whereabouts unknown. Twenty-seven have no legal residence and are therefore untraceable. Two are missing after recent natural disasters."

Firebrandt scowled. He didn't like this Spencer Conklin. Something about him seemed wrong. Not all work was good or glorious, but it could be found. Even someone like Computer served a purpose. One didn't have to go back many generations to find people like Computer in institutions being cared for continuously. Now Computer was a valued member of his crew. If Conklin were telling the truth, why did he continue to drift? "We found a stowaway aboard the Alpha Coma freighter named Spencer Conklin who claims to be from Epsilon Indi. What's the probability he's telling the truth?"

"Impossible to calculate. He could simply be lying." Computer's eyes again stopped roving. He looked at Firebrandt. "I could determine if he was from Epsilon Indi if I had a DNA sample. DNA is recorded as part of the planet's census data."

Firebrandt nodded thoughtfully as Computer resumed scanning. Turning around, the captain activated a video screen and watched as the crew brought the pods and crates aboard the Legacy. Satisfied that all was proceeding as it should, the captain activated the com and called the kitchen. "Juan, this is the captain."

"What can I do for you, sir?"

"Is your medical kit handy?"

"Yeah, you got something wrong?"

"Nothing like that," said the captain. "We're going to have a guest aboard, soon. Go over to the Alpha Coma ship and have Roberts introduce you to Spencer Conklin. Get a blood sample and deliver it to Computer. If Conklin asks, tell him it's a routine health check."

"Aye aye, Cap'n."

With that, Firebrandt turned off the intercom and resumed watching the operation on the video monitors.

An hour and a half later, the *Legacy* detached itself from the Alpha Coma freighter and began making its way toward the jump point for Sigma Draconis. Leaving the command deck in Roberts' capable hands, the captain made his way below decks. He found Spencer Conklin in the ship's mess. Two empty plates were pushed to the side and he literally shoveled food into his mouth from a third. Suki sat across from him, sipping green tea.

"How are you doing, Mr. Conklin?" asked the captain.

"Fine, except for my arm." Conklin paused eating long enough to rub his right elbow. "Took that doctor of yours five times to hit a vein and get that blood sample for the exam. He's a damn fine cook, though." He paused and looked over his shoulder toward the counter, behind which, Juan de Largo was working on supper for the crew.

"Well, I'm glad to see you're availing yourself of our hospitality." The captain turned toward Suki. "Could you take a walk with me, please?"

Suki nodded and stood. "Excuse me," she said to Conklin as she followed the captain.

They walked down the corridor a short distance. "Do you believe his story? Is he really from Epsilon Indi?"

Suki nodded. "He talks the talk as they say. He knows the world well and his story holds up. He says he was working as a clerk at a factory that went out of business. He left the planet to find a new job."

"If he has a family, why didn't he bring them along?"

"He planned to send for them once he settled down." She inclined her head. "It's easier to stow away on a ship alone than with an entourage."

The captain nodded. "I suppose that makes sense." The deck rumbled, as though the engines had increased power.

"Roberts calling Captain Firebrandt." His voice sounded from the ship's speakers.

Firebrandt stepped over to the intercom panel. "This is the captain, go ahead."

"We have an Alpha Coma ship making a bee-line for us and they're closing," said Roberts.

"Have you tried evasive maneuvers?" Firebrandt scowled.

"I don't think it would do any good. It's like they know exactly where we are."

"I'll be right up." Firebrandt hit the intercom switch and turned to Suki. "Get Conklin. Bring him up to the command deck."

"Why?" Suki's brow furrowed.

"I have a feeling he knows something about this." He turned and strode down the corridor.

Arriving at the command deck a moment later, the captain evaluated the information presented in the holographic tank. "How long until the warship intercepts us?"

"Six hours, twenty minutes," reported Computer.

"And we're a little over eight hours from the nearest jump point." Roberts anticipated the captain's next question.

Firebrandt folded his arms. "How soon until we can make another intrasystem jump?"

"We can do so now, sir," said Computer.

The captain looked at Computer. "Plot a course that gets us as far away from that ship as we can and toward a usable jump point."

Computer's eyes shifted back and forth a few times. "We can jump to a position some distance above and behind the Alpha Coma warship. Going there will put us on a course for a jump point to New Earth. We could jump there in about five hours."

Suki and Spencer Conklin stepped onto the command deck as Computer finished his report.

"Send the data to the helm." Firebrandt pointed to Suki. "Get the intrasystem jump engine ready to go." He turned to face el-Din. "Jump as soon as you can."

The helmsman nodded, then watched the data on his screen. "Tracking course," he announced a minute later. "Ready to jump as soon as Miss Mori gives the word."

Suki's hands played across the computer console. She frowned, made an adjustment and then turned to el-Din. "Ready now."

Firebrandt grabbed onto the rail at the side of the command deck. Lowry jumped up from the gunner's rig and ushered Conklin to a position behind the captain. Just as Lowry returned to her station, el-Din initiated the jump. As usual, reality seemed to collapse as the ship sidestepped into the fourth physical dimension. Firebrandt sensed that Conklin had lost his grip on the rail. When the ship came out of jump and the captain's senses functioned again, he saw the tramp sprawled on the floor across the room.

Conklin blinked a few times, rose to a sitting position and then gripped his stomach. First there was a belch, then the hastily consumed meal from earlier came up and splattered on the deck.

"Let's get a mop and bucket up here right away!" Roberts placed his hand over his mouth, as though he was about to lose his own lunch from the smell.

"Alpha Coma warship is turning." Computer's eyes tracked back and forth, as though he was oblivious to the jump and the smell that now pervaded the command deck. "They appear to be moving toward an intercept course."

"How could they lock onto us so quickly?" Firebrandt's brow furrowed as he dug in his pants pocket for a pipe.

"It's as though we missed a locator beacon in the cargo," said Roberts as two men arrived with a mop and bucket. The first mate pointed them to the sloppy mess on the deck.

Firebrandt lit his pipe and watched as Suki helped Conklin to his feet. "I helped your crew find all the locator beacons." The tramp's voice wavered.

"Did you?" Firebrandt looked over to Computer. "Have you completed the analysis of Conklin's blood?"

"Negative," responded Computer. "Nanodevices in subject Conklin's blood have interfered with genome matching."

The captain blew out a cloud of smoke, his eyes wide.

"Nanodevices? What kind?"

"Unknown."

"Could such devices generate a signal?" The captain took a step toward Conklin, evaluating him keenly.

"Negative." Computer's eyes stopped roving and looked directly at the captain. "However, they have a unique low-level energy signature. A ship scanning for such a signature could locate and pinpoint its source very quickly." Computer's eyes roved the deck again. "Alpha Coma warship is on course for us again, sir."

Firebrandt bit down on the pipe stem with an audible crack.

"Let's space him, and get the hell out of here," suggested Lowry.

Firebrandt nodded. "A very good idea."

"No!" Suki stepped between Conklin and the captain. "Ellison, I believe he's really from Epsilon Indi and he's really trying to help a family. He's a victim of Earth's struggle with Alpha Coma as much as you are."

Conklin wrung his hands and looked down at the deck. "I told the truth. I was a stowaway." He drew in a deep breath and let it out slowly. "What I didn't say was that they captured me. They injected me with something and said I could stay in the hold. I would be free to leave the ship when they reached their destination. They would deposit money in my account back on Epsilon Indi." He looked up and met the captain's eyes. "They didn't tell me what they injected me with."

Firebrandt shook his head, then took the pipe from his mouth. He brushed past Conklin and sat down next to Computer. "The shielded room," he said quietly. "Will it keep the Alpha Coma ships from sensing this low-level energy signature?"

Computer nodded. "The signature is quite weak. I calculate a ninety-seven point eight percent chance of success."

The captain looked up at Roberts, who was standing behind Conklin. "Stun him with your hepler gun and help me get him below."

Conklin's brow furrowed. "Stun? But high energy pulsed guns don't have a stun setting?"

Just then, Roberts cracked Conklin over the head with the butt of his gun. The tramp crumpled to the deck.

Firebrandt looked from Suki to Roberts. "Get him below decks and place him in the room. You know the one I mean."

The two looked at each other, then set to work, dragging Conklin off the command deck.

Firebrandt looked down and scowled at his cracked pipe stem. "Computer, I want you to plot a series of intrasystem jumps that won't drain our engines too low for a jump to Sigma Draconis or New Earth. Begin execution as soon as our passenger is secure and Miss Mori confirms engine readiness." The captain checked that the tobacco in the pipe was no longer lit, then shoved it in his pants pocket. He looked at the Alpha Coma warship's position in the holo-viewer and hoped they would have time to get away.

☠

Spencer Conklin awoke with a splitting headache in a completely darkened room. He started to sit up, but a wave of nausea overcame him again and he thought better of it. He lay in one place until the nausea receded. Finally, he made his way onto his hands and knees, picked a direction and crawled. He stopped when he came to a "wall" of plastic. Feeling around in the dark, he discovered it was a box—possibly a shipping container like the one he had hidden in aboard the Alpha Coman freighter. He turned and found another container next to the first.

Edging his way along the containers, he finally came to a metal wall. He eased his way to his feet and found that there was a door near the place he stood. He felt along the side of the door, trying to find a control that might open it, or at least turn on the lights. He moved to the other side of the door and found a control panel. With a swallow, he pushed one of the buttons.

A shrill alarm blared from a nearby speaker and the door remained shut, but the lights popped on. Looking down at the control panel by the door, Conklin noticed there were a total of three buttons. He wasn't sure which one he had activated, but the shrill alarm discouraged him from trying more. He was on a privateer vessel, after all. He might discover one of the buttons was rigged with something worse than an alarm. Also, given the alarm, he figured someone would arrive in short order anyway.

Turning around, Conklin took stock of the room. As he suspected, he was in a room full of storage containers. Taking a few steps further into the room, he noticed a set of stasis containers with paintings inside. One of them was a realistic painting of a woman in a strange, black dress and a beguiling half-smile. Uneducated in the arts, he didn't recognize the small painting and wondered about its significance.

Just as he turned his attention to the next painting in the line, the alarm shut off and the door slid open. Captain Firebrandt and his first mate, Roberts entered the room. Conklin raised his hands. "I didn't touch anything. I swear!"

"You touched the light switch and set off the alarm," said Roberts. "That was plenty to agitate an already shaky crew."

"How ... how are we doing?" asked Conklin. "Have you ... have we gotten away from the warship."

Firebrandt nodded thoughtfully. "We've put some distance between us and that ship, but I'm not ready to say we're safe just yet." He turned. "Follow me." The captain strode down the corridor.

Conklin stood his ground until Roberts produced a hepler gun. "Move," said the first mate.

The tramp nodded hastily and scooted by the intimidating, bald man who looked all too ready to use the weapon he held. He caught up to the captain. "What are you going to do? Shove me into space like your pilot wanted?"

Firebrandt pursed his lips. "Not exactly. Lucky for you, Computer was finally able to get a genome match. He confirmed you really are from Epsilon Indi ... and Prospero before that ... and Earth's asteroid belt even before that. You've been dragging your poor family with you the whole way. Despite what Suki said about traveling with an entourage, I'm surprised you don't have them now."

"I wasn't sure what I'd find. You hear stories about Alpha Coma ... they don't like outsiders."

"But you risked going anyway?" Roberts narrowed his gaze.

Conklin nodded and frowned. "Industry is thriving on

Alpha Coma. I haven't been able to find a job anywhere else."

Firebrandt paused at a heavy door and looked into Conklin's eyes. "Unable to find a job, or unwilling? There's always a shortage of miners in the asteroid belt. Prospero has good farms."

"I was an office worker," complained Conklin. "I don't know anything about mining and farming."

"I'm sure you could learn. It's better than being a traitor to the homeworld." Firebrandt activated a set of controls next to the door. It hissed open and Firebrandt disappeared inside. Roberts still aimed the hepler pistol at him. He swallowed and darted inside behind the captain.

Looking around, Conklin realized they were in the outer section of an airlock. He fell back against the inside wall, heart pounding a staccato and eyes wide with terror. "You're gonna space me after all!"

Firebrandt shook his head and pointed to a lifepod from the Alpha Coma freighter on the floor.

"You see, with those nanodevices in your bloodstream, that warship should find you in no time," explained the captain.

"What if they don't?"

Firebrandt shrugged and shook his head. "Not my problem." He stepped close to the tramp. "I recently told Suki that a victim has two choices. They can hide and hope not to be attacked again or they can go on the offensive." He snorted. "You've made me realize there's a third choice. You can sell yourself to those who would make you a victim." The captain lifted his chin. "You see, you're a tramp in every sense of the word. You're a stowaway, a hobo, a shiftless wanderer ... and a man who will sell his body to the highest bidder."

"But I'm doing it for my family!" protested Conklin.

"If you live, go home. Find a better way to make money and a home for your family."

Conklin opened his mouth to respond, but the captain shoved him backwards into the lifepod. Roberts secured the latches and the two stepped from the airlock. The inner door closed and the outer one opened. The air shot out into space carrying the lifepod and Conklin with it. Tumbling end over end, Conklin's sensitive stomach rebelled and he vomited into the pod. The smell made him gag, but there was no more food in his belly to come up. A bright flash lit up the pod's interior. Conklin guessed *Legacy* had jumped. He was truly alone. Finally he tore his eyes away from the spinning stars and looked down at the oxygen gauge.

Realizing Firebrandt was right, he prayed the Alpha Coma warship would find him before he ran out of air. He wanted more than anything to get back to his family and make a better life for them. Being a farmer or a miner might be hard work, but it was better than whirling through space, lost and alone as he was now—and really, as he had been for the last several years of his life.

Chapter Five
The Convoy

Helmsman Kheir el-Din brought the star vessel *Legacy* into a low orbit around the planet Kolkhoz while first mate Carter Roberts checked the chronometers. "We're right on time," reported Roberts. "They're scheduled to launch the cargo pod in three minutes."

Captain Ellison Firebrandt nodded his approval. He studied the image of the forested world below in the holographic display. "I've heard there are some nice lakes and rivers on Kolkhoz … good fishing. Too bad we don't have time to visit."

Roberts and el-Din exchanged a glance.

"I have a hard time picturing you with a rod and reel, Captain." The console lit the first mate's face from beneath, lending his skull-like features a spectral quality.

Firebrandt stroked his beard and nodded. "It would probably be funny to watch. I've never fished in my life … but it would be nice to be in one place long enough to learn how."

Roberts sighed. "You'll have no argument from me on that score, Captain."

Computer interrupted their musings. "Ground control reports they've launched the cargo pod." He pointed to the holographic projection and a dot appeared on the planet surface. He then ran his finger through the air and a course projection was shown.

"Moving to intercept." Kheir el-Din stood at the helm console in the center of the command deck wearing only a vest on his upper body. His muscles rippled almost as though he were grappling a ship's wheel at sea instead of typing on a computer display.

As el-Din maneuvered *Legacy* toward the cargo pod, Suki Mori entered the command deck. Firebrandt smiled and gestured for her to join him at his side. "Not much to see. This is pretty dull and routine."

"Dull and routine is a refreshing change from what life has

been like since I came aboard the *Legacy*," she said. "It's nice to see us doing something legal for a change."

Firebrandt scowled. "We operate under a letter of marque. What we do is completely legal."

"All right," Suki amended. "It's nice to see us doing something that doesn't involve us shooting at someone ... and someone shooting back."

The captain nodded in agreement, then looked forward. The cargo pod appeared in the display. Kheir el-Din fired thrusters until the *Legacy* matched the pod's speed and trajectory. Roberts opened cargo doors in the ship's belly and deployed grappler arms.

Suki folded her arms. "What exactly are we bringing on board, anyway?"

"Kolkhozian lumber is highly prized back on Earth," explained Firebrandt. "The climate is predictable, and the soil nutrients are well balanced, leading to wood with exceptionally even tree rings and coloration."

"So we've come all the way to the far side of the galaxy to haul a load of logs back to Earth?"

Firebrandt shrugged. "There aren't many trees left on the mother planet itself."

Roberts looked up from his console. "Cargo is aboard and secure."

"Excellent," said the captain. "Set course for the nearest jump point on our route back to Earth."

"Aye aye, sir." The helmsman fired thrusters dropping *Legacy* into a hyperbolic orbit. The ship swung around Kolkohz and accelerated toward its destination.

Firebrandt glanced up at the chronometer. They had a couple of hours until they reached the jump point. He held his hand out toward Suki. "Shall we have some dinner?"

She unfolded her arms, but took a step back. Her eyes flickered around the room, but a moment later, she nodded and took his hand. The captain worried she was having second thoughts about their growing relationship. Not surprising given both her history and the fact that personal intimacy had grown unfashionable. Still, as they grew closer, he found himself longing for contact. Together the two strode toward the corridor with only a few furtive, curious glances from the crew.

"I sense a ship approaching," said Computer before they reached the door.

Firebrandt sighed, the moment broken. He gave Suki's hand a squeeze, then released it and spun around. "Who are they? Battleship?"

Roberts shook his head as he studied the readouts. "No, they seem to be a cargo transport bound for the same jump point as we are."

"We're receiving a signal from the ship," said Computer. "I'll put it on the holo."

The image of a stout woman in a plaid shirt and a cowboy hat appeared. "This is Captain R.J. Driscoll of the transport *Big Ben*. We saw you pick up a shuttle pod in orbit. Where you bound?"

"Ellison Firebrandt of the *Legacy*, with a load of lumber bound for Earth," responded the captain.

"Hope you don't mind company," called Driscoll cheerfully. "We've got a load of livestock we're takin' to the mother world."

Kheir el-Din waved the captain over to his console and pointed to the display. It showed the course projection of both vessels. They converged at the jump point.

Firebrandt grinned. "The more the merrier, as long as you can keep up." He nodded to the helmsman, who put on a burst of speed.

"You won't lose me that easy," said the captain of the *Big Ben*. She pointed to her own helmsman, who fired thrusters and easily pulled alongside.

"Good to see a captain who keeps her ship in tip-top condition," said Firebrandt.

"Likewise, Captain." R.J. Driscoll winked, then signed off.

☠

Suki and the captain retired to his quarters for dinner.

The captain eyed Suki over a glass of wine. "Were you parents romantically involved?"

She blinked. "They were fast friends. They held hands and hugged all the time."

Firebrandt blew out a deep breath. "I mean sexually."

When her eyes widened and she scooted back from the table, he held up his hands. "My parents were. I gather I was conceived the old-fashioned way."

She leaned forward, studying him as though she might discern some telltale just by looking. "Really?"

"Really." He sipped his wine. "And there's nothing wrong with me."

She narrowed her gaze. "Why are you bringing this up now?"

He set down the wine glass. "It always seemed ... nice. It seemed like my parents were closer than other people's parents."

She snorted. "I thought you said your mother left your father."

The truth of the statement stung. The captain sat back and folded his arms, realizing that part of why her leaving stung was precisely because the two had seemed so close. "I don't know what drove them apart, but it was nice while it lasted. I always thought it would be nice to be intimate with someone, to share that depth of contact and love, maybe even make a life someday without the interference of doctors and techs."

To his relief, she actually considered that. Then her eyes widened again. "You mean with me?"

He held up his hands. "Don't feel pressured. If you don't want to, I understand."

Suki resumed her meal. "You know, there are planets where you can be arrested for even posing this topic."

He pointed to his chest. "Pirate, eh?"

She laughed and it was the most wonderful sound he could imagine.

After dinner, Firebrandt returned to the command deck to supervise the jump to the next system on their route. Gravity waves converging from different stellar systems defined jump points. Too far away and a star's gravity is too week to form a jump point. So, ships had to jump from system to system, like playing hopscotch across the galaxy.

Once the *Legacy* and the *Big Ben* jumped into the new system, Computer scanned for the next jump point. A course projection and an estimated travel time appeared in the holographic tank. Seeing that the next jump point was a few hours distant, the captain left el-Din in charge and went to his quarters to get a few hours' sleep.

Suki had already returned to her quarters. He took off his jacket and boots and climbed under the blanks, then set the alarm. As he drifted off to sleep, he wondered what it would be like to fall asleep with Suki in his arms.

☠

It felt like he had just closed his eyes when the alarm went off. It took a moment for him to realize they approached the next jump point. He padded over to the coffee maker and set a cup brewing while he retrieved his jacket and boots. He turned on a light over the sink and tried to put his long, red hair back in order. Not entirely satisfied, he retrieved the coffee cup, then stalked back to the bridge.

Nicole Lowry had taken over Kheir el-Din's place at the helm. She nodded when the captain stepped up beside her. "Right on time, Cap'n. We're only two minutes from the jump point."

He sipped his coffee, then nodded. "Sound the jump warning and ready the scanners."

"Scanners are ready," reported Computer, who rarely left his post on the command deck.

Firebrandt took another sip of coffee, then closed the lid and slipped the cup into a holder near the bow. He grabbed hold of a wooden rail that ran the length of the room. A blinking dot in the holographic tank indicated they had reached the jump point. The captain nodded to the helmsman and closed his eyes as she executed the jump.

Because the ships left normal three-dimensional reality, jumps were disorienting. There was no good sense of direction or balance. It was like free fall, but without the visual and auditory clues that would normally serve as a frame of reference.

"Jump complete," reported Computer a moment later.

The captain opened his eyes slowly. The room spun and his stomach threatened to give way, making him grateful he had waited before eating breakfast. He took several deep breaths, then retrieved his coffee cup. After a couple of sips, he felt better. By then the crew came around as well. Computer seemed completely unfazed. His eyes darted back and forth as the ship's scanners explored the system.

"Sir," said Computer, "we've jumped near the planet Banaadir. There's a ship in orbit under attack."

"Can you get me a visual?" Firebrandt took another sip of his coffee.

Computer nodded. A moment later, an image of a freighter similar to the *Big Ben* appeared. Two small gunboats fired at the larger, unarmed ship.

"Any official markings on those smaller ships? Is that an orbital patrol of some type?"

Computer's brow furrowed as he checked the ship's database. "Unlikely. They bear no official markings nor match designs in use by Banaadir officials. They appear to be small personal boats equipped with military hardware."

"Pirates," growled Lowry. "True pirates."

"What about the freighter?" Firebrandt stepped toward the holographic display.

"The freighter is from Earth," reported Computer.

Firebrandt sighed. "Sounds like it's our duty to save the day. Set course for Banaadir."

Lowry nodded and the *Legacy* peeled away from the *Big Ben*.

"Sir," interjected Computer, "we're getting a message from Captain Driscoll. They're asking if we would like assistance."

Firebrandt's brow creased. "Are they armed?"

Computer's eyes moved back and forth for a moment then he shook his head. "No, sir. They carry no large armaments."

"Then tell them to hold their position." He faced the holographic display. "Open a channel to those marauders."

"Channel open," said Computer.

"This is Captain Ellison Firebrandt of the *Legacy* calling unidentified craft. Break off your attack or we will destroy you." He looked at Nicole Lowry who nodded, confirming she was charging the high-energy pulse cannon.

"We have an incoming visual message," said Computer.

"Show me."

In the holographic display, was a close-up of a hand, the middle finger extended.

"All right, they asked for it." Firebrandt nodded at Lowry who fired the pulse cannon. The blast vaporized one of the small ships. The other small ship fired its thrusters and retreated back to the planet.

"Shall I let them have it?" asked Lowry.

The captain shook his head.

"I have an incoming message from the Earth vessel," reported Computer.

"Let's hear it," ordered the captain.

"This is Rafael Melendez of the *Silver Cloud*. Thanks for coming to our rescue, *Legacy*. That's some fire power you have."

"The pleasure is ours," said Firebrandt. "Where are you bound for?"

"Back to Earth, we're hauling Quinnium."

The captain's eyebrows shot up at the mention of the highly volatile substance that was used as fuel for both star vessels and weapons. He looked over to Lowry, whose mouth had fallen open. Firebrandt took another sip of coffee while he regained his composure. "Shouldn't you have an armed escort *Silver Cloud*?"

"Those gunboats attacking us *were* our escort," said Melendez. "I'm guessing they got a better offer from Banaadir than they had from our company."

"A share in the profits, no doubt." Firebrandt scowled. "Come with us. The *Legacy* and the *Big Ben* are traveling to Earth in tandem. The three of us make a convoy. We'll look out for each other."

"Much obliged, Captain. We'll be happy to take you up on that offer."

☠

The next jump took the three ships to the outskirts of a system with a red giant star and no inhabited planets. Firebrandt invited the captains to come aboard the *Legacy*. Rafael Melendez was the first to arrive. He was wiry with black hair turning silver. R.J. Driscoll arrived next. Although her smile revealed dimples, Firebrandt thought he saw sadness in her blue eyes.

The privateer captain invited the freighter captains to his cabin where Suki and Roberts waited. On the table were bowls of chicken curry and rice along with an assortment of chutneys.

"I hope you enjoy it. I grew up in South Africa and curries are still a favorite."

"It smells wonderful," said Captain Melendez. "We've been looking forward to getting back to Earth so we can restock."

R.J. Driscoll nodded slowly. "Money's been pretty slim on the *Big Ben* lately. It's been a while since we've had a really good meal, too. I just wish Benjamin could be here to join us."

"Benjamin?" asked Suki.

Captain Driscoll blushed. "Benjamin's my husband. I named the ship after him. Kind of silly actually."

"Not at all." Firebrandt's eyes flitted to Suki and he wondered briefly if Ben and B.J. were intimate in the way he wanted to be with Suki. Realizing the answer was none of his business, he allowed the thought to drift away as he sat down and indicated the other chairs. Roberts passed a bowl of rice and Firebrandt tossed a salad.

"So, is Benjamin back home?" asked Suki. "Wherever home is…"

"Home's on Earth," Driscoll looked down at her bowl as she took the rice, "but Benjamin's on the ship."

"You should have invited him along," said Melendez with a broad smile. "I'm sure Captain Firebrandt wouldn't have begrudged his company."

"I'm sure you're right." Driscoll sighed and passed the rice along. "It's just that Benjamin ain't been feeling too good lately. The med scans show intestinal cancer and it looks like it's spreading."

Firebrandt, Suki, and Roberts exchanged glances, then the captain turned to Driscoll. "Haven't you seen a doctor? You just need nano treatments to repair the cells…"

Driscoll shook her head. "We don't have money for nano treatments much less a doctor's visit." The captain understood. He dreamed of a job big enough that would give him money to pay for a proper ship's doctor instead of relying on the dubious ministrations of the ship's cook. Driscoll took a deep breath, then blew out a sigh. "There's a great cancer center on Alpha Coma Berenices and we've almost saved enough money, but the orbital taxes for our ship … the customs duties … even paying the crew while we're at the hospital would be a challenge."

Firebrandt took the bowl of curry and served a generous portion, then passed it along. "Roberts and I have a few connections." He looked at the first mate meaningfully.

Roberts nodded. "Indeed. I think we could find a place for you to park your ship a while and some work for your men ... at least till your husband's recovered."

Melendez smiled. "I could help a little with the medical bills, especially since I don't have to pay those two worthless escort captains!"

Captain Driscoll blinked back a tear. "It's no fair, Captain Firebrandt. I don't want hope where there is none. There's still the matter of actually getting to the hospital. If we go with our ship, there's all those issues I mentioned. If we dock at Earth, we'd still have to pay for a star liner ticket to Alpha Coma, not to mention the time it would take to make arrangements ... then there's the issue of getting a visa."

Firebrandt spooned chutney on his curry, then handed it to Roberts. "None of that sounds insurmountable, does it?"

"Not at all, Captain."

Suki reached across the table and took Driscoll's hand. "Never give up hope, especially when you're among friends."

☠

Two days later, Firebrandt stood on the *Legacy's* command deck. The holographic display showed views of the other two ships' command decks. Captain Melendez stood on the *Silver Cloud's* bridge. The command chair of the *Big Ben* was occupied by Driscoll's first mate, a man with long mouse-brown hair and a silvering beard named Williams. "You know what to do," said Firebrandt. "This is going to require precise timing."

"Those customs officials will have a lot to inventory over here on a Quinnium freighter," said Melendez with a smile. "The safety regs will add some time."

"If those customs officials aren't real careful," said Williams, "those pigs will start running loose all over the ship and it's damn near impossible to keep count of 'em all."

"Perfect," said Firebrandt. "As soon as you've got them occupied, signal us and we'll make our move."

"All righty," said Melendez and both ships signed out. The *Big Ben* moved forward first and winked out as it jumped to

Alpha Coma. A moment later, the *Silver Cloud* followed.

Firebrandt crossed the command deck to Roberts' console. He reached down and activated the intercom. "Everyone ready down there in the launch boat?"

"Captain Driscoll and her husband are settled in nice and cozy," said Kheir el-Din.

"Don't let them get too cozy. They're going to have to move fast before long."

"Miss Suki's all set to help them."

"Remember, no gun play unless it's absolutely unavoidable," said the captain.

"Aye, aye, Cap'n. I figure that's why Miss Suki's along, to help remind me o' my manners." There was the sound of a slap and Firebrandt could easily imagine her whacking him in the arm. The captain smiled.

"You're absolutely right about that, el-Din. Mind your manners and bring her back safe. Understand?"

"Aye, aye, sir."

Firebrandt signed out, then scanned the command deck, eyes roving from Computer to Lowry at the helm, to the chronometer. "Message from the *Silver Cloud*," said Computer. "They have guests aboard."

Firebrandt pointed to Lowry. "That's our cue."

The *Legacy* moved forward and jumped across thousands of light years into the Alpha Coma Berenices star system, one of the oldest and most prosperous human colonies in the galaxy. A ship with the green stripes of Alpha Coma customs was docked to the *Silver Cloud* and a second one maneuvered toward the *Big Ben*.

"We're receiving a message from Alpha Coma customs," reported Computer.

"Ignore them, proceed with our plan," said the captain, staring into the hologram.

Roberts reached over and activated a series of commands on his console. The *Legacy's* hatch opened and they carefully removed the shuttle pod of lumber, which left a mass where the customs officials were no doubt scanning for one. As soon as the grappler arms were stowed and the hatch closed, Lowry activated the intrasystem jump engine and jumped directly into Alpha Coma's orbit.

Firebrandt toggled the launch boat intercom. "Go!"

Aboard the launch boat, Kheir el-Din released the clamps hold-ing it to the ship and dropped down into Alpha Coma's atmo-sphere. Suki looked over at Benjamin and R.J. Driscoll, holding hands. She could tell that Benjamin had once been a robust and big man, but his unshaven face had become pale and drawn. R.J. reached out and stroked Benjamin's hair. Suki wondered if her mother would touch her father like that and she began to understand there could be value to intimacy. When Suki looked up, she saw the resolve and hope in R.J.'s eyes.

Kheir el-Din homed in on the cancer center in Alpha Co-ma's capital city of Shangri-La. He darted through traffic and shot between buildings. Suki thought for a moment Benjamin would throw up. Then she realized she might be the one to get sick, the way el-Din was flying. Finally, the helmsman brought the launch boat to a smooth landing at the cancer center's emergency launch pad.

Suki unstrapped herself from the seat, then she and R.J. helped Benjamin stand. Together, they guided him into the emergency reception area of the Alpha Coma hospital. Once the hospital staff got over the shock of the appearance of a non-emergency vehicle, they began asking routine questions about payment and addresses. Suki loitered just long enough to make sure the payment cleared and the visas Roberts forged for the Driscolls passed muster. As soon as she could, she gave R.J. Driscoll a quick hug, then ran back to the launch boat.

Ellison Firebrandt paced the *Legacy's* deck, glancing frequently at the chronometer, then checking the holographic viewer for any sign of police traffic or a battleship. He breathed a sigh of relief when he saw the launch boat's trajectory displayed in the holographic viewer. "Move to intercept," he ordered.

Nicole Lowry did as she was ordered. Ten minutes later Roberts looked up. "They're aboard."

"Back to the convoy," ordered the captain.

The *Legacy* jumped back to the other ships, still engaged

with the customs officials. They retrieved the shuttle pod of lumber, then immediately made for the nearby jump point. The customs ships soon disengaged and pursued the *Legacy*. Firebrandt ignored them as he gave the order to jump. Within five minutes, the *Big Ben* and the *Silver Cloud* appeared by the *Legacy's* side.

"I think it's time to finish this journey and drop off our cargo at Earth," said the captain. "Hauling freight is proving to be a little too hair raising for me," said the captain.

"Me, too!" Roberts rubbed his hand over his bald head and the two friends laughed at the old, shared joke.

☠

The next day, Ellison Firebrandt stood with Suki on the *Legacy's* command deck. They watched as the *Silver Cloud* and the *Big Ben* peeled off, going their separate ways. Good as his word, Roberts found dockside jobs for the crew of the *Big Ben*, who promised to contact the *Legacy* if they needed any help retrieving their captain and her husband.

"You know, that was a noble thing for a pirate—" she stopped short at the look he shot her "—for a privateer to do."

Firebrandt pursed his lips as he considered that. "In a very real way, this shows the difference between the two ideas. You see, a privateer is not merely a pirate hiding behind an official letter from the government. If I wanted to steal, I would be happy to do so without Earth's permission. I'm perfectly capable of stealing without getting myself hung, shot or vaporized, thank you very much."

Suki's eyebrows came together. "Then why not just be a freelance shipping merchant like the Driscolls or Captain Melendez?"

"Because the universe—and humans in particular—aren't always just. Sometimes, it takes a privateer to set things right."

She reached out and took his hand. "Is it wrong of me to hope for a day when that's no longer true?"

He squeezed her hand and looked out at the Earth below and the stars beyond. "Not at all. I hope for it all the time."

Chapter Six
Gun Runners

A knock sounded at the captain's door.

He looked up and rubbed tired eyes. He'd just been going over accounts, his least favorite part of being a ship captain. He'd much rather face down an angry, well armed merchant crew than balance the books. "Come in."

Suki entered the cabin holding a bottle and wearing a stylish, long coat reminiscent of the one he owned. "I bought you a present down on Earth."

She handed him the bottle. He shook his head, not able to read the language on the label. "Alcohol of some kind, I take it?"

"Sake," she explained with a grin. "I was just down in Japan, doing some shopping." She walked over to the captain's cabinet and retrieved two glasses.

The captain scowled and set the bottle down on his desk. "I've never acquired a taste for sake, to be honest."

"So you told me." She grabbed the bottle and filled the glasses with milky liquid. "This is different. It's nigori—unfiltered sake."

The captain lifted the glass, took a sip and smacked his lips appreciatively. "I do like that better than other sakes I've tried. It's just a little sweeter."

Suki took off the coat, sat down on the couch, and beckoned the captain over.

"Are you trying to get me drunk and have your way with me?" The captain lifted an eyebrow and took another sip of the nigori, glad to be distracted from the accounting.

"Perhaps." Suki gave him a wry smile. "While I was on Earth, I made some discrete inquiries…"

The captain stood up from the desk and shook his head. "This isn't about the paintings in the hold again, is it?"

She sipped her sake, then set the glass down on the table beside her. "Why do you resist doing anything about the paintings?"

He sat down on the couch beside her. "It's easy to find people who will take the paintings. It's even easy to find people who will spend a lot of money for the privilege of being their caretaker. The hard part is finding someone who has the right facilities and the ability to keep them safe for generations. I have people investigating. We need to be careful."

She reached into the pocket of her new coat and retrieved a data chip. "Now you have a few more contacts to investigate."

Firebrandt took the chip. "I'll check them out, but I make no promises."

She took another sip of the sake, then leaned against the captain.

He sighed and forced himself to relax. It wouldn't hurt to have more possible buyers. He'd go over them himself, then forward any that looked promising to his contact on Earth. He put his arm around Suki's shoulder.

Before they progressed to anything more intimate, the intercom sounded. "Sorry to interrupt, sir," said the first mate, Roberts. "We just received a funeral announcement … I thought you should know."

"Funeral announcement?" The captain sucked in air and extracted his arm from Suki. There was only one funeral announcement he cared about that might arrive while they were in Earth's system. "Relay it down here."

The captain took a gulp of the nigori, set the glass down, then walked over to his desk. Suki followed and stood beside him. He reached up and she took his hand. A holographic image of a man in a tailored black suit and sunglasses appeared. "My name is Wilbur Wright. I am sending this message to all who knew and worked with my brother Orville. He recently passed away and we are holding services for him on Luyten b. He left a valuable legacy behind and it's critical that all who knew him travel to Luyten b in one week's time to participate in the funeral so his heirs may have closure. There will be just compensation."

Suki yelped and the captain realized he held her hand in an iron grip. He let go. "Sorry."

"I take it this wasn't news you expected." Suki rubbed her hand.

The captain shook his head. "I feared this day would come all right." He tapped the intercom button. "Roberts, take a look at that funeral announcement, I'm on my way to the command deck."

Without waiting for a reply, the captain left his quarters with Suki trailing behind him. He noticed she left her coat behind. He hoped that was because she planned to return and not mere forgetfulness. They reached the command deck just as the man in the tailored black suit said, "There will be just compensation."

"I presume Orville was your contact back on space station Xiūxí qū sān," said the captain.

Roberts grunted. "The ubiquitous Mr. Wright," he affirmed.

Firebrandt turned to face Computer. "How'd we get the message? Was that a general broadcast?"

The wraith-like man with stringy hair sat stock still. His eyes scanned lazily from side to side. "Tight beam aimed directly at the *Legacy*."

"No doubt coded for the benefit of anyone listening in." Firebrandt planted his fists on his hips. He turned to Suki. "How's that second intrasystem jump engine coming?" He referred to the nodal point generator that allowed any ship to make short faster-than-light jumps within star systems.

She narrowed her gaze. "Not as well as I'd like. There are some chips in the device I'd have to make from scratch. I'd need some time in a top-notch electronics lab with a laundry list of materials."

The captain quirked an eyebrow. "And you're presenting me with a list of … art collectors?"

She shrugged. "My shopping list is on the chip I gave you, but I knew you were busy doing accounting. I figured that could wait."

Firebrandt rubbed the bridge of his nose. "I'm afraid it can't wait anymore. Wilbur expects us to bring him the jump engine."

"I take it Wilbur Wright isn't a relative or close friend."

Roberts inclined his head toward the still image of the man in the holographic tank. "His 'brother' is the reason we have the nodal point generator in the first place. They've figured out we have it."

"And they want it back," finished the captain.

"If I had an unlimited budget, I could get you something in about a month."

The captain grimaced thinking about his accounting figures. "What does your current version do?"

She shrugged. "It'll open a nodal point and allow a ship to jump out of normal space. After that, it depends on how it's programmed. Most people who use it won't be coming back."

"For these people, I think that will be good enough. I doubt they'll test it themselves and if they do … they won't be our problem anymore."

She shot him a horrified look.

He reached out and took her hands. "Look, I don't know who these people are. If I'm hesitant to give the artwork in the hold to the first people I meet, you can bet I'm even more hesitant to hand the intrasystem jump engine over to just anyone who might have heard of it and have the resources to track it down. How long will it take you to polish up what you have, make the displays work correctly and look as correct as possible."

Suki swallowed. "I think I can do it in three days."

"We have a week," said the captain. "I think that gives us time to sample a little more of that fine nigori before you get to work."

Roberts reached out and grabbed the captain's arm. "Are you sure trying to trick these people is wise? It might be better to hide."

"We can't afford to hide," said the captain, "and these people knew just where to send their message. I hope giving them something will buy us some time. What's more, they say there's a reward." The captain lowered his voice and whispered in Roberts' ear. "We need anything we can get to pay the crew."

Roberts nodded, but his frown stayed in place.

Firebrandt patted him on the shoulder, then led Suki back to his cabin.

Suki sat at a computer console near the counterfeit nodal point generator. She ran a simulation. A holographic schematic appeared. The machine generated a divot that would allow a space ship to jump beyond normal space. Everything looked correct to that point.

She then simulated the machine's functionality in the beyond. That's when things went wrong. In the beyond, time no longer behaved like time, but like length, width, and height. The true nodal point generator used crystals found on high gravity, hot worlds. When Quinnium particles were fired through them, microprocessors could convert time as measured in the beyond to time as measured in normal space.

She substituted a normal microchip timer for the special timer and the simulations produced near-random results for the same passage of time. The formulas required to generate the return nodal point needed to measure time precisely. If only a little time passed, a nodal point solution converged and the ship could move back into normal space. It might be a rough ride, but the crew would survive.

Most of the time, the ship moved too far. Sometimes it shot far away from the star where the nodal point solution would not converge, trapping the crew in the beyond forever. Other times, it slung the ship back toward a system's largest nodal point, the star itself.

The graphic simulation was clean, but every time the dot which represented the ship bounced into the nearby sun, she cringed.

Nicole Lowry walked in during a failed simulation. "That doesn't look good." She glanced over at the device. "That, on the other hand, looks excellent. It would fool me."

"That's the problem." Suki shook her head. "I could imagine someone installing this in a ship to test it out. According to my simulations, five times out of six they're going to die a horrible death. It would be kinder if I just pointed a hepler at them and blew their heads off."

"Dice roll of one in six. Those ain't bad odds." Lowry shrugged.

Suki shot her a withering glare then held up her hands. "I don't want to be responsible for those lives."

Lowry held Suki's hands and shushed her. "My own hands have taken far more lives than I want to count and yet you don't shudder when I touch you."

Suki squeezed Lowry's hands hard. "Thing is, I don't know who is going to test this engine. More than likely they're on our side from Earth."

"Our side?" Lowry shook her head. Suki released her hands and Lowry pulled up a stool next to the workstation. "We're pirates, love. No one's on *our* side."

Suki sniffed and choked back a gasp. "What about the captain's letter of marque?"

"The captain makes a big deal about his letter of marque, but truth be told, the people who issued that scrap of paper would come out and cheer us on as we danced from the gallows just as much as the people they're fighting against." Lowry turned her head and it looked as though she would spit. Instead, she just snorted a bitter laugh. "All the letter of marque really gives us is some guaranteed business. It only protects us when it's convenient for Earth to protect us."

Suki closed her eyes and collected her thoughts. "So it wouldn't bother you if a shipload of engineers and scientists vanished while attempting to use my counterfeit generator."

Lowry took a deep breath then shrugged. "Depends on whether I knew them or not." She walked over and put her hand on the counterfeit device. "Truth is, I don't think this is an Earth device."

Suki agreed with that assessment. The device would need truly expensive materials to duplicate. That pointed to Alpha Coma, or private industry—possibly illegal industry. No trademarks or ownership information adorned the device. Governments insisted on stamping their ownership on items that belonged to them. What's more, she'd checked the news feeds about the device. It was the best kept secret she'd seen.

If a government had built the generator, they shouldn't have needed pirates to transport it from one point to another—unless that government had spent all of its money on the parts. Suki chewed her lip as her doubts resurfaced.

Before Suki could find words to answer Lowry, Roberts appeared at the door. "We're getting close to Luyten b. Captain wants to know if the device is ready."

Suki couldn't bring herself to answer or even nod. Lowry

folded her arms and grinned. "Looks just like the real thing to me."

Roberts pursed his lips and frowned. He took a step closer. "May I check?"

Suki stood up and gestured for him to take the chair. Instead of sitting, he approached the device and activated the small keypad next to a view screen. He nodded to himself. "I wouldn't be able to tell the difference between the real one and this one without performing a scan for the rare components."

Suki caught her breath. "Do you think they will?"

"Not unless they think we're playing them false." Roberts shook his head. "If they're smart, they'll scan it before they try to use it. Even then, I suspect they'll just think we stole the components and substituted them. They'll probably replace them before they try to use it."

"You think so?" The words came out like a relieved sigh.

"If they're smart," reiterated Roberts. He looked from Suki to Lowry. "Now get this thing unplugged from the test apparatus and bring it down to the launch bay."

"Yes, sir!" Lowry gave the first mate a sharp nod.

Two hours later, Roberts ran through the preflight checks aboard *Legacy's* launch boat. Nicole Lowry sat beside him and the counterfeit nodal point generator was strapped to the wall behind them. Once they received word from the command deck, they released the docking clamps and floated from the launch bay.

Below them rotated Luyten b, a rocky world covered in a gray haze of pollution from the mines and factories that dotted its deforested surface. Beyond the planet, Luyten's Star glowed bright red, as though angry at what humans had done to the world that circled it every eighteen days.

The launch boat descended to an abandoned factory sitting on a salty, unnaturally still ocean's shore. Another launch boat waited on the tarmac beside a monolithic concrete structure with broken-out windows and crumbling walls. Roberts touched down, then slumped in the seat, feeling the so-called super earth's extra gravity, over twice Earth's gravity. Most colonists who moved to Luyten b developed good leg and arm muscles in short order.

With a force of will, Roberts unbuckled the restraints, then went back to the nodal point generator. Lowry followed and retrieved an antigravity sled. Heavy under normal gravity, the nodal point generator was almost too heavy for just the two of them to manage in Luyten b's gravity.

They both sighed relief once they wrestled the generator onto the antigraviton sled. Roberts opened the door and both coughed at the noxious air that entered. Roberts' eyes watered and he scrubbed them with his sleeves. It wouldn't do for the buyers to perceive tears.

Roberts trudged out onto the tarmac. As they strolled toward the other ship, men swaggered toward them. A man in a tailored blue suit and sunglasses stepped away from the others. Despite his forced swagger, he seemed to have as much trouble negotiating the high gravity as Roberts. Clearly these men weren't settled colonists. No surprise there.

The man removed his sunglasses briefly. His eyes were red from the pollution, but he did bear an uncanny resemblance to the man called Mr. Wright they'd met on space station Xiūxí qū sān. Was it possible they really were brothers?

Without prelude, "Wilbur Wright" stepped up to the nodal point generator and activated the touch pad next to the screen. He browsed through the menus. He tapped in a couple of commands. Lowry backed up a couple of steps. Roberts shot her a cold glance, to remind her not to telegraph this was a counterfeit.

Wright summoned one of the other men forward. He held a handcomp and walked along the generator. He nodded to Wright, who shut down the device.

"This is satisfactory." Mr. Wright reached for the handle on the anti-gravity sled. Roberts put his hand on top of the mysterious stranger's.

"There's the matter of payment."

"Ah yes, I almost forgot." Mr. Wright nodded to his companion, who tapped the handcomp.

Roberts' own handcomp beeped. He retrieved it and stared at the numbers displayed there with a furrowed brow.

"The numbers are coordinates to a cache of forgotten

weapons here on Luytens b," explained Mr. Wright. "Take
them to space station Xiūxí qū wū and redeem them for your
payment."

"If they're weapons, what's to stop us from finding another buyer?" Lowry's brow furrowed.

Wright shrugged. "They're mostly outdated hardware.
Take 'em wherever you like, but you'll get what you truly deserve from the people waiting at the space station." Wright
reached for the anti-gravity cart again.

Roberts shook his head. "You can do better than that."

Wright nodded to his companion again, who again typed
on the handcomp. Roberts checked his display. This time he
noted a nominal payment added to one of *Legacy's* unmarked
bank accounts. It would be enough to pay the crew for a week
and cover fuel to the space station. Not great, but not bad—especially if the weapons haul worked out. By this point, Roberts
figured he'd protested enough to convince Mr. Wright and his
companions that the nodal point generator was authentic.

Wright reached for the anti-gravity cart a third time.

Again, Roberts put his hand on top of Wright's. "The cart's
ours."

Wright inclined his head, then beckoned his people over.
They hefted the nodal point generator off the cart. Apparently
a couple of these people were used to Luyten b's gravity. They
seemed to have little trouble hauling the device over to their
ship.

Roberts and Lowry returned to the launch boat. Once they
were aboard and airborne, Lowry leaned over the armrest.
"What do you think of that? Ripped off, if you ask me!"

Roberts shook his head. "I don't know what to think, other
than feeling like it's worthwhile to see what these weapons are
like."

They circled the planet until they came to a muddy bog.
Trapped gas under the bog occasionally broke free with a sp-
loosh. The *Legacy's* first mate searched around for a dry spot.
Failing to find one, he settled on hovering as close to the coordinates as he could manage.

He opened the launch boat's back door and the rotten-egg
smell of sulfur wafted in. Roberts pulled his undershirt up over

his nose and looked out. A pair of cargo crates jutted from the mud. He could just reach the handle of one. Hefting as hard as he could, he just made the crate move. He called Lowry over, who helped him heave the crate into the shuttle. They repeated the maneuver with the second crate.

Foul-smelling mud oozed to the deck. Roberts did his best to find the crate's lid. Opening it, he discovered top-of-the-line hepler rifles. "Outdated hardware my ass," said Roberts.

"They're just giving us this stuff?" Lowry shrugged.

"Looks like a dumped shipment to me. I'm guessing Mr. Wright and his buddies got a line on it and found a buyer. Saves them having to pay much for the nodal point generator and gets us out of their way."

"So, back to the ship?"

Roberts scanned the crates to make sure they didn't contain any locator beacons. At last he nodded. They closed the launch boat's hatch, then resumed their seats.

On the way back to *Legacy*, Roberts called Firebrandt and briefed him.

"We don't have any enemies in that sector of the galaxy," said the captain. "I think we should find out what the buyers are willing to give us."

"I don't like it. I think this is a setup," said Roberts. "I think we should dump the guns where we found them."

"That's probably the smart choice," Firebrandt conceded as the launch boat approached the ship. "Thing is, I'd like to know who's paying Mr. Wright. I think we might get a clue when we meet the gun buyers. The information alone might be worth more than the engine or the guns."

"This could be an elaborate setup to get rid of us," muttered Roberts.

"They could have destroyed us here at Luytens b if they wanted that," suggested the captain. "They still want something."

Roberts turned off the intercom, his gut churning. It seemed likely Mr. Wright and his friends knew they'd been given a counterfeit engine and were after the real one.

"So, I guess we're gun runners now," said Lowry.

"We're running all right. I just wish I knew what we'll find at the end of the race," grumbled the first mate.

Firebrandt watched station Xiūxí qū wū on the holographic viewer at the front of the command deck as *Legacy* approached. Like its sister station, it was a lusterless, pitted silver wheel. Ships occupied all the docks save one. Although of different makes and models, the ships all appeared to be a similar recent vintage and high quality manufacture—much too nice to be doing business at such an old station. Also, there seemed too many ships to just purchase a couple of crates of hepler rifles, no matter how new.

The captain looked down at his boots and considered a strategic retreat, but when he looked back up, he could picture all those ships pursuing him. All those ships that probably knew he shouldn't have a nodal point generator aboard.

The captain glanced over at his first mate. Roberts crossed his arms and glared. The captain didn't have to hear it. He could imagine Roberts saying, "I told you so."

"Any chance of tapping into the computers of the ships docked at the station?" Firebrandt waved his hand at the holographic display.

Roberts shook his head. "Locked down tight." Just like the man's clenched jaw.

"What about the station?"

Roberts relaxed at that and nodded slowly. "Now there's a thought, let me see what I can do."

His first officer occupied, Firebrandt turned his attention back to Kheir el-Din. "Bring us in to the open docking bay."

The helmsman nodded and executed the commands. Half an hour later, the docking clamps locked onto *Legacy*'s bow. Firebrandt pointed to Lowry. "Let's get those hepler rifles and see who our buyers are."

Lowry gave him a curt nod and went to the docking bay.

"I have no idea who those ships belong to," reported Roberts, "but they all docked within the last day. They're working together."

Firebrandt frowned and left the command deck. He climbed down a ladder and entered the docking bay. There, he grabbed a hepler, made sure it had a full charge, then tucked it into his coat pocket. He decided not to take a sword. After all, this was supposed to be a friendly meeting.

Lowry and one of her assistants pushed the hepler rifles into the docking bay on anti-gravity sleds. They opened the door and entered the space station. The place could do with a good paint job. A lightbulb overhead flickered.

A moment later, the door at the other end of the docking bay opened. A dozen men came through and took up positions, each holding hepler rifles. A moment later, a man in a fashionable brown suit and slicked-back hair entered. Firebrandt's blood ran cold.

Chris Bowman from Epsilon Indi.

"What a nice load of arms." He walked forward and opened one of the crates. He took out one of the rifles and examined it. "Premium merchandise."

"I trust we will receive payment in full," said the captain, putting his hands on his hips, letting them sit close to his own hepler pistol.

Lowry's gaze shifted from Bowman to the captain.

Bowman laughed. "For this, no. I can do as well ordering this stuff legally from a dozen arms merchants." He walked over to Firebrandt. "Besides, you owe me for that little power outage you arranged. Caused me no end of trouble."

"At least as much as that Gaean Alliance cruiser you called in to give me trouble, I'll wager."

"Oh, more than that." Bowman shook his head. "I didn't expect you to be the type to be taken in by a pretty face." He gazed over at Lowry. Firebrandt frowned, wondering if Bowman even remembered what Suki looked like. After all, Suki was Asian, while Lowry's ancestors were African.

"A sharp mind means more to me than a pretty face." The captain cocked his head. "If I just liked pretty faces, I might ask you to dinner."

Bowman barked another laugh. "That's what I like about you, Firebrandt, you've got a good sense of humor." He leaned close. "Here's the thing, I hear you have some rather remarkable treasures aboard your ship. I have some collectors here willing to give them a good home. I'll even split the take with you." Bowman made a show of running figures on his fingers.

"Say ninety percent for me and ten percent for you."

"Treasures?" Firebrandt narrowed his gaze. "I don't know what in the universe you're even on about."

"Don't play coy with me," growled Bowman. "The Mona Lisa, Bathsheba at her Bath, La Mousmé Sitting. I almost sense a theme and yet you didn't appreciate the gift I gave you." Again he cast a glance at Lowry. "Or maybe you appreciated it too much."

Firebrandt nodded. "All right, I'll sell them, but the split will be Fifty-fifty."

Bowman tutted and waggled his finger. "Twenty-Eighty."

"I'll consider forty-sixty, given that you brought the buyers."

"Thirty-seventy since I also have the armed soldiers."

The captain nodded. "I'll just go in and get the paintings."

Bowman grinned. "My friends here will accompany you." He stepped over to Lowry and grabbed her hand. "And your friend here will accompany me."

Firebrandt narrowed his gaze. Lowry gave him the briefest of nods.

"Very well," said the captain as he walked backwards toward the airlock. The soldiers followed. As the captain reached the ship, he turned around and pushed a button beside the airlock door. A moment later the soldiers entered as he continued through the airlock's second door. Both doors slammed shut and Firebrandt grabbed onto the wall as thrusters fired and the ship rolled away from the station.

The captain hit the button evacuating the airlock, which propelled the ship away from the station even faster. Fortunately, with no air, he couldn't hear the screams of Bowman's hired soldiers. For that, he was grateful. He strode back to the ladder and climbed up to the command deck.

He looked over to Roberts. "You heard."

"Bowman got word of some of our cargo somehow," said Roberts.

"I have an idea how, and I will tend to it."

He looked around and noticed Suki sitting at the engineering station, her shoulders hunched over and her hands folded in her lap. She understood that her inquiries may have tipped off Bowman.

"Nevertheless, this gives us an opportunity to do some pest control," said the captain.

"Shall I prepare the intraship jump engine?" Suki's question was almost too quiet to hear.

Firebrandt shook his head. "No, we want to move away at normal speed. They know enough as it is."

"Ships are starting to pursue," reported Computer.

Firebrandt looked to Roberts. "You have control of the station's computers?"

Roberts nodded.

"Take care of those ships."

Suki gasped. "Isn't Nicole aboard?"

Firebrandt didn't answer. Instead, he turned his gaze toward the holographic viewer at the front of the command deck. Ancient gunports on station Xiūxí qū wū opened and fired on the ships. The captain pointed to his gunner. "Open fire on pursuing ships as well."

The gun turrets on *Legacy* turned to the rear and opened fire. The first few shots bounced off electromagnetic shields, but the sustained fire from both the station and ship soon proved too much for the ships. One exploded in a bright flash, followed by a second. Soon other ships broke off and moved toward distant jump points.

"We don't dare let them get away," said Roberts, "not with what they know."

Firebrandt shook his head. "That's something we'll have to deal with later." He cast a meaningful glance at Suki, then turned his attention to the helmsman. "Take us back to the space station."

They docked within the hour. Firebrandt, Suki and Roberts entered the station. The captain patted the cases of guns left behind in the airlock. "We should get these back aboard. We should be able to sell them to someone for a decent profit."

Roberts nodded. "On it." With that, he returned to the ship.

Firebrandt strode forward to the corridor beyond the airlock. Suki followed. "I'm sorry I took matters into my own hands with the paintings."

"Now you know why I'm very careful with my inquiries."

"But Nicole … Did we have to sacrifice Nicole to that monster?" A tear fell from Suki's eye as they reached the space station bar.

Nicole Lowry sat at the bar nursing a drink. She looked up, shot back the drink, then made a face. "Thank god you came back, Cap'n."

Suki ran forward. "You're okay!"

"No thanks to the Cap'n here."

Firebrandt stepped forward and put his hand on Lowry's shoulder. "I knew you could handle Bowman."

"Oh, Bowman was no problem. The minute he heard you were bailing out, he ran to his own ship." Lowry made a face at the empty shot glass. "I'm talking about the booze on this station. Tastes like rocket fuel. You owe me some decent rum, Cap'n."

"It's a deal," said Firebrandt. "Just as soon as we sell those guns we acquired."

Chapter Seven
War Zone

Captain Ellison Firebrandt frowned at the graphical display of the ship's manifest that hovered over his desk. Roberts sat beside him, evaluating the information with his arms folded. They only had supplies to last another month and none of their contacts had sent them a new mission. That meant the privateer vessel would have to find its own supplies or return to an Alliance planet and release the crew from service until they received a new mission. Such a possibility could be disastrous, as most of the crewmembers would seek employment on other privateer vessels before *Legacy* was sent out again.

"What systems are in range?" asked the captain, stroking his bushy, red mustache.

"Sigma Draconis, Draperia, and Epsilon Eridani are all in jump range, but they're all strict, law abiding Earth colonies." The first mate pulled up a holographic chart, showing systems they could reach with their Erdon-Quinn engines. "They're all off limits unless we want to be hanged by our own government as pirates."

Firebrandt rubbed his neck, even though he knew it was far more likely they'd be vaporized than hung. He studied the map. Small labels floated near numerous star systems. Most of the labels indicated that the associated stars did not have habitable planets. The most interesting thing one was likely to find in those systems would be heavily armored robotic mining facilities where one would have to battle for hours in the confines of spacesuits. There certainly must be easier prey. The captain continued his examination and finally pointed at one of the stars. "What about this system?"

"Villanueva?" Roberts shook his head. "Only a madman would try to raid ships in that system."

"Why's that?" The captain narrowed his gaze and touched the system's holographic label. The hologram expanded, showing a yellow-orange star with eleven planets. Two of those planets were habitable by humans.

"Villanueva's a war zone. The two colony worlds in that system have been at each others' throats for nearly two centuries." Roberts shrugged. "I'd rather go to Draperia and see if someone needs a load of cargo taken somewhere, no questions asked."

"Those jobs never pay well." Firebrandt stepped over to a nearby bookshelf. He selected a pipe from a small rack, then tamped in some tobacco and lit it. He looked around his comfortable wood-paneled cabin while he savored the pipe smoke and considered his options. "War salvage pays a lot better than cargo runs."

"I really wouldn't advise going into a war zone, sir."

"Set course for the Villanueva system, Mr. Roberts. Let's find out what's worth fighting about for two centuries." The captain turned his back and continued smoking the pipe, his mind made up.

Roberts sighed. "Very well, sir."

A week later, Captain Firebrandt paced in front of the command deck's holographic tank, smoking his pipe, his hands clasped behind his back. The hologram showed the system's two worlds, Prosperity and San Miguel. Prosperity was a blue-green world, not dissimilar to Earth. San Miguel was a little closer to its star—a desert world with a handful of large lakes. It reminded Firebrandt of Mars after it had been terraformed. What the holographic viewer didn't show was any wreckage that could be salvaged. Moreover, the viewer showed no ship traffic at all.

Suki Mori eyed the tank with her head inclined. "Do you suppose they killed each other off?"

Roberts, sitting at his station, shook his head. "No. We're picking up transmissions from the two planets. There are people alive on each of them and the transmissions are completely mundane—news of elections, the occasional robbery, weather forecasts, sporting events, things of that sort." He touched a control and displayed one of the newscasts on his monitor. "Something does seem out of place, but I can't quite put my finger on it."

Firebrandt took a puff of the pipe, then exhaled a smoke ring toward the holographic display of the two worlds. The ring moved around the planet called Prosperity. "There aren't any ships, but that doesn't mean there's nothing at all. Scan the planets. Is there something besides ships near them? Satellites? Radiation? Energy?"

Roberts activated the ship's scanners—an action he'd avoided up until that point, since it could give away their position. His forehead creased and he nodded slowly. "There's some kind of strange time-warp signature near each planet. It's like the EQ field our engines generate, but stable. Nothing's actually moving. The areas of time disturbance seem to be orbiting each of the planets."

A grin slowly formed under Firebrandt's mustache. "That doesn't sound like any technology available in the Gaean Alliance. I wonder what it's for?"

Roberts stood and stepped toward the captain. "So far, the only applications of EQ technology have been faster-than-light travel and weapons—and all the weapons applications have been banned—for good reason, I might add."

Firebrandt nodded and clasped his pipe in his teeth. The problem with EQ weapons was their inherent instability. You could make things disappear in time, but you never knew where they would reappear. To make things move in space as well as the temporal dimension, you needed a container—such as the Erdonium hull of a spacecraft. "Well, whatever it is these people are doing with time warps, they appear to be stable. I think it's worth checking out."

Roberts folded his arms, but nodded slowly. "I agree, but we need to be very careful."

"I'm always careful, Mr. Roberts," said the captain. "Set course for Prosperity. It has the ring of good fortune to me."

The *Legacy* arrived at Prosperity later that day. The black privateer vessel slipped into an easy orbit. Normally it was something of a challenge to find a stable orbit around an inhabited planet when the ship didn't call for clearance ahead of time. However, nothing orbited the planet other than the strange time bubble—and that was easy to avoid.

Firebrandt held onto one of the rails that lined the command deck while Roberts scanned the planet and the time bubble. The first mate rubbed his hand along his bald head. "There seems to be a whole network of facilities on the planet generating a considerable amount of EQ energy. My guess is they're related to the time bubbles somehow."

The captain nodded. "Have you formed any theories about what the time bubbles are actually for?"

The first mate licked his lips and sat back. "No. I have no idea what they're for, but I have discovered one thing. They're not perfectly stable."

Firebrandt's eyebrows came together. "Is there a danger?"

Roberts stood and joined the captain in front of the holographic display. "I don't think so. The bubbles are growing very slowly. It's slow enough I missed it at first."

"At what rate?" asked the captain.

Roberts shook his head. "It's not a constant growth. Just every now and then, the bubbles expand, maybe a thousandth of a percent."

"That's tiny," declared the captain.

"Relatively speaking," said Roberts. "The bubble around Prosperity is the size of a large moon—somewhere around the size of Ganymede or Titan in the home system, I'd guess."

Firebrandt was silent for a time as he studied the images of the planets. "So, you think this network of EQ generators is related to the time bubbles?"

"I can't think what else they'd be used for unless the people here are trying to move their planets, but all data indicates the planets are right where we expect them." Roberts stepped back over to his console and checked the display. "It looks like one of the EQ generating facilities just crossed the terminator into night. That would be a good one to check out."

"Let's do it," said the captain. "Assemble a landing party. I'll be at the launch bay in a few minutes."

The captain strode from the command deck to his quarters. Inside, Suki read one of the captain's leather-bound volumes. She put a marker in the book and looked up. "Well, what's the verdict?"

Firebrandt explained about the EQ generating facilities

Roberts discovered. "We're going down to investigate." He opened the closet and retrieved a belt with a holster and a scabbard. Then, he retrieved a saber and slid it into the scabbard and picked his favorite hepler pistol.

Suki stood. "Could I come along? We don't get many chances to leave the ship. It would be good to stretch my legs."

The captain started to protest, but cut himself short. There were no war ships or signs of battle on the planet. He really couldn't see any danger at all. "Very well, but you'll need to be armed. There may be some kind of danger we don't know about."

Suki swallowed hard, but nodded. "Very well, Captain."

Reaching into the closet, he retrieved another holster and sidearm and passed them to Suki. "Have you ever fired one of these before?"

Suki studied the gun. "Not this exact model, but my dad used to take me out target shooting with high-energy pulsed rays."

Firebrandt frowned. "This might have a little more kick than you're used to. Use it only if it's an emergency. When we get back, I'll take you to the ship's firing range."

"I'd like that," said Suki.

Together, the two left the captain's cabin and went to the ship's launch bay. Roberts had a crew of three assembled. "I've briefed the crew," he said. "For now, we're just going down to see what's on the surface we might be able to use."

The captain studied the faces of his crew to see if anyone had a question. Satisfied that they understood, he opened the launch's door and ushered the landing party inside. Settling into the pilot's seat, Firebrandt initiated the launch sequence. The man known as Computer called from the command deck and gave them the all-clear. Firebrandt guided the small craft out of its pocket on the side of the privateer vessel.

Through the window, the captain could see the bright blue-green world. In many ways it reminded him of Earth. As they crossed the terminator toward the planet's night side, he realized something was very different and he had missed it when he'd studied the holographic representations of the planet. Few visible lights dotted Prosperity's night side. Usually that implied a rather small population or a primitive colony. Of course, if Prosperity hadn't been trading with other worlds, it certainly could have reverted to a rather primitive state. However, that didn't mesh with the network of EQ generators on the planet.

Firebrandt guided the craft to a grassy field near the coordinates Roberts had given him. Performing a quick scan, Roberts confirmed what the *Legacy's* instruments had reported. The atmosphere was perfectly breathable. The captain opened the launch's hatch and stepped onto the ramp.

Grassy parkland with shrubs and a few trees surrounded the shuttle. Overhead hung a black sky dotted with stars. "Something doesn't feel right," he said. He reentered the launch and pointed to Roberts and three of the crewmembers. "You four come with me." He looked at Suki, then pointed to a young pilot, Alberto Rodriguez. "You two stay with the launch. Have it ready to go, just in case."

Suki stood and stepped up to Firebrandt. "What's the matter?" She looked around him through the door at the darkened parkland. "It looks perfectly safe."

"Looks can be deceiving." He rubbed the back of his neck. "Something's giving me goose bumps and it's not even cold outside. We'll look around. If it's safe, I'll come and get you or send Nicole Lowry for you."

Seemingly satisfied, Suki nodded.

Firebrandt led the rest of the crewmembers down the launch's ramp onto the grass. Roberts checked his portable scanner and pointed. After walking fifty yards in the direction he indicated, there came a crackling and a blue glow from behind followed by a loud pop.

The captain whirled around. "The launch! Where's the launch?" He ran back toward the place they'd left the small landing boat. Roberts and the others followed close on his heels.

Roberts checked his portable scanner. "I don't find any trace of it at all, aside from some cellular damage and fuel residue in the grass."

Firebrandt knelt down and touched the place where the landing pads had rested. It was clear the ship had been there. "They didn't take off, did they?"

"Not possible," said Roberts. "We would have felt the blast

from the rockets and seen them airborne if they had." The first mate shook his head then checked his scanner again. "I'm picking up some chronoton particles—like you'd find in the wake of an EQ jump."

Firebrandt pursed his lips and nodded. "Like an EQ jump," he repeated. "We were on our way to investigate a nearby EQ generator. I think that's the best place to find some answers."

"Agreed," said Roberts.

Firebrandt stood, straightened his jacket, pulled his side-arm and strode toward his original objective, trusting his crew was close behind.

Two hundred yards later, the ground began to slope downward. The captain paused and studied his surroundings. At the bottom of a depression stood a domed building with a large dish-antenna on top. Easing their way around the depression's rim they came to a place where they saw a covered doorway. Two guards with holstered side arms stood within the doorway talking to each other. Firebrandt pointed to the two men. Roberts grabbed a device from his belt and hurled it toward the guards. They looked down at it dumbfounded. A moment later, a sonic pulse knocked them off their feet.

The privateers ran down the side of the depression, and looked around. No more guards appeared and no alarm sounded. Checking the entry, Roberts found a button and pushed it. The door slid open.

No people occupied the domed building, just computers and electronics racks. Firebrandt ordered his men to drag the unconscious guards inside the building. Roberts stepped up to one of the computer consoles and began typing. "If I didn't know better, I'd say these people never expected to have their systems compromised. There are no passwords—no encryption of any kind. The only security seemed to be those two men outside."

"And they didn't look like they expected trouble." Firebrandt's eyebrows came together. "So who runs this place?"

Roberts opened a file and read the contents. "It seems this complex along with the others in the network are controlled from a city about five miles away. I think that's where we'll find the people behind this."

"And what exactly does this facility do?" asked the captain.

"As best as I can tell, it controls the time warp around San Miguel," said Roberts.

"San Miguel? But we're on Prosperity!"

Roberts simply nodded. "I think we'll need to go into town to get the answers we're looking for."

The captain considered that, then nodded. "Well, let's get going then."

☠

The walk to the nearby city was time-consuming, but walking took less time than waiting for the *Legacy* to send down the other launch. Also, sending down the second launch did not seem prudent until they knew what had happened to the first one. As they stood on a rise overlooking the city, Firebrandt noticed faint lights glowing from within many of the buildings, but there were no streetlights.

"It would seem no one goes out after dark," commented Nicole Lowry.

Firebrandt nodded and his mind turned over the possibilities. Had Prosperity developed a religion that prohibited people going out after dark? Could there be some danger their scanners had not detected?

"I just realized what seemed strange about the newscasts from this planet," declared Roberts a few minutes later as they reached the city's streets. "Every image was taken inside. I saw no pictures of anyone outside a building at all. Not for the sporting events, not for any of the on-the-scene crime reports..."

"Why don't they go outside?" asked Kheir el-Din, the other man in the party.

Nicole Lowry pointed to a sculpture in the middle of a park. "They've clearly put a lot of effort into making this a nice place to live."

A little further on, they passed a fountain made of a translucent, marble-like rock, but drained of all water. Kheir el-Din rubbed his hand around the inside, then pointed. "No coins on the bottom. This fountain hasn't been used in a long time."

"How close are we to the control complex?" asked the captain. "I think I'd like to get inside sooner than later."

Roberts nodded. "It's right around the corner."

The privateers passed one more building and Roberts pointed to a structure that seemed little different from others they had passed. There was a faint glow of illumination from within and they saw the first people they'd encountered aside from the guards at the EQ generator complex. One smoked a cigarette and another leaned against the inside of the enclosed doorway reading a book. The one who smoked looked up and started to speak just as Roberts and Firebrandt crept close and knocked them unconscious.

Roberts found the door unlocked. Stepping in, the privateers found a room filled with computer monitors. A group of people in brightly colored business suits had gathered around one big, central screen, studying it intently. The screen displayed a map. A symbol that looked a little like the top of the *Legacy's* launch was there and then vanished.

"If it was a San Miguel ship, why did they fire on it?" asked one of the assembled men.

"If it wasn't a San Miguel ship, who did it belong to?" asked another.

Firebrandt cleared his throat and the men in business suits turned around.

"Ah," said a man in a purple suit, "I gather you must be from the ship that landed in the woods."

Firebrandt leveled his sidearm at the man who spoke. "We are," he said. "That ship vanished. I want to know what happened to it."

The man who spoke took a step forward and raised his hands to indicate he was unarmed. Gray strands shot through his fair hair making it look a little like corn silk. Firebrandt gathered he must be the leader. "You are strangers to Prosperity?"

Firebrandt smirked at that remark, but nodded.

"I am General Szerbo and this is my staff." He indicated the men surrounding him. Firebrandt eyed them warily, but none of them made a move to attack. They just seemed perplexed by the strangers in their presence. "Do you mind telling me who you are?" asked Szerbo.

"We're ... travelers. Just passing through," said Firebrandt.

"Do you have a name?" asked Szerbo, narrowing his gaze.

"I do," said Firebrandt.

Szerbo pursed his lips, but did not pursue that line of questioning further. Instead, he pointed toward the door. "Are the guards dead?"

"No," said Firebrandt. "Merely knocked out." Even in these strange circumstances, the captain avoided killing unless necessary. He didn't want to alienate potential allies.

"Please bring them inside. They are in danger, exposed as they are," said the general.

Firebrandt nodded affirmation to Lowry and el-Din, then turned his attention back to the general in the brightly colored business suit. "What exactly is going on here?" asked Firebrandt.

"If you can't tell me your name, I really don't see why I should tell you anything about us," said Szerbo.

The captain drew his hepler pistol. "Hepler guns at close range are quite destructive and I want my property back."

The general sighed and indicated a table at the center of the room. "I assure you that won't be necessary. I'm unarmed, as is my staff. Let's sit and talk like civilized men."

Firebrandt nodded and holstered his hepler, but with a glance indicated that Roberts should stay ready. The first mate kept his hand on his pistol, as did the other two privateers.

Szerbo and Firebrandt sat at the table. "I thought everyone in the galaxy knew that we are at war with our neighbors on San Miguel," said the general.

Firebrandt shook his head. "We'd heard that, but there's no damage outside, no cratering, no evidence of fires. How are you at war?"

"We use EQ transmitters, like the one you landed near, to take anyone who happens to be in range and pull them out of time. We'll continue doing this until one side or the other has an advantage and then the winning planet will take over and all the prisoners in time will be released."

"Prisoners in time?" asked Roberts. "Is that what the time bubbles are that we sensed around your planet and San Miguel?"

"Indeed," affirmed General Szerbo. "We have created the perfect means of warfare. No one actually dies. No property is damaged. The only people at risk of becoming casualties are those outside—and hardly anyone goes outside."

"Why do you do this?" Roberts shook his head. "Why fight a war like this?"

The general held up his hands and shrugged. "You were outside. You've seen how we've been able to preserve the buildings and our art."

"But no one can enjoy them," said Nicole Lowry, a little sadly.

The general inclined his head. "But no one dies. When the war is over, the people will be back and we can enjoy them anew."

"Then Suki and my launch … they're inside one of these time bubbles?" Firebrandt sat back and rubbed his chin.

The general nodded. "If this Suki was aboard your vessel then yes and there they will remain until the war is over."

Everything they'd seen now made sense to Firebrandt. These people were at war, but the war was like a game. They didn't kill. Perhaps they didn't know how to kill. The launch was a big stationary target, so of course it had been grabbed. No one went outside, unless they had to, but the war continued, because occasionally people would have to go outside to repair something or take care of some task. It was so rare, though, that the war could go on almost indefinitely. It could be centuries before Suki would be free if he did not act. Firebrandt leaned across the table. "You will return my boat and my crewmembers now."

"I'm afraid I cannot," said the general. "They were captured by San Miguel. Their coordinates within the bubble are not in our computers. They're in the enemy computers."

Firebrandt drew his hepler pistol. "I demand you contact the San Miguel military. I want my launch and my crewmembers back. We're not part of your crazy war."

"I'm afraid I can't do that," said the general.

"Afraid you can't do that?" asked Firebrandt. The privateer captain gestured toward the general's staff with his gun. The privateers drew their swords and each one grabbed a member of the staff. "What you're afraid of is blood, and guts and the horror of war. With an order, I can have your people killed and it will not even be a clean vaporization." With a nod from Firebrandt, Lowry and el-Din pushed their hostages against the wall and held them at sword-point.

The remaining staff members backed away and General Szerbo's eyes went wide. "What are you doing?" he cried.

"I bet my three people can do more damage in one night than you and San Miguel have done to each other in two centuries." Firebrandt leveled his pistol right between General Szerbo's eyes. "You *will* contact the enemy, sir."

Szerbo looked down at his hands and finally nodded. "Very well."

He stood and went to a console. After a moment, a man with dark hair appeared on the computer screen. The man scowled. "General Szerbo, what is the meaning of this? Do you have any idea what time it is here?"

"We have a … situation here," said General Szerbo, sounding more embarrassed than anything else. He entered a command into the console and cameras moved. Firebrandt guessed that Szerbo must be sending a picture of the staff members at sword-point to the enemy general.

Firebrandt nodded to Roberts. The first mate stood and made his way to a different computer console. One of Szerbo's staff stepped up to him. "What do you think you're doing?"

Roberts put his hand on the man's sternum and shoved him to the floor. "Nothing you should concern yourself with."

The staff member started to stand and Roberts pulled his hepler. "I want you to sit right there and take it easy," said the first mate.

When the staff member relaxed, Roberts turned his attention to the computer.

"I'm sorry, General Velasco, but as you can see, we're under siege." Szerbo held his hands out to his side.

Firebrandt stepped up next to Szerbo and shoved him out of the way. "You have taken my ship and I understand you have the coordinates. I want it back!"

The man called Velasco shook his head. "The only way I can do that is to release all the time prisoners. I can't do that. We would lose the war."

The privateer captain leveled his hepler pistol at Prosperity's war computers. "If you don't do it, I'll destroy the computers here. If I understand correctly, that would be a death sentence for your people."

Velasco laughed. "Destroy a few computers in a network with backed-up information? Surely you must think I'm an idiot."

Roberts stood from the console where he was working and moved next to Firebrandt. "True, destroying these computers won't wipe out the data, but if I activate the virus I just programmed into the system, it will." The first mate looked at his captain. "Plus, I traced the call. I have the coordinates of General Velasco's headquarters."

"Very good, Mr. Roberts. You've just earned your pay for the week," said Firebrandt. He activated his commlink and called the *Legacy*. "Computer, I want you to make an intersystem jump to San Miguel. Mr. Roberts will transmit coordinates. Lock all weapons and destroy that facility on my mark. Do you understand?"

"I do," came the response from the man named Computer.

Velasco's eyes went wide. "What is the meaning of this?"

"How the planets in this system fight war is your business." Firebrandt folded his arms across his chest. "But once you've taken a member of my crew hostage, you've declared war on me. I don't intend your war with me to take two hundred years," he growled.

"Coordinates have been sent to the *Legacy*," reported Roberts.

"Very good," said the captain. He lifted his commlink and opened his mouth to speak his next order when General Velasco held up his hand.

"Stop! You win, Captain Firebrandt. We'll release those captive in the time bubble."

"Then that means we won, too," said Szerbo, with a sneer. "We'll have the forces to invade San Miguel."

Firebrandt sneered and held up his hepler pistol. "No, I think it's only fair that you both release all the prisoners."

Szerbo held his head up high. "I refuse to do that."

Firebrandt fired the hepler pistol, boring a hole through Szerbo's head.

He turned the hepler toward the others. "Anyone else have any high-minded ideas about who won this war?"

Szerbo's staff and even Velasco on the screen all shook their heads no.

"Then let's get to work," said Firebrandt.

Two hours later, Firebrandt and his crewmembers made their way through a city crowded with all the people who had been returned from captivity. Around the city, speakers announced that an armistice had been reached and the war was over. The walk out of the city took much longer than their walk through empty streets, but they finally reached the parkland and began the hike through empty countryside to the launch.

The captain breathed a relieved sigh when they found the ship where they left it. Suki stood in the doorway looking perplexed. "Where did you go? What did you find?"

Firebrandt rushed forward and grabbed Suki up in an embrace and kissed her deeply. She blinked at him and looked at Roberts. "What's going on?" she asked.

"Time would have stopped for her while she was in the bubble," said Roberts. "I'm guessing she has no clue what happened."

The captain nodded. "That's probably just as well." He looked at Suki. "What we found were a bunch of fools who treat war like a game. The problem is that if you get good enough, you find yourself in perpetual stalemate."

"Actually, both sides would have eventually lost," said Roberts.

Firebrandt's eyebrows came together in an unspoken question.

"The time bubbles represented huge entropy fields," explained the first mate. "It was only a matter of time before they imploded taking both planets with them."

Firebrandt shook his head and clucked his tongue. "Then we saved these planets from themselves," he said. "Too bad we didn't get more for our efforts."

Nicole Lowry and Kheir el-Din stepped forward and opened bulging pouches. "It wasn't exactly for nothing, Captain," said Lowry. "All those people in the street…"

"Pretty easy pickings, Cap'n," said el-Din.

Firebrandt's lips turned up in a wide smile. "I love me

crew," he said. He looked over to Roberts. "Still, I think we're going to need to find another job."

Roberts nodded. "Just promise me, no more war zones."

"Agreed," said the captain. With that, he led Suki back into the launch. The crewmembers followed with their loot and the door closed. Firebrandt activated the thrusters and the privateers flew into the sky, glad to leave Prosperity behind.

Chapter Eight
Jump Point Blockade

The privateer *Legacy* hung a short distance away from the asteroid designated MX-271. The asteroid housed an automated mining operation owned by the Xerolith Corporation based on New Earth. The *Legacy's* first mate, Carter Roberts, led the landing party. Roberts hacked into the mine's computer network and unleashed a virus he hoped would knock out the defense grid.

Nicole Lowry piloted the craft. She checked the scanners. "The asteroid's shields are disabled. I see no indication of weapons being powered up."

Roberts nodded, acknowledging the report, but he did not relax. Instead, he double-checked the readings himself. Once satisfied, he turned to Lowry. "Take us in, but be careful."

Lowry pulled back on the joystick and activated the landing rockets. "Your virus programs haven't let us down yet. I'm not worried."

"Neither am I, but that's no excuse to let our guard down." The first mate kept his eyes on the scanner readouts.

A few minutes later, the pilot pushed the joystick forward and shut off the rockets.

"So far, so good," said Roberts. He commanded the station's docking tunnel to extend and mate with the launch's airlock. Unbuckling his harness, he turned around and faced the landing party. "Let's see what goodies the New Earthers have left us." He drew his sidearm and opened the hatch.

Cautiously, Roberts crept into the docking tunnel. His nose wrinkled at the still, stale air. The only sounds he heard were the footsteps of the landing party behind him.

A lone defense robot, its weapons pointed impotently at the floor stood just within the airlock. The first mate remained silent, while his eyes roved the room. Occasionally mining complexes left a few defense robots unjacked from the network, to keep them immune from viruses. Such robots were usually sound activated.

Satisfied no defense robots prowled the entry area, Roberts indicated a door at the far end of the room with his hepler pistol. Nicole Lowry crept beside him and peered down the corridor, then activated a handheld computer. She nodded and gave a thumbs-up, signaling both a clear path and that they were heading in the right direction.

They proceeded down the corridor until they came to a gaping door that led into a vast, darkened space. Lowry activated a button just inside the door and banks of overhead lights flickered to life revealing a warehouse-like space containing processed bars of erdonium ore neatly stacked on anti-graviton carts. Roberts looked around to make sure no unjacked defense robots patrolled the storage area. Finally, he relaxed and holstered his hepler pistol. Turning to face the landing party, he smiled. "This should pay our salaries for a few months."

"All right, you swabs," called Lowry. "Start moving those anti-grav carts to the launch. Step to!"

Just as the *Legacy's* crewmembers began to fan out, the door to the storeroom slammed shut.

On *Legacy's* command deck, Computer stood against one wall. His eyes roved back and forth under a curtain of stringy hair as he communicated with the ship's computer under the metal grating beneath his feet. A moment later, his eyes ceased their near-constant motion and he turned to face the ship's captain, Ellison Firebrandt. "A New Earth battleship has just entered the system."

The captain—his long, red hair worn loose about his shoulders—spat a curse. "Contact Roberts. Tell him to get back to the ship as fast as he can."

Computer's eyes roved back and forth for a moment. "Sir, Mr. Roberts is calling us."

"Put him on," ordered the captain.

"Captain, something's gone wrong." Roberts's voice came through the intercom. "We just located the processed erdonium when the doors to the storage facility closed behind us. We're locked in. I've double checked the computer here. The virus is still active and defense systems are shut down."

"Could they have been commanded from outside?" asked Firebrandt.

"I suppose it's possible." Roberts sounded uncertain.

"A New Earth battleship just jumped into the system." Firebrandt stepped toward the front of the command deck and looked into the holographic tank. He saw a three-dimensional representation of a nondescript black cylinder hovering near a gray potato-shaped rock—the *Legacy* next to the mining asteroid. Some distance away, a marble-sized blue sphere that indicated the position of the New Earth battleship moved toward them.

"How could they know about us?"

"I don't know," said the captain. "Hang tight. We'll find a way to get you out of there."

"Captain, you should leave. We'll be okay till you get back."

"I'm not leaving you, Mr. Roberts."

A new voice cut in on the transmission. "This is Captain William R. Stewart of the Battleship *New New Jersey* calling the unidentified ship at MX-271. State your purpose in this sector." In the holographic tank, the blue sphere morphed into a menacing black cylinder bristling with gun ports. *Legacy's* scanners had obtained a clear reading of the ship.

Firebrandt scratched his beard and considered his previous encounter with Captain Stewart of the *New New Jersey*. He turned toward Computer and instructed him to open a channel. A moment later, Computer nodded.

"This is the Earth vessel *Dragonfly*," said the captain. "We've sustained micrometeorite damage and sent a party down to the asteroid to look for repair parts."

Firebrandt's transmission was greeted with silence. He stepped back toward Computer and made a slashing motion across his throat, then turned to face the helmsman, Kheir el-Din who stood at the ship's wheel console. "What are they up to?"

"Scanning us, I'll wager," said the helmsman. "Checking to see if we really are the good ship *Dragonfly*."

"What are they even doing here?" Firebrandt's eyebrows came together. "I thought the New Earthers were tied up with that stupid blockade of Alpha Coma Berenices's jump point to

Rd'dyggia. That's what made this seem like such a foolproof plan."

"The New Earthers say the Rd'dyggians are making weapons for the Alpha Comans." Kheir el-Din toyed with a short string of beads strung in his long, black beard. "I thought you would support the blockade."

The captain shrugged. "The Rd'dyggians make weapons for everyone. I have no objection to the blockade. I just don't see how it will do any good."

"MX-271 is on the jump path from the New New Jersey's patrol sector to the blockaded jump point," reported Computer.

The captain huffed and nodded. "They must have been summoned to the blockade."

"The *New New Jersey* is powering up weapons," said Computer. In the holographic viewer, a translucent sphere appeared around the battleship indicating the range of its guns. *Legacy* was nearly within that sphere.

The captain pointed to the helmsman. "Call Suki to the command deck. Prepare for emergency intrasystem jump."

"Yes, sir," said el-Din.

"This is Captain Stewart of the *New New Jersey*. We have scanned your vessel and determined that you are, in fact, the fugitive Gaean Privateer *Legacy*. Captain Firebrandt, I am authorized to destroy your vessel."

Firebrandt looked at the helmsman and mouthed the words, "Don't wait for Suki."

The helmsman swallowed, ran over to the engineering station and activated the intrasystem jump engine. He held up ten fingers, indicating that they would jump in ten seconds.

Stewart continued speaking. "Be advised that we have control of the computers on MX-271. If you attempt to flee, we will flood all the chambers with poison gas."

Firebrandt shook his head. "Belay emergency jump." He gathered his long, red hair into a ponytail and tied it behind his neck. "Captain Stewart, we surrender. Under the terms of the treaty between the Gaean Alliance and New Earth, we demand a trial."

"You are already fugitives, Captain Firebrandt. There's no need for a trial—and no time."

Firebrandt heard the urgency in Stewart's voice and thought fast. "Then take us with you," said the captain.

"What?" Captain Stewart shouted so loudly, the speakers crackled in response.

Firebrandt retrieved a pipe from his coat pocket, then a pouch of tobacco. "I'm sure you could use more ships to blockade the jump point at Alpha Coma. We'll join you. Once the blockade is over, we'll stand trial."

"Why should we bother?" Captain Stewart sounded skeptical.

Firebrandt tamped the tobacco into the pipe. "Mr. Roberts have you been listening in?"

"I have been," said the first mate. "I've been scanning both vessels. My scans show *Legacy* has not powered up her weapons and has lawfully requested a trial. I can transmit that data to Titan and the Gaean Alliance as soon as the *New New Jersey* engaged. That should start a pretty little diplomatic incident."

"A diplomatic incident for which the captain would be held responsible." Firebrandt put the pipe to his mouth and lit it.

"I can untangle a diplomatic incident and you'll be dead." Despite the coldness of the words, Firebrandt thought he heard a quaver of uncertainty in Stewart's voice.

"Is that really the best course of action?" countered Firebrandt. "After all, we are offering to help you."

Stewart remained silent for a few minutes. Firebrandt made the slashing motion across his throat again and looked at el-Din. "Don't shut down the emergency jump engines. I don't want to lose Roberts and his team, but we can't help them if we're dead."

"I'll slave them to my station." el-Din nodded and began preparations.

"We accept your offer," said Stewart.

Firebrandt smiled and signaled for Computer to turn on the microphone. "Then release our men. As soon as they're aboard, we'll follow you to Alpha Coma."

"No," said Stewart. "Your people stay where they are. There are rations at the mine that will last for a week. That's our rotation period at the blockade. Once the week is up, we'll escort you back here to retrieve them, then take you to New

Earth for trial."

"All right, we'll play it your way." Firebrandt clamped his teeth on the pipe stem and signaled for Computer to end the transmission.

"We're following Billy Bob Stewart where?" Suki Mori looked over the dinner table at Firebrandt.

"We're joining New Earth's blockade of Alpha Coma's jump point to Rd'dyggia." Firebrandt served himself rice. They sat at a table in the captain's wood-paneled quarters at *Legacy's* heart. Bookshelves lined two walls and an antique, brass lantern illuminated the room.

Suki shook her head. "But the *Legacy* displays the flag of the Gaean Alliance. Neither New Earth nor Alpha Coma are friendly with the Alliance. Is our involvement in their conflict even legal?" Eyes hardened by her time on crime-infested Epsilon Indi 2 bored into the captain.

Firebrandt shrugged. "As far as I could tell, the choice was get involved or be destroyed." He took a bite of bobotie—a dish of ground meat, fruit, nuts, and spices from his native South Africa—and washed it down with a sip of wine.

Suki leaned forward. "We're joining a blockade force, Ellison. Didn't it occur to you that we could be destroyed there just the same?"

"Of course. But the blockade's been going on for weeks with no sign that the Alpha Comans are challenging the New Earthers." Firebrandt took a bite of his rice and chewed it thoughtfully. "I'm sure the Alpha Comans are finding other ways to import their guns. Blockading the jump point doesn't prevent trade, it just causes the Alpha Comans to use a bit more fuel to get what they want."

Suki frowned. "Some of humanity's biggest wars have been fought over fuel and the right to possess weapons."

"You worry too much." The captain smiled and pointed to Suki's plate with his fork. "Eat, before your food gets cold."

"Captain." Computer's voice came over the intercom. "We're within scanning range of the blockaded jump point. We've received coordinates for our position in the blockade."

"Very well," said Firebrandt. "I'll come up and take a look."

He wiped his mouth with the napkin and stood. "Would you care to come and see our surroundings for the next week?"

Suki followed Firebrandt to the command deck. In the holographic tank, a floating golden sphere marked the jump point. Battleships, destroyers and dreadnoughts formed a greater sphere around the point in space where the temporal-gravitational tides came together to allow a direct jump from Alpha Coma Berenices to the planet Rd'dyggia.

Forming up in a ring outside the spherical blockade of New Earth ships was the Alpha Coma Navy. Firebrandt looked at the numbers displayed in the holographic tank. As far as he could tell, a large percentage of both navies were present.

Suki's eyebrows came together. "Why are the Alpha Coma ships in a ring? Why aren't they in a sphere as well?"

"Intimidation, Miss Suki," explained Kheir el-Din. "They hope to force the New Earthers into a single plane of combat. If the New Earthers move some of their ships, that'll create a hole the Alpha Comans can exploit to break the blockade."

"And if the New Earthers don't move?" pressed Suki.

"Then the Alpha Comans would hope to use their firepower to blast a gap in the New Earthers' sphere."

The *Legacy* followed the *New New Jersey* into the sphere. The *New New Jersey* took a position in the sphere. The *Legacy* flew past the battleship to a position facing an Alpha Coman heavy cruiser.

Suki folded her arms across her stomach and glared at Firebrandt. "Looks like we're right where the Alpha Comans will start blasting that gap. Billy Bob's using us as a shield, isn't he?"

"Well, we can always hope the Alpha Comans won't try to break the blockade before the *New New Jersey's* rotation is up," said Firebrandt with forced enthusiasm.

"There is a fleet-wide transmission," said Computer. "In light of Alpha Coma's increased presence in the area, all regular rotations out of the blockade have been canceled until further notice." Computer stood silent for a moment. "New Earth is diverting as many of their ships here as possible."

Suki shook her head. "Fuel … and weapons … and you didn't think the Alpha Comans would take the blockade seriously?"

Firebrandt nodded slowly. "I guess the Alpha Comans

were a little more put out than I thought." He turned to Suki. "I'll think of something."

She looked at the holographic tank and sighed. "I hope so—for all our sakes."

A week later, the situation remained unchanged. Ellison Firebrandt paced the length of the command deck, from the holographic viewer in the bow to the gunner's rigs, aft. He knew time was running out for his people at the mining asteroid. He had to get back there somehow. He pointed at Computer. "Open a channel to the *New New Jersey*."

"Yes, sir."

A moment later, the forward hologram dissolved into an office aboard the New Earth battleship. A young woman with blond hair sat behind a gray, metal desk that flowed out from the wall. "May I help you?"

"I would like to speak with Captain Stewart. This is Captain Firebrandt of the *Legacy*."

"May I inquire as the nature of the call?"

Firebrandt rolled his eyes. "Captain Stewart said we would only be here a week. I have a landing party on MX-271 that's nearly out of food. I request permission to retrieve them before they starve to death."

"Very well, Captain Firebrandt, I will inform Captain Stewart." The woman pushed a button on her desk. She then activated another button and spoke, but her words weren't audible. Apparently she had muted the conversation. After she delivered her message, she listened for a moment. Her eyes widened just a touch, but finally she nodded and spoke again. At last she pressed the button she had used to mute the call. "Captain Firebrandt, I'm afraid Captain Stewart is occupied. He reiterates that we have been ordered to hold position until we receive further orders."

Firebrandt narrowed his gaze. "Anything else?"

The woman swallowed and nodded. "He says your crew are nothing but a bunch of no-good pirates, what does he care if they starve? He said he didn't mind if I quoted him."

Firebrandt pursed his lips and nodded. "Thank you for your candor. Please give my regards to the captain." He turned to Computer. "Close the channel."

"Well, that's a right fine mess," growled Kheir el-Din.

"But not entirely unexpected," said the captain.

"What I don't understand is why nothing's happened this whole week." el-Din shrugged. "We've just been standing here staring at each other."

Firebrandt shook his head. "Neither fleet wants to be the first to fire. None of the captains are willing to risk their ships in combat." He turned and looked at the system schematic in the holographic viewer. They were only a few thousand kilometers from a jump point. It wasn't a jump point to a place they wanted to go, but they could easily find a jump path back to the asteroid. The only problem was the New Earth battleship that sat between them and the jump point.

Firebrandt considered the problem further. In a situation where neither side wanted to be the first to fire but nerves were on a razor edge, what could the *New New Jersey* actually do to prevent them from leaving? He looked back at Kheir el-Din. "Helmsman, plot a course to the jump point. We'll go to Rd'dyggia. From there, we'll find our way back to the asteroid."

"But sir, what about the *New New Jersey?*" asked the helmsman.

"I'm gambling if she fires on us, she'll have a whole lot more than us to deal with."

The helmsman flashed a toothy grin. "I like the way you think, sir." He set to work. A few minutes later, he looked up. "I have a course plotted."

"Shields to maximum. Back slowly toward the jump point. Once we're alongside the *New New Jersey*, begin powering up the jump engines," ordered the captain.

The *Legacy's* thrusters engaged and the ship slid toward the *New New Jersey*.

A moment later, Suki Mori strode onto the battle deck. "What's going on? I felt the engines engage."

"We're leaving," said the captain.

"We got permission from Captain Billy Bob?"

Firebrandt smirked. "Not exactly."

"We're getting a call from the *New New Jersey*," announced Computer.

"On audio—I want to keep an eye on what's happening," said the captain.

"This is Captain Stewart of the *New New Jersey*. Captain Firebrandt, you are ordered to return to your position."

"Ah, so now you'll talk to me," said Firebrandt. "A few minutes ago, we were nothing but dirty pirates."

"Return to your position, or I'll blast you out of the sky," growled Captain Stewart.

"I'd like to see what happens when you try," said Firebrandt.

"Sir, the *New New Jersey's* pulse cannons are tracking us," reported Computer.

Suki grabbed Firebrandt's arm. He sensed a silent plea not to provoke the battleship's captain further. He put his hand on hers, a gesture of reassurance, then he led her over to the wooden handrail at the side of the command deck and had her grab on. He did so as well.

"This is your last warning, Firebrandt!" barked Stewart.

"Let's see what you've got," said the Legacy's captain.

In the holographic tank, red letters flashed, indicating the *New New Jersey* had fired. A pulse blast shuddered through the privateer vessel. Suki fought to keep her grip on the railing.

"Our shields are down sixty percent," reported Computer.

Firebrandt didn't need any further explanation. Another blast like that would collapse the shields and breach the ship's hull. He watched the holographic display intently. Then, he saw exactly what he wanted, motion from the Alpha Coma ring.

"An Alpha Coma frigate has opened fire on the *New New Mexico*," reported Computer.

Firebrandt gritted his teeth. Pinpricks of light pulsed in the holographic viewer where the two warships exchanged fire. Other Alpha Coman ships approached. It was like a tightening collar.

"This is your last warning," said Stewart, apparently oblivious to the results of his actions. "Return to your position in the line."

A voice on the other end spoke. "Sir, the Alpha Coman heavy cruiser is advancing."

"All weapons forward," called Stewart. The channel abruptly shut off.

Firebrandt punched the air. "Let's get to the jump point before things get too hot."

"With pleasure," said el-Din.

The holographic viewer revealed weapons' fire erupting all around the Alpha Coma ring. The blockade sphere eroded as New Earth vessels moved in to assist those already engaged in battle. In the meantime, fast, lightly armored Alpha Coma ships shot away from the back of the ring and arced toward the jump point. However, they were sufficiently far away, they wouldn't reach the jump point before the *Legacy* did.

The *New New Jersey* had advanced and sat broadside-to-broadside with the Alpha Coman heavy cruiser. Shields had collapsed on both ships and hull plating whirled off into space as the ships unleashed their pulse guns at each other. Firebrandt wondered if the *New New Jersey* would survive the encounter. He would shed no tears if Billy Bob Stewart was a casualty of war.

"We're at the jump point," announced el-Din.

"Let's go get our people," said Firebrandt.

Three days later, the *Legacy* arrived at MX-271. The captain prayed they weren't too late. He was pleasantly surprised when Computer announced that Roberts signaled from the mining facility.

In the holographic viewer, a lounge with couches, comfortable chairs and holographic entertainment units appeared. Three of his crewmembers were gathered around a holo viewer watching an old movie. Lowry and Alberto Rodriguez sat hunched over a chessboard.

"Glad to see you all are having a nice shore leave. I thought Captain Stewart said there were only a week's rations at the station," said Firebrandt.

"In the warehouse area, yes," said Roberts. "There are also cutting tools. We were out of there a few hours after you left. Between the rations on the launch and the additional rations in the crew quarters here, we could have gotten by for at least two more weeks before we were worried."

Firebrandt nodded. "Well, I'm glad to see you're all right."

"Same here," said Roberts. "We've monitored the news frequencies. It sounds like the battle at Alpha Coma was rather nasty. Each fleet lost nearly half their ships before the New Earthers finally withdrew."

"Any word about the *New New Jersey?*" Firebrandt retrieved his pipe and began packing it with tobacco.

"Apparently Billy Bob Stewart is facing a board of inquiry. They say he fired the shots that started the battle."

"Couldn't happen to a nicer guy."

"In the meantime, we have a pretty cargo of erdonium all ready to bring up to the ship."

"Very good, Mr. Roberts." Firebrandt lit the pipe. "Care to try your hand at raiding any more of these New Earth asteroids while they're off licking their wounds?"

"I'm game, Captain—" he held up a foil ration pouch "—as long as we pack some better food next time."

"Oh no," said Firebrandt. "Next time, you get to go to the blockade, and I'll take the vacation!"

Chapter Nine
Between the Devil and the Cold Black Void

An enormous planet with bands ranging from lavender to deep violet hung in the holographic display at the front of *Legacy's* command deck. A swirling, oval storm danced across the planet's surface. An ID code that read OGLE-2008-BLG-92LAb drifted in the upper right corner of the holographic display. Suki Mori walked forward and put her hand on Captain Firebrandt's shoulder. "It's beautiful, but what are we doing here?"

The captain shrugged as the ship eased across the terminator to the planet's night side. "I have no idea why Earth command wants us here." As the ship continued its orbit, a pair of stars, little brighter than those in the background, became visible. The Neptune-sized planet orbited one of the two stars in the distance. The second star spun around the first in an orbit much closer than the planet's. "There's nothing here anyone seems to want. No colonies, no bases, no mines."

"How long do we wait?"

Firebrandt turned and pulled Suki close. "Until something happens."

"Eventually we'll run out of food," grumbled Roberts from his station. "I suspect the crew would like us to leave before that happens." He looked serious, but the captain recognized his friend's dry sense of humor. He chuckled in response even as he knew the truth in the statement.

Computer sat at his station, eyes roving back and forth as his mind interfaced with the ship's computer. His brow furrowed and his eyes stopped moving. "Sir, a ship has just jumped into the system with us."

Roberts checked the scanners. "Confirmed, and they're not sending out a transponder signal. No idea who she is."

"Well, we aren't broadcasting a transponder signal either," said Kheir el-Din at the helm. "Fair's fair, I suppose."

"I guess this means something's happened." Suki's voice

held a bittersweet note.

The captain gave her a gentle squeeze then released her and strode over to the wheel console. "Swing us around and see if you can get a visual on that craft." He held up his hand. "Keep some distance, though. I want some maneuvering room if this is a trap."

The helmsman nodded as he fired thrusters and adjusted the ship's orbit around the planet. "I'll keep us in the lunar ecliptic. If they spot movement, hopefully they'll think we're just another moonlet."

Firebrandt turned to Computer and Roberts. "Avoid active scanning. I don't want them knowing we're here. Learn what you can from visual readings."

"Aye, aye, sir," said Computer as his eyes resumed their slow side-to-side sweep. Roberts gave a curt nod.

Firebrandt strode back toward the holographic viewer.

Suki narrowed her gaze as she looked from Firebrandt to the display. "Do you think this is a hostile?"

"I don't know what to think. Earth command just told us to come out to this backwater." He reached into his pocket, retrieved a rubber band, and tied his red hair into a ponytail. "I don't know whether we're here to meet someone or conduct a raid." He shrugged. "For all I know, it's some kind of elaborate trap."

"I've got a visual," said Roberts as he activated a control. A black cylinder appeared as a structured lump against the black background. "Not close enough to read hull markings, but she's entered orbit around the planet. That gives me a mass—we're looking at about 50 million kilos."

Kheir el-Din whistled from the helm. "Sounds like a warship to me. I'd say we're out of our league."

"Keep closing." The captain kept his voice calm and steady. "Present a minimal profile to them. I don't want them reading our hull markings, either."

The crew on the command deck fell silent and watched the black cylinder on the screen as they grew closer. Firebrandt reached out and took Suki's hand. She trembled. He turned his head and gave her a reassuring smile.

"That's the goddamned *Unification*," hissed el-Din. They

hadn't approached close enough to read the white letters and numbers of her registration on the ship's flank. "I recognize her profile." He pointed to the screen. "She's just like other Earth heavy cruisers, except for that bump on her belly. That's the admiral's yacht."

Firebrandt pursed his lips and nodded. A few more minutes passed and they could make out the code on the hull.

"Confirmed," reported Computer. "Ship is the ASV *Unification*."

"What's Earth's flagship doing out here?" Roberts narrowed his gaze. "And without an escort?"

Computer turned to face the captain. "We're receiving a tight-beam radio message, sir."

"Radio?" Suki shook her head. "Who uses radio anymore?"

"Someone who doesn't want their signal intercepted for a very long time." Firebrandt folded his arms. "What's the message say?"

"Captain Ellison Firebrandt is hereby ordered to report at once." Computer blinked as though checking to make sure he'd received the entire message. Without another word, his eyes began roving the deck again.

"Respond via tight beam radio that I'm on my way." Firebrandt swallowed, then turned to Roberts. "Make sure the launch is prepared. I'll leave as soon as I'm changed."

"Aye, sir," said the first mate.

Firebrandt turned on his heel and strode from the command deck. Footsteps clanked on the deck behind him. He turned around and faced Suki.

"What's going on?" she asked. "Why are you flying over to that ship?"

"The ASV *Unification* is Earth's flag ship. It's the command center of Admiral Luke Williams, the man who issues letters of marque for the Alliance." The captain paused for a moment. "The only person in the wide universe I answer to."

Her eyes widened and she gave a smile he thought was supposed to be reassuring, but looked nervous. She reached out, squeezed his arm, then returned to the command deck.

The captain continued to his quarters. He hoped his tone hadn't frightened her, but he was just as glad to be alone with his thoughts as he grappled with the reasons Earth's most senior field officer had flown off to a remote star system to meet with one pirate captain. He didn't like any of the possibilities that came to mind.

He stripped off his jacket and trousers, then took a moment to wash his face, and comb his hair, putting it into a neater, more presentable ponytail. As he did, he considered the possibility that Williams had somehow learned about the intrasystem jump engine and wanted to get his hands on the real one. As he donned his best trousers and jacket, he wondered if those people had been working for Williams.

Firebrandt stepped back and examined himself in the mirror. A red stripe adorned the trousers leg and a brass skull and crossed swords were on the jacket's left breast. The skull wore an earring, a nod to one of Firebrandt's heroes, Captain Henry Avery, sometimes known as 'the successful pirate.' He grinned, thinking he'd pass muster on a military ship even if his beard could use a trim. He pursed his lips. He'd kept the admiral waiting long enough. He strode from the cabin to the launch bays near the ship's stern.

Nicole Lowry met him at the launch with an appreciative wink. "Looking sharp, sir. The launch is ready to go."

The captain acknowledged the report with a brief nod then entered the craft. The door sealed behind him with a hiss. A moment later, the bay door opened and Firebrandt activated thrusters sending him across to the admiral's flagship. At that moment, the captain thought about the paintings hidden in his hold. If the admiral had learned about them, he certainly wouldn't be pleased. Aboard the flagship, Firebrandt could easily be arrested and the *Legacy* commandeered. If Williams attempted that, would Roberts cooperate or run?

The first mate had been loyal to the captain ever since they met as deckhands aboard Captain Cheryl McCall's *Nightrider*. They'd been captured during a raid on a freighter. Working together, they'd broken out. Along the way, they'd discovered the freighter had a secret room loaded down with illegal pharma and tech. It's what gave Firebrandt the idea for the secret room aboard *Legacy* and it also garnered both men their first promotion.

Despite those pleasant memories, Roberts could earn his own letter of marque if he cooperated with Admiral Williams against Firebrandt. He might even take command of the *Legacy* if he could get enough support from the crew. The captain fought to push those thoughts aside. Carter Roberts had never once worked against him. If Roberts said he wanted a ship, Firebrandt would stop at nothing to assure he got one.

The captain's launch docked with the *Unification*. A moment later, the airlock opened and Firebrandt entered a pristine, gray corridor. A neat row of conduit pipe ran along the ceiling. Below his feet, the deck shone from a recent swabbing. A lone boatswain piped him aboard. The captain thought it would be bad form to cover his ears against the shrill sound. "Please follow me," said the boatswain as he lowered the whistle.

Firebrandt followed him through the flagship's neat and orderly corridors. The captain couldn't help but notice no crew walked through the ship. Had the path been cleared? Perhaps no one was to know he was there. Surely the ship's captain must know about his visit, but what other officers needed to know?

They entered a lift and went down one deck, then passed two doors. At last, the boatswain pushed a chime beside the door. "Come," called the admiral in a booming baritone.

Who says 'come?' thought Firebrandt as the boatswain stepped aside and allowed him to enter. *Normal people say, 'Come in' or 'Door's open.'*

Admiral Luke Williams sat behind a tan desk. He wore a neat, white beard. His dark hair was combed back over his head. Firebrandt wondered whether the admiral dyed his hair or if his beard just turned gray before the rest of his hair. Williams stood and walked around the desk. The man towered a good four inches over Firebrandt's six-foot height. He held out his hand and the two men shook, then Williams offered a chair. "Coffee?" He barked the question like a command.

"Thank you, I'd like a cup," said Firebrandt as he sat.

"Cream or sugar?"

Firebrandt shook his head.

The admiral walked over to a wall unit and pushed a

button. A door slid open revealing two cups. "What do you know about the aid New Earth has been giving the separatists on Yaroslavl 3?"

"They say it's humanitarian aid." Firebrandt sipped his coffee. "Nothing but medical supplies."

Williams stepped around the desk, swung his leg over the chair and sat. "What if I told you those 'medical supplies' could be used to make biological weapons?"

The captain shrugged. "Most medical supplies could probably be made into biological weapons of some kind."

The admiral shrugged. "True enough, but we have reason to believe the Yaroslavl separatists are doing just that."

Firebrandt pushed his coffee aside and looked into Williams' intense blue eyes. "So why would Earth care? Yaroslavl has been an independent colony for two centuries."

Williams grinned and sipped his coffee. "The Yaroslavl government has been making overtures to the Earth Alliance. We think we can bring them to the negotiating table if we can get the separatists to stop making biological weapons."

Firebrandt snorted. "Are you sure this isn't just a ploy to keep the separatists from getting aid?"

"If we tried to stop the deliveries in a formal way, that's exactly how it would be played in the media." The admiral's tone sent a shiver down the captain's spine.

He retrieved the coffee and took a sip. "So, that's why you want a privateer vessel to handle this."

The admiral nodded once then took a sip of coffee. He retrieved a data chip and pushed it across the table to the captain. "We have word that a New Earth transport will be passing through the Wray 17-96 system in two days. You can reach it in two jumps. It's an active system, which will wreak havoc with sensors. The transport will have three escort ships. Agents have found computer passcodes for two of them."

"Presuming they haven't changed their codes, that would leave one we have to fight directly."

Again, the admiral nodded.

Firebrandt picked up the computer chip and waved it at the admiral. "All of this could be transmitted by courier or encrypted messages. Why are you here in person?"

The admiral leaned forward, his intense ice-blue gaze boring into the captain. "To emphasize just how very important this mission is to the Earth. You're a privateer. Most missions are, shall we say, optional. We would take it amiss if you should decide to be somewhere else when that transport comes through."

"And just how would you show your displeasure?"

The admiral sat back and folded his arms. "I believe your letter of marque is up for renewal soon."

Firebrandt sighed. "That's a decent stick, do you have a nice carrot to encourage me. We're not exactly on salary and it's been a while since my crew has had a good job. We might do better going rogue."

"Get those medical supplies, bring them to Earth, and we'll pay you three times their value."

Firebrandt whistled long and low. "That's a pretty nice carrot. You must want those supplies stopped very badly."

"We want you to get them without being noticed or traced." The admiral's smile reminded Firebrandt of some sharks he'd seen. "Think you can handle the job?"

"You say that as though I have a choice."

"Then we understand each other."

Firebrandt finished his coffee while the admiral turned his attention his comp screen. "Do we have further business?" asked the captain.

The admiral dismissed him with a wave.

Firebrandt, stood and left the cabin. The coffee churned in his stomach as the boatswain led him back to the launch.

Two days later, the privateer *Legacy* held position between two jump points in the Wray 17-96 system. The system's active star meant the holographic display jumped and flickered occasionally. Computer did his best to steady the image. Despite that, Firebrandt held the wooden railing at the command deck's wall in a white-knuckled grip as he watched for any changes.

Behind the captain, Kheir el-Din stood at the wheel console, ready to pounce on any target the captain ordered. Nicole Lowry awaited a target at the gunner's rigs. Suki sat at the engineering console in case the intrasystem jump engine was needed.

The captain and Roberts decided to keep the engine off line for this raid unless they needed it to finish the job or run. Roberts agreed with Firebrandt that this seemed like all too good a setup to make them reveal the engine. Despite that, they needed the pay and going rogue would only result in them being hunted by the people who provided them their safe harbor.

One possibility that occurred to Firebrandt was that Williams knew he had the engine, but was happy to let the captain use it for Earth's benefit. That possibility bothered him most of all. If they succeeded here, what other missions would Williams devise for them? If they failed, they might find the engine taken and all Earth jobs dried up. For all he knew, Williams might revoke the letter of marque. The captain was caught between the devil and the cold black void.

Roberts looked up from his console. "Chronoton emissions from the jump point."

"It's show time, folks," called the captain. He loosened his grip on the railing, relaxing a bit now that the moment of truth had arrived. He chanced a glance back at Suki. She chewed her lower lip and her eyes widened. He wanted to take her in his arms and comfort her, but this wasn't the time.

Four ships appeared at the jump point as expected—a freighter and three escort ships. Firebrandt nodded to Roberts who set to work hacking the ships' computers. Their goal was to silence the ships and lock them on course to the jump point, so it wouldn't alert the third ship to a problem.

"So far, the admiral is as good as his word," reported Roberts. "We've compromised two of the vessels."

Firebrandt pointed to el-Din. "Intercept course for the freighter." As the engines came to life, he turned to Roberts. "See if you can hack the third escort. I would rather not fight her unless we have to."

Roberts nodded. "I'm also working on gaining access to the freighter itself."

Computer looked at Firebrandt. "One escort ship has changed course." His eyes tracked back and forth twice. "They are on a course to intercept us."

"Damn," muttered the captain. "How soon will they reach us?"

"We'll be near the freighter's position." He paused as though consulting the ship's computer. "About twenty minutes."

Firebrandt smiled in spite of himself. Computer might seem like a machine much of the time, but he could interpret the computer's results and give him responses without stating more significant figures than was helpful.

The captain released his hold on the railing and studied the holographic viewer. "Show me positions and course projections of all ships."

Computer obliged and a series of arcs appeared in the holographic display. Three of the arcs moved from one jump point to the other. Two moved headlong toward each other. The captain considered jumping past the intercepting ship, but wasn't ready to go there yet. He strode back to the gunner's rig. "What's your assessment of their armaments?"

"Typical destroyer escort. She has four banks of pulse cannons that would take out our main engine if we showed our back to them. We're at our best defensively if we remain nose-to-nose. We're a small target that way."

"And they're a small target to us." The captain nodded, then walked over to the wheel console. "In five minutes, feint to starboard, make it look as though we're going to do an end run around them."

The helmsman nodded.

Firebrandt turned back to Lowry. "If I can get them to show their rear quarter, think you can make a few shots count."

"I'll goose 'em so they know it, sir." With that, she turned her attention back to the targeting computer.

Firebrandt took a moment to walk over to Suki. "How are you holding up?" he asked quietly.

"Okay," she said, but didn't sound as though she meant it. "Better being here and seeing what's happening than waiting to die in the cabin."

The captain held his finger to his lips. "Let's not have talk like that. This is not a good day to die. I have too many plans. I'll run before we get into trouble."

She looked as though she wanted to say something, but held her tongue. Suki was becoming a good pirate. Don't show too much concern or cowardice in front of the crew. "You would give up the reward?" she finally asked.

Firebrandt nodded. "I don't want to, but I will if it means I get to live another day."

"Adjusting course," announced el-Din from the wheel console. He eased a joystick to the right. The captain thought he felt the ship list to one side, though he knew inertial dampeners kept gravity firmly in place unless they were disrupted.

"She's falling for it," called Roberts. "She's adjusting course to intercept."

"How long until she's in range?" Firebrandt leapt to his feet and grabbed the railing at the front of the command deck.

"If we straighten our course, two minutes," announced Lowry.

Firebrandt looked back to el-Din. "Give us one minute, then return to our original heading." He looked past the helmsman to Lowry. "Keep your guns locked forward until they're in range."

Computer put a countdown clock in the corner of the holographic display. Another reason to appreciate a human who interfaced with the computer. He could anticipate the captain's needs better even than an AI.

As soon as the countdown clock reached one minute, he turned back and nodded at el-Din, who took the ship back to port. The other ship fired thrusters, attempting to return to an intercept course. The minute required for *Legacy's* pulse guns to come into range crept by all too slowly. Again, the captain grabbed the handrail at the side of the command deck.

"We're in range," announced Lowry.

"Target their rear flank and fire," called Firebrandt. The ships exchanged fire. The escort's first few shots missed. Two hit their mark on *Legacy's* forward shields, sending a shudder through the deck. The captain bent his knees and rolled with the ship.

"The escort's rear shields are down," announced Computer.

Three more shots hit *Legacy.* The last one rocked the ship hard enough that Firebrandt had to struggle to keep his hold on the rail. "Can we evade?"

"Not without showing them more of our flank."

Just as el-Din answered the question, the escort's engine glowed bright blue as several of Lowry's shots struck home. The holographic display indicated the ship was now locked on a course that would carry them past the *Legacy*. They could recover and maneuver somewhat without their main engine, but it would take time—time the *Legacy* could use to capture the freighter.

"Plot an updated intercept course for the freighter, Mr. el-Din," called the captain. "Keep us out of the escort ship's range." He shot a hopeful glance toward Roberts.

"That freighter is locked down tight. We're going to have to knock down the shields the old-fashioned way." He ran his hand over his bald head. "I've fed the location of their shield generators to Lowry's targeting computer."

Firebrandt nodded, then looked back to Lowry. "Stand by to attack that shield generator as soon as we're in range." He turned around and noticed the countdown clock had been re-set to show when they would be close enough to fire on the freighter. "Will we make it to them before they reach the jump point?"

Computer gave a sharp nod. "We'll reach her with thirty minutes to spare."

The captain turned back to Lowry. "Does that give you enough time?"

"Easy peasy." Lowry gave the captain a wink.

The captain released the handrail, retrieved his pipe from his pocket, packed a small amount of tobacco and lit it. The scent of the pipe smoke relaxed him as the clock counted down their approach. His thoughts grew more ordered. As he finished the pipe, red letters began flashing over one of the escort ships. The captain made sure the pipe was extinguished as he walked forward. Either the crew of the escort had regained control or they had been faking. The escort ship rolled out of formation and assumed an intercept course.

"Roll to port," called the captain. "Let's see if we can fake this guy out."

The helmsman did as ordered and *Legacy* executed a neat turn.

Roberts shook his head. "We're going to lose our time

advantage, and this guy's not falling for it. He's barely adjusted course. He knows we're on the clock."

The captain nodded. All the escort had to do was delay them and the freighter would be safely on its way through the jump point. Firebrandt swore under his breath. If they engaged the escort and the battle took any time at all, they'd lose their prey. He turned to Suki. "Activate the intersystem jump engine. Put me in a position just off their flank, so we can take out their shields and engines."

Suki nodded and began the power-up sequence, while Computer handled the complex spatial calculations.

"Second escort ship will be in range in two minutes," announced Computer.

"I'm ready to go," said Suki.

"Sound the warning," called the captain. Klaxons sounded from the ship's speakers. Firebrandt gave his crew a good thirty seconds to prepare, then pointed at Suki. "Jump!"

She activated the engine and the world descended into sensory chaos. Firebrandt saw the rail as a laser beam in his hands guiding their way. He felt as though he tumbled through a rabbit hole of extra-dimensional space, then was yanked back to reality as the jump completed.

Before the holographic display came to life, he sucked in a deep breath and yelled, "Fire!"

Lowry punched the fire controls even before she aimed the pulse cannons. She blinked several times as she focused, then brought the guns to bear first on the jump engine, then on the shield generators. A bright flash in the holographic display indicated she'd hit her mark.

"Second escort ship is coming about to intercept," reported Computer.

"I'm on it," said Roberts.

Firebrandt pointed to el-Din. "Bring us about."

As the helmsman executed the maneuver, the second escort ship exploded in a bright flash.

The captain blinked back the spots before his eyes. "What the hell just happened?"

Roberts sat back, folded his arms and grinned. "They weren't faking. My earlier hack had been successful. They're good enough that they regained control, but didn't think to lock me out. I ordered their engines to overload."

Firebrandt nodded. He hated to kill in combat, but he had to admit, Roberts had come up with a brilliant solution. It would look like the captain of the second escort had pushed his ship too hard and blew it apart himself.

Roberts only took a moment to look proud of himself before turning his attention back to the console. "I'm shutting down the third escort's engines, shields, and weapons. That should give us time to get what we came for."

"Freighter has just passed the jump point without attempting a jump."

"All right," said the captain, "let's lock on, get what we came for, and get out of here."

As the crew set to work, Firebrandt blew out a sigh and walked over to the engineering console to drop into a chair next to Suki.

"Damn it!" called Roberts.

Firebrandt's head shot up. "What's the matter?"

"It's the first escort," said the first mate.

"Did they regain control of the ship?"

Roberts shook his head. "No, but they just sent out a tight beam transmission."

"Who did they send it to?" Firebrandt's brow furrowed.

"No idea."

Firebrandt nodded. "Nothing to be done for it now. Let's get what we came for and get the hell out of here."

Later, *Legacy* cruised between a pair of jump points on the way to Earth with a hold full of medical supplies and pharma. Captain Firebrandt sat in his wood-paneled cabin and sipped a glass of velvety Cape port wine. Suki stood behind him, rubbing the tension from his shoulders.

"What's on your mind?" asked Suki.

"I'm trying to decide if I should continue on to Earth, or if I should run as far and as fast as I can." He shook his head.

"I have to admit, I was impressed by how things went today." Suki reached out and took Firebrandt's glass of port, took a sip and then set it aside. "You analyzed the situation carefully and made the best decisions possible to keep the crew safe while achieving the mission's objective. In a lot of ways, it reminds me of the scientists I grew up around."

"So you see some good in this old pirate, after all." Firebrandt dared to lift the corner of his mouth in a half-grin.

Suki reached out and took the captain's hands. "You do your best with the choices you're given. I see the way you care not only for me, but for Roberts, Computer, el-Din, and Lowry. They're your family and you're just as loyal to them as they are to you." She swallowed.

Suki's words prickled Firebrandt's conscience. Although he'd kept it to himself, he'd questioned his first mate's loyalty. Had his first mate deserved that? "I don't know what will happen when we get to Earth." Firebrandt shrugged. "If the admiral played *straight* with me, we could get a nice payoff and be on our way. If the admiral *played* me, we could find a boarding party searching the ship for the intrasystem jump engine."

Suki's eyes widened and she squeezed Firebrandt's hands. "Couldn't you just hide the engine in the secret compartment with the paintings?"

Again Firebrandt shrugged. "I could, but it won't keep the admiral from tearing my ship apart searching for it. It won't keep him from arresting me if he thinks he has evidence of wrongdoing on my part." He sighed. "Perhaps I should run as far and as fast as I can."

"Whatever you decide—whatever happens—I want to go with you."

Firebrandt narrowed his gaze. "You're already part of the crew. You've proven yourself. You'll definitely come with us."

"You don't understand." She leaned forward, gazing intently into the captain's eyes. He could smell her scent and feel the heat of her lips near his. "Whatever happens, I want to go with *you*." She leaned in and kissed him.

The kiss continued even as she began unbuttoning his jacket and Firebrandt stopped worrying about the future.

Chapter Ten
A Vanishing Past

Captain Ellison Firebrandt sat dozing in his wood-paneled cabin aboard the privateer *Legacy*, a half-empty glass of wine on the desk beside him and smooth jazz on the speakers. The ship orbited Earth. Lowry and Roberts had delivered the medical supplies and the ship's coffers were filled as promised. It all seemed far too easy, but the captain knew if there was a next move, Earth would have to make it. Meanwhile, most of the crew enjoyed shore leave on the planet below. A knock at the door roused him.

"Come in," he said.

Suki, wearing a form-fitting dress, entered.

The captain lifted an eyebrow and smiled. "I thought you would be planetside with the rest of the crew."

She stepped over to a cabinet and retrieved a glass, then helped herself to the captain's wine. She sat down in a chair across from him, then swallowed a gulp. "I'd really like to see my parents."

The captain frowned. Over the last few months, his relationship with Suki had grown. He wanted to make her happy and she had made the intrasystem jump engine work. He owed her more than cold cash. Despite that, he needed to analyze any move he made for potential traps.

She pressed on in the wake of his silence. "They're on Ceres. Roberts tells me it's only a few hours away in the solar system's current alignment."

"I remember." The captain's eyes remained half closed and he smiled as he considered a coincidence he'd never spoken aloud to her. Then again, the coincidence wasn't that extraordinary. Millions of humans lived and worked in the belt and Ceres was the belt's largest body.

Suki took another gulp of wine. "Surely you know by now you can trust me. I don't plan to run away."

Guilt stabbed at Firebrandt's conscience as she pleaded

with him. Trust wasn't the issue. There once was a time she would have run. Even now, she didn't seem entirely comfortable making a living raiding other ships. He took a drink, then shook his head. "It's not a matter of trusting you or of distance. Ceres is … difficult for me to visit."

"How so?"

Firebrandt poured a fresh glass of wine and stared into the distance. Finally he took a sip. "My father lives on Ceres."

"Really? Just like my parents?" Suki's breath caught. "You've never said much about your father. He's a miner, right?"

The captain gave a slow, shallow nod.

"Nothing wrong with that. Does he make a good living?" Suki sipped her wine.

Firebrandt snorted. "The money's adequate for his needs. Living?" The captain shrugged. How could he explain without getting into more personal details than he wanted? By the same token, he saw no reason to deny her request. He reached over and activated the intercom. "Mr. Roberts, think the skeleton crew would mind a little field trip over to Ceres? We can pick up some fuel while we're there and Miss Suki has requested shore time."

"You should take some for yourself, Captain," suggested the first mate.

The captain narrowed his gaze and frowned. The first mate also knew about his father, but avoided making a more direct suggestion. A knot formed in the captain's stomach. "Set out when ready."

"Thank you." Suki finished her wine and stood up. As she strode past the captain, she stopped, bent over, and kissed him on his cheek. He felt his face warm but willed himself not to react further. His walls had already crumbled too much.

The next morning, Suki strolled down a familiar, beige corridor in the chemistry lab at Occator Crater. She'd walked these halls with her parents many times, wrinkling her nose as the strange smells and peering in at test tubes, beakers, and holographic displays which revealed details about the rocks of Ceres.

She passed a lounge where white-coated scientists clustered

around a holo display holding a passionate yet quiet discussion about the chemical processes that pushed distinctive, bright mineral salts to Occator's surface. The discussion seemed so alien after three years teaching computer classes on an impoverished world far from Earth and several months on a pirate ship where boisterous men and women drank and played games of chance to pass the time between raids.

At last she reached her mother's office and knocked on the door. No one answered. She swallowed and realized she should have checked the station roster to make sure her parents still worked at Occator. She double checked the nameplate on the door and it was her mother's. If they had taken a new assignment, it was a recent change. She tried to open the door, but found it locked.

Suki swallowed, then walked further down the corridor to her father's office. Again she knocked. This time a familiar, if distracted, voice answered. "Come in."

Suki entered. Kinji Mori looked up from a computer screen then donned a pair of glasses. He blinked twice, then sat back wide-eyed. "Suki?"

"Papa." Suki barely choked out the word.

Suki's father stood, ran around the desk and gathered his daughter up into a hug. "Where have you been? Last we heard was a missing person's report from Epsilon Indi 2." Mori shook his head. "We feared you'd been caught up in the gang activity there."

"In a way, I was, but I'm safe now."

"Why haven't you called or messaged? What's been happening?"

"That's not altogether easy to explain." Suki had envisioned this meeting many times, thought about many things she would say to her parents when she finally saw them, but it all flew out of her mind as she stood in her father's strong embrace. "Where's mom? I knocked on her door, but she didn't answer."

Kinji Mori stood back, holding Suki's arms and looking into her eyes. "I wish you had called. I so wish you had sent a message to tell us where you were." He shook his head. "She's gone to Epsilon Indi 2 to look for you."

☠

Firebrandt waited by AB Mining Co's airlock in the Dantu pressure dome on Ceres. A bored man with several days' stubble walked up to a control board and checked the stats, then glanced up at the captain. "Can I help you?"

"My father is Bradbury Firebrandt. He's working the shift that gets off soon."

The man at the control board grunted and returned his attention to his work. Fifteen minutes later, a light next to the airlock cycled from red to green and the door rolled open with a hiss. Several men and women wearing dust-encrusted space suits passed through. Most unclasped their helmets the moment they stepped through the door.

One figure continued through the staging area toward the locker room. The man at the console smiled, shook his head and jogged over to the man. "Brad!" He shouted so the man could hear through the helmet. "Your son is here."

The man turned around and finally reached up and unclasped his helmet. He lifted it off and narrowed his gaze. His face was very much like the captain's with deeper furrows. White stubble covered his face and the top of his head as though someone had simply taken a razor and cut it all to the same length. "Home from school, boy?"

Ellison Firebrandt smiled in spite of himself. "It's been a long time since I've been in school, dad. Get out of that suit and I'll walk you home."

The old man's brow furrowed, but he nodded and disappeared into the locker room. Fifteen minutes later, he reappeared, this time wearing a pair of orange coveralls, frayed at the cuffs and worn at the knees and elbows. He turned right and entered a tunnel without stopping for his son.

Ellison hurried to catch up with him. "Thought you were going to leave without me?"

The old man turned his head, eyes narrowed. A moment later he brightened. "Home from school, boy? You need a haircut."

The captain grimaced, then self-consciously ran his hands through his long, red hair. His father suffered from dementia, though the mining operators never bothered to determine its exact cause. It could be Alzheimer's or he might have suffered a mini-stroke, or any number of other conditions. Despite the dementia, his father's muscles knew how to operate laser drills and sonic blasters. The mining company had invested money in augmenting those same muscles with nanofibers to keep them strong. They just couldn't be bothered to invest in diagnosing his mind and even a fairly successful privateer captain didn't make enough to send his father to a quality neuroclinic for further evaluation. "I've been out of school for a long time," said Ellison. "My ship's orbiting Ceres. I'm taking some shore leave."

"Quit school, did you?" asked Bradbury.

"Finished school a long time ago," said Ellison. "I'm captain of a ship now."

The old man's brow furrowed. "Seen anything of your mother?"

Ellison snorted. "I'm the one who doesn't remember her."

Bradbury nodded slowly. "That's right. She run off when you were a baby." He looked off into the distance. "Barbara was so beautiful, but she always had itchy feet and big dreams. She never liked being the wife of a miner."

They entered a corridor and passed several doors. Finally, Bradbury stopped and blinked several times. He extracted an electronic key from his pocket and tried it on the locking plate of the nearest door. The key and the plate both blinked red.

Ellison gently extracted the key from his father's hand. It had the number 13 on it even though they stood before apartment 15. "I think we passed your door."

They walked back a door and Ellison tried the key. The door opened to a neat little one-room apartment. "Good afternoon, Brad," chimed the computer. "Your medication has been dispensed. Please let me know what you'd like for dinner."

"Gimme a hamburger and a chocolate shake."

The computer paused a moment. "Will add suitable nutrients to bring requested food up to appropriate dietary standards."

"Yeah, yeah, whatever." Bradbury crossed the room to the small kitchen nook, retrieved the pills and some water and swallowed them down. When finished, he looked up at his son.

"Ellison? How nice to see you. Home from school?"

The question was getting old. "Just visiting. I'm here with my ship, the *Legacy*. Roberts is aboard keeping an eye on her."

"Robert? Who's Robert?"

"Just my best friend since my days in the merchant service."

"Merchant service? When did you join the merchant service? Did you quit school?"

The captain rubbed the bridge of his nose. Every time he visited his father, he felt like a piece of his own past vanished. His father remembered his mother—the mother who abandoned them both—with clarity, but he could barely remember the son who stuck with him for sixteen years after she left.

"Would you like something to eat?" asked the old man.

Ellison sighed, not really wanting synthesized food, but feeling obligated to stay, at least for a while. "I'll take a salmon salad with spinach leaves and onions, drizzled with a light vinaigrette."

"Not your kind of food at all," remarked Bradbury. "You hate vegetables."

"I *hated* vegetables ... when I was a kid."

Soon, a wall panel opened, delivering the food for both men. Bradbury took a seat on a tattered sofa, while Ellison sat in an adjoining chair. They each lifted tabletops built into the furniture. Bradbury turned on the holo screen, letting a news channel play while they ate.

"So you say you're aboard a ship now?" The old man took a bite of his burger, then focused on the chocolate milk shake. He took a sip, made a face, then took another sip.

"I own a ship. I call her the *Legacy*."

"Nice name. Freighter?"

"We haul cargo from time to time." The captain hesitated discussing his career as a privateer captain in depth. He hated to expend the energy explaining something his father would forget in ten minutes.

Satisfied with the brief explanation, the old man returned to his burger. He finished about half of it, then lit a cigarette. He sat back, and watched the news for a while, then turned to Ellison and smiled. "It's good to see you, son. You say you're aboard a ship now?"

Ellison sighed. "Yes, the *Legacy*."

Bradbury nodded, oblivious to having heard the answer recently. "Gotta be careful when you captain a ship here in the asteroid belt. Accidents happen."

The captain's brow furrowed. The conversation had taken an interesting turn. "What kind of accidents?"

"You remember Mathilde?"

Firebrandt thought back to his youth and remembered a rundown pressure dome where the other kids called him a shrimp. He learned to fight on the asteroid Mathilde. "Miserable little hunk of rock," muttered the captain.

"Remember that big crater? Scientists used to think another asteroid collided with it—reasonable in the belt—but sonic imaging found something else. We found a Rd'dyggian treasure galleon down there. Old one, too. They used to make their currency out of rhodium. We found huge heaps of it in the hold."

Ellison looked up from his salad. "The ship was intact? How did it survive the crash?"

Bradbury shrugged. "They must have screwed up their hyperspace jump calculations and plowed right into the asteroid before they jumped fully into the beyond. We dug a tunnel, but we were only able to get a few of the rhodium coins out."

The captain reached into his coat pocket and retrieved a pipe and tobacco pouch. An ancient Rd'dyggian galleon would be worth a small fortune, especially if it still held a cargo of rhodium coins. "Couldn't you blast it out of the rock?" He began packing the pipe.

The old man shook his head. "The ship was too fragile. We'd have destroyed it if we tried to blast. Besides, that would have drawn attention to the ship. We weren't about to tell the mine owners, or else they'd claim everything for themselves."

Ellison Firebrandt lifted his pipe to his mouth and lit it. He smoked for a few minutes, thinking. The intrasystem jump engine might be able to extract the galleon from the asteroid. Played out, no one should be watching the area. "If I took you to Mathilde, do you think you could lead us to the tunnel you dug?"

"Are you kidding? I remember it like it was yesterday."

They turned their attention to the news for a while. His pipe finished, Ellison stood and collected his father's dishes. The old man blinked at his son, startled.

"Ellison? Home from school?"

The captain closed his eyes, feeling vulnerable despite the excitement of the quest.

After dinner, Suki made excuses and went to her old room. Her parents left it much as she remembered. Scattered on the walls were holo-posters of bands and movies she once liked—relics of a young girl's interests. On the vanity was a photo of a young man whose name she struggled to remember. She wondered where he'd gone. He looked so young and insecure next to Captain Firebrandt.

Over an uncomfortable dinner, Suki learned that her mother had traveled to Epsilon Indi 2 to see if she could learn anything from the local authorities. She had checked in just the day before to let her father know she'd arrived safely. Father didn't expect to hear another message until mother had some news.

"I could send a message to her hotel to let her know you're safe."

Suki shook her head. "I don't know if that's a good idea. It might be better to wait for her to call, then encourage her to return without telling her anything." Suki hated to reveal all that had happened. It humiliated her to think about being tied up naked and shivering in a warehouse. It was even worse to think about her mother in the same situation

She made up a half-truth about how she found a job as an engineer for a space salvage company. She formulated a story about being unable to call because of the proprietary nature of salvage work. Her cheeks warmed just thinking about revealing intimate details of her relationship with a pirate captain to her father.

Once she was alone in the room, she opened the blinds and looked out at the desolate, gray surface of Ceres. She brought out her comm unit and contacted Firebrandt.

"This is why I needed to get a message to them," she growled. "Surely between Roberts and Computer, you could have figured something out."

A long silence followed on the comm line and she feared the signal had been interrupted for some reason.

"You're right," he said at last. "We should have found a way to get a message to them."

"She'll probably inquire at the college where I taught and talk to the police station." Suki shook her head. "I don't know whether Bowman would monitor for anyone snooping around for me."

"You're right. Her inquiries probably won't trigger anything. His people will just treat you as one of many who just vanished."

"What if her inquiries do trigger something?" Suki gripped the comm unit tighter.

"It'll take resources to extract her." The captain remained calm and cool, infuriating her. "More resources than I currently have, but I may be able to fix that if you can return and help me."

Suki didn't even pause to consider what kind of scheme the captain may have hatched. "Count me in," she said.

The asteroid Mathilde expanded to fill the *Legacy*'s holographic viewer. The captain pointed to a large depression on the asteroid's surface. "Scan there and see if you can find evidence for this ship my father's talking about."

The man known as Computer closed his eyes for a moment. When he opened them, they drifted back and forth. Finally, they locked on the captain. "There's a hollow space under the crater, like a small cavern."

A three-dimensional schematic appeared, overlaid on the asteroid's image. Roberts crossed his arms over his barrel chest and shook his head. "Doesn't prove anything. It could be a natural cavern that formed under the crater somehow."

"Unlikely," responded Computer. "Mathilde is composed of metal-rich carbonaceous chondrites. Few natural caves have been recorded."

Firebrandt nodded. "Compare the cavern to schematics we have of old Rd'dyggian galleons circa twelve hundred years ago."

A series of ship schematics appeared in the holographic

viewer. One separated from the others and oriented itself over the cavern. The area and shape were a near perfect match. The captain nodded slowly as he stepped over to the intercom and called the engine room. "Suki, have you disconnected the nodal point generator from the engine?"

"Almost there," she said. "It should be ready to go in about fifteen minutes."

"Perfect. Let me know when you're ready and meet me in the launch bay."

"You know, my dad says I should ask for a raise," said Suki.

Firebrandt barked a laugh. "Parents are like that." The captain turned off the intercom.

Roberts approached. "So, what exactly do you plan to do? Even if you do find a twelve-hundred year old ship buried in the asteroid, it's not like it'll have a working engine. The ship can't jump from where it is."

Firebrandt grinned and patted Roberts on the shoulder. "The ship won't have to jump. The nodal point generator will allow the ship to drop into the beyond for a time. We'll just let the asteroid continue its orbit. The generator will disable itself after about half an hour. The ship should appear in normal space where Mathilde had been. Nice, calm, and quiet. Shouldn't draw any attention to ourselves."

Roberts blinked at the captain, then ran his hand over his bald head. "That's either the most brilliant or the craziest idea I've ever heard."

"You're not going to try to stop me?"

Roberts shrugged. "If you're right, we could have a small fortune. If you're wrong, I guess I'm in command of the *Legacy*. I don't see how I lose."

On Mathilde, a domed ghost town called Brisbane huddled near the crater Damodar's vertex. The air generation plant had been shut down years ago. Roberts shuttled Suki along with Ellison and Bradbury Firebrandt to the surface, where they donned space suits and hiked across the surface. Roberts returned to the *Legacy*.

Captain Firebrandt pointed out places where someone had

taken potshots at the transparent dome, leaving scorched holes.

"This place was always a dump," said Bradbury. "The mines played out in just a few years."

The old man led the way through a hole in the dome where an airlock had been cannibalized. Suki carried the nodal point generator in a chest pack, which counterbalanced the air pack on her back. Though heavy in normal gravity, it was easy to manage on the potato-shaped space rock. As they walked through the old town, Bradbury pointed out places he remembered. "There's the old general store." He turned around. "I used to live in an apartment up that street. I wonder if it's still there."

The captain studied the abandoned buildings. The faint light of the distant sun cast long shadows. Despite the eerie setting, Ellison smiled at his father's apparent lucidity. He seemed much more in the moment than he had in earlier conversations. "We don't have much time. Do you remember the way to the tunnel that leads to the abandoned ship?"

Bradbury's brow furrowed. "We need to get into the mine." He led the way to the center of town where a metal pillbox-shaped building stood. The old man tried the handle but found it locked.

Ellison motioned for him to stand clear. He drew his sidearm and blasted the locking mechanism. He leaned on the door and pushed it into a dark space. The captain's helmet lamp illuminated a lifting platform. He wondered if there was any way to supply power to it.

His father eyed the elevator. Stepping on, he opened a hatch in the bottom of the floor and shone his helmet lamp on a set of wall rungs. "The personnel lift broke down a lot. We had to climb down all too often. Sometimes we'd sneak aboard the ore lift outside the dome. They never let that one break down."

With that, the three clambered through the hatch and climbed down into the subasteroidal chambers. At the third level down, Bradbury paused. "Most of the time I worked here. I wonder if any of our old gear is still around."

"You were going to show us the way to the tunnel," said the captain.

"Tunnel?"

"Yes, the tunnel that led to the buried treasure galleon."

A silence ensued which lasted long enough that Ellison began to question the quest's sanity. Could his father focus long enough to see the mission through?

"How did you know that?" asked Bradbury. "We never told anyone about the ship we found. There's no way to get it out."

"You told me about it yesterday," said Ellison. "Just lead the way."

"We should go take the ore lift. That always has power," remarked the old man.

"Not anymore," said Suki. "Nothing has power here."

"I wonder why that is." The old man continued climbing down the ladder. As they climbed, the only sounds Ellison heard were the rhythmic steps on the metal rungs and labored breathing transmitted through the suit speakers. The captain's muscles began to burn. He knew his father's nano-muscular implants would allow him to keep going, but he worried about Suki. They climbed past several dozen levels until they dismounted on rough laser-carved rock.

The captain looked up and estimated they'd climbed down nearly a kilometer. There was no way they could have endured the climb in Earth's gravity. Firebrandt felt warm and assumed it was from the exertion of the climb since there was no atmosphere to transfer the small amount of heat generated from subsurface rocks.

"I've only been down here a couple of times," remarked Bradbury. "Usually I worked up on the third level, but some of my friends showed me the ship they'd found down here. Did I tell you about that?"

"Yes, dad, you did," said the captain. "Can you show us which way it is?"

Bradbury Firebrandt looked around, then pointed to a tunnel that led away behind them. "We should have taken the ore lift. It always has power."

"Nothing has power right now," said Ellison.

They followed the tunnel past abandoned laser drills and emptied emergency medical kits. Finally, they came to a place where a large steel sheet painted with graffiti leaned against the wall. "Help me with this," said the old man.

The captain grabbed one end and his father took the other and they hefted it to the side. The captain sensed his father actually took most of the weight. He began to think nano-muscular implants could be handy. A narrow tunnel twisted downward.

"The geologists discovered the ship when they were doing scans. They thought they'd found a cavern, but what really grabbed their attention was the erdonium deposit." The old man referred to the metal used to build starship hulls.

"The erdonium must have been from the Rd'dyggian ship's hull," remarked Suki.

"How do you know about the Rd'dyggian ship?" asked Bradbury. "I never told anyone about it. Didn't think they'd believe me."

Ellison ignored his father and led the way down the winding, twisting tunnel until it opened into a large area. Exposed deck plating canted at a sharp angle. Across the way, strapped into a dust-covered chair were the mummified remains of a seven-foot tall Rd'dyggian warrior with a hole in his chest. Trapped in the asteroid with atmosphere failing, he no doubt took his own life rather than await suffocation or starvation. The captain shivered in spite of himself.

"These old ships used to carry coins made out of rhodium," said Bradbury, repeating information he'd relayed back on Ceres.

Suki retrieved a portable scanner from her belt. "I do detect rhodium in the holds." She shook her head. "A lot of the erdonium hull plating is gone, though. It's like whoever found this cut it out from the inside as much as possible."

"Erdonium brings in more money than rhodium," explained the old man, nothing wrong with his professional knowledge. He led the way up the canted and buckled deck of the Rd'dyggian treasure galleon to a door that had been forced open. Inside, a small fortune in rhodium doubloons had spilled against the near wall.

Ellison Firebrandt smiled.

"If most of the hull plating is gone, how do we get this ship out of here? Won't the coins just drift away?" Suki closed her porta-scanner and placed it back into its carrying case.

"The nodal point generator creates a field doesn't it? Make sure the field includes the surrounding rock. I'm sure a museum will be interested in this ship and the cargo," said the captain.

"Help me with this pack," said Suki.

The captain helped her lift off the carrying case. Despite the low gravity, it proved awkward work balanced between the wall and floor of the trapped alien vessel. They extracted the nodal point generator. Ellison pulled off his own chest pack and produced a small portable power supply. They connected it and Suki began programming. "I wouldn't recommend staying aboard the ship when the field activates. Without the erdonium plating, the radiation from the EQ-field could be deadly. How long should we allow to get out of here?"

"How far away do we need to be?" asked the captain.

"I'd like to be at the top of the ladder and out in the mining camp, at least," said Suki.

"Set it for two hours."

She set the timer and then looked up. "Okay. Time to get going."

With that, the captain looked around for his father. He was no longer in the room with them. "Dad?" called the captain. There was no response.

Suki pulled out her porta-scanner. "He's not in the ship, but the surrounding rock is making other readings difficult."

"Could he be...?" Ellison hated to speak the rest of the question.

"No. I'd still read his suit if he were dead." She didn't add that he'd need to be nearby to do so.

The captain blew out a breath, then nodded. He motioned for Suki to follow. His dad must be out in the mines somewhere. He only hoped they would catch up to him before it was too late. They followed the winding tunnel back up to the main part of the mine then returned to the elevator shaft. Suki scanned again but didn't get any readings.

Firebrandt looked around and considered his father's words. He could imagine his father returning to the third level where he once worked, or even to the surface to try to find the old apartment. Searching either location would take a while. Just then, he remembered the ore lift. He looked around. Besides the dead-end tunnel they exited, there was only one other tunnel on the bottom level. Firebrandt followed it with Suki on his tail.

A thousand feet down the tunnel, Suki scanned again. "I register a human life form just ahead."

Firebrandt smiled and bounded forward in the low gravity. They found Bradbury Firebrandt at the ore lift, fumbling with some corroded battery leads, trying to get the lift operational again. He'd just reached out to remove the gauntlet when the captain put his hand on his dad's forearm.

"We don't have much time," warned Suki.

"Can we get this lift operational?" asked the captain.

Suki scanned the battery. "It does have some residual charge left." She reached into her pouch and took out a small tool that let her grab the wires and attach them to the lift controls. Once done, she threw the lever and blew out a breath when the ore lift started moving. It came down to their level and stopped.

The three climbed aboard and Bradbury threw the lever and the lift carried them toward the surface. "We used to use this lift when the main elevator would break down," he said.

"Ellison! Home from school?"

Ellison Firebrandt stood outside his father's apartment on Ceres. A woman in a green lab coat stood next to him.

"Who is this? A new girlfriend?"

Ellison and the woman smiled at each other as Bradbury Firebrandt stood aside and indicated they should enter. "Dad, this is Dr. Apolinaria Apodaca. She'll be looking in on you from time to time."

The doctor lifted a medical scanner. "May I?"

Bradbury Firebrandt's eyes shifted nervously from side to side. "I don't have money for a doctor's visit, especially not a house call."

"Oh yes you do," said Ellison. The Rd'dyggians paid a tidy sum for the remains of the craft salvaged from the interior of Mathilde. Embarrassed that one of their captains would steer a ship into an asteroid even twelve hundred years ago, they were willing to pay to make that part of their past vanish. They didn't even question why the holds had been emptied of the ancient rhodium coins, probably assuming the miners who stripped the vessel of its plating had emptied the hold years before. Firebrandt had already sold a few on the collectors market and figured he'd parcel out the rest as needed in the years to come. He could use the coins to help Suki's mother if needed. He really hoped it wouldn't be needed.

Dr. Apodaca looked up from her scan. "Mr. Firebrandt, may we sit."

"Of course," said the captain and miner together. They all shared a chuckle.

"You're suffering the degenerative effects of Alzheimer's. I can slow it down, possibly stop it, although I don't think I can undo any damage that's already been done."

Bradbury's eyes sharpened. "Is that why I keep saying the same thing over and over again?"

The doctor nodded.

"Do what you can to help me out."

She opened a pouch, attached a vial to a hypo and pointed it at his arm. A faint ping indicated the medication had been injected into his bloodstream. "That should help."

"Dr. Apodaca will check on you once a week. I also have a housing agent who will help you find some nicer quarters," said the captain. "If you decide you want to retire, they'll even help you move back to Earth."

Bradbury Firebrandt sniffed. "Thank you, son. I don't know how you can afford all this."

The captain snorted, glad most of his crew had been on shore leave and had no idea how much money the captain had acquired when he extracted the ancient, alien galleon and presented it to the Rd'dyggian embassy on Titan. "You earned it all yourself, dad. I'll look in on you when I'm back this way in a few months."

Bradbury blinked a few times and nodded. "You're not in school anymore are you?"

"No," said the captain.

"Be careful out there and I'll try to hold onto my memories."

Captain Firebrandt smiled and pulled his father into a hug, feeling a little less vulnerable, hopeful that his own past had ceased to vanish.

A moment later his comm unit chimed. He stepped back and answered.

"Ellison," came Suki's voice, "I've just been watching the news. There's been a series of warehouse explosions on Epsilon Indi 2."

The captain waved to his father and the doctor, then stepped out into the corridor. "You're afraid your mother might be in trouble?"

"I'm afraid my mother might be responsible."

Chapter Eleven
Sins of the Mother

Sumika Mori had grown concerned when she hadn't heard from her daughter for a month. Nearly instantaneous EQ communications across the galaxy were expensive and generally reserved for wealthy industrialists or the military. Letter packets could piggyback onto EQ carrier waves for much less money and while teaching classes at the Institute of Computer Studies on Epsilon Indi 2, Suki had generally sent a note home every couple of weeks Earth time.

When three months had passed, Sumika had grown truly worried. She sent a communique to the Institute of Computer Studies. The response had chilled her. Suki simply stopped coming to work. Sumika had followed up with more inquiries to the school and to the police, but no one could give her any more information.

After six months, Sumika could stand by no longer. She took a leave of absence from her job as a chemist on the asteroid Ceres and caught the first available starliner flight to Epsilon Indi and that's where the trouble began.

Once she arrived on Epsilon Indi she checked into a motel in the city of Palomar near the Institute of Computer Studies. Scantily clad human women and men plus a couple of other species loitered nearby. When she turned down an offer of an hour's "entertainment" from one of the men, a Rd'dyggian prostitute approached her. She scowled and walked steadily on to the institute.

The secretary in the front office gave Sumika the same answer she'd received from her electronic mail packets. Suki had taught there, but simply did not arrive for class one day. "Did you follow up at her home? Ask any of her students about her?"

The secretary shook his head. "No, ma'am. It's Institute policy to simply terminate an employee who has three unexcused absences. We don't look into their personal affairs."

"Well, can you give me a list of her students and maybe

some contact information?"

"That information is confidential, ma'am," said the secretary.

"May I speak to the dean?"

"You may make an appointment." A holographic datebook opened over the secretary's computer dais. "The dean is off world right now. The next available appointment is next week."

Sumika cursed under her breath. She hadn't expected to be away that long. "Can you at least tell me where my daughter's classroom was?"

The secretary pulled up a holographic map and pointed to a room in the building. "Room 153." He pointed to a hallway behind the desk. "Down this hall and to the left."

"Thank you." Sumika gave a brief bow and then walked down the brick-lined corridor to the classroom. Inside, students paid attention to a lecture. She pulled out her handcomp and checked the time. It was near the top of the hour local planetary time. It seemed possible one of the students or the professor might be able to tell her something. She pulled up a hologram of Suki.

Five minutes before the hour, the classroom door opened. Sumika felt like a pathetic fool standing in the hallway with a hologram of her daughter. Most of the students simply ignored her, but one young woman stopped. "My God, that's Miss Mori."

"You know Suki Mori?" Sumika's eyes widened.

The girl nodded. She grabbed Sumika's arm. "You'd better turn that off before anyone else notices."

Sumika complied and the girl led her around the corner and into an empty classroom. "I don't know how much you know, but Palomar is a bad city. The government is under the thumb of gangsters posing as legitimate businessmen. Miss Mori joined a political group trying to change all that. She joined a protest march calling for an investigation of a businessman named Chris Bowman. One of the networks interviewed her for broadcast. She was gone the next day."

"What do you mean, 'gone'?"

"Disappeared, vanished, never to be seen again." The student shook her head. "It's happened to a lot of women. Men, too, for that matter. You don't stand up to Bowman and remain free."

Sumika ground her teeth but nodded. "What's your name, young lady?"

The student shook her head and backed up. "Names are dangerous. I don't know who you are, not really. You look enough like Miss Mori that I think you must be related. Everything I've said is part of the public record. I don't dare say anything more." With that, the girl ducked out of the room.

Sumika took a step to try to stop her, but ultimately decided to let her go. Fear and tyranny—couldn't humans get beyond that? As she taught her daughter, the only answer was to stop living in fear and stand up to tyranny.

She returned to her motel room, passing the gantlet of prostitutes. This time, instead of viewing them with disgust, she felt a certain pity for their plight. In the room, she searched for information about Chris Bowman. She discovered he owned a set of warehouses near Palomar's space port. He also had a few ships for short cargo runs out of the system, but mostly his business was renting warehouse space to other shipping companies.

She found contact information for Bowman Enterprises. "Is it possible to make an appointment with Mr. Bowman?"

"What would you like to speak to Mr. Bowman about?" asked the clerk who answered the call.

"My daughter, Suki Mori, was last seen in the company of Mr. Bowman. I was wondering if she'd had an appointment and what they discussed." Sumika made up the part about Suki actually being seen with Mr. Bowman, but thought that might be the quickest way to cut through the bureaucracy.

"And when did she meet Mr. Bowman?"

Sumika checked her computer records. She took a chance and suggested the day after she'd last heard from Suki. When she received a blank stare from the clerk, she converted the date to local time.

The clerk checked records off screen, then nodded. "Yes, Mr. Bowman did hold one of his galas that day, but I don't see your daughter's name on the guest list. Is it possible she accompanied one of the invited guests?"

Sumika tried not to show her pleasure at how well this was going. "Yes, it's possible."

"I'll leave a message for Mr. Bowman and someone will get back to you if there's any more information." With that, the clerk abruptly terminated the call. It occurred to Sumika that he didn't ask for contact information. He either brushed her off, or he read the contact information from the call records and didn't inform her. She didn't know which option irritated her most.

She heard nothing more for the rest of the day. She pulled back the blankets of the room's bed and growled when she saw bedbugs. Too tired to do more, she slumped in the room's only chair and fell into a fitful slumber.

Later that night, she woke to a glow from the holographic terminal. She opened her eyes. The display showed the image of a chair in the middle of an empty warehouse office. A door in the corner of the room burst open and two men pushed her daughter inside. Her clothes were in tatters. She fought and screamed. She tried to scratch the eyes of one of the men. The other grabbed her arms and forced them back. The first man tore the remaining clothes from her body. Sumika forced herself to hold back a sob as she continued to watch.

The men forced Suki into a chair. She struggled and rolled out of their grasp, onto the floor. One of the men clocked her across the back of the head, driving her face into the concrete. They yanked her up into the chair, unconscious and bleeding, then tied her up and left. The image froze on her daughter's battered form.

"Your daughter is now gone," came an anonymous male voice from the holographic console's speaker. "Continue to pursue her here and you will be gone too."

With that, the holographic console shut off.

Sumika's heart pounded with equal parts fear and rage. She never gave in to fear, so rage took over. She knew where to find Bowman's warehouses. As a chemist, she knew ways to level buildings inexpensively. She wasn't certain how much she could hurt Bowman, but she hoped she could keep this from happening to another mother's daughter.

She took her handcomp off the network and began making plans with information stored on its internal memory.

☠

The Privateer *Legacy* jumped into the Epsilon Indi system. As the crew recovered, Computer announced an incoming message. Captain Firebrandt frowned as he leaned back against the wall and let his stomach settle. "Someone's expecting us," he said.

"So it would seem." Roberts rubbed the bridge of his nose, then blinked as he focused on his display.

"Put the message in the holographic viewer," ordered the captain.

Chris Bowman stood in the room of a warehouse. He wore an impeccable gray suit with matching shirt and tie. As a result, he nearly blended in with the walls behind. "Captain Firebrandt, so terrible of you to keep me waiting."

"We did our best to get here as fast as we could." The captain narrowed his gaze, studying as much of the room behind Bowman as possible. It looked nearly identical to the one where Suki had been held captive just a few months before.

"I didn't like that double cross you did to me at station Xiūxí qū wū. We're no longer playing around. You have something I want and I have something you want. We'll do a straight exchange and you can go on your merry way. If we do this right, I'll refrain from ruining your reputation on the nets."

"I have a reputation on the networks?" Firebrandt chuckled to himself.

Instead of answering the question, Bowman stepped aside and revealed a woman tied up in a chair. Behind the captain, Suki gasped. Bowman approached the woman and removed a blindfold. Then in a fast rip, he tore a piece of tape from her mouth. The woman blinked and her eyes widened as Suki rushed up behind Firebrandt.

"Suki?" she asked.

"It's me, okaasan," squeaked Suki. She grabbed Firebrandt's sleeve and held tightly as a tear rolled down her cheek.

The captain wanted to pull her into an embrace, but forced himself to glare at Bowman. "How do I know you'll play fair?" They had come to Epsilon Indi to look for Sumika Mori. Suki feared her mother had been behind a series of warehouse explosions on the planet. Firebrandt wasn't sure whether to believe that or not. He'd hoped they'd simply find Suki's mom and go home. Things didn't look so simple anymore.

"I never said I play fair." Bowman shrugged as his lips turned upward. He walked around Sumika Mori like a predator circling prey. He undid the braid at the back of her head and started running his fingers through her silver-black hair. Suki's mom shuddered. "What you do know is that the longer you take, the more fun I'll have with Dr. Mori. When I grow bored, I have lots of people who will help me keep her entertained."

To her credit, Sumika Mori didn't cry or scream out. Her jaw tensed and Firebrandt sensed if she were released, Bowman would have a difficult fight on his hands.

Suki's grip tightened on the captain's shoulder. "Ellison, you have to do…"

Firebrandt put his finger to her lips, then turned to the display. "What are the coordinates for the exchange?"

"Appended to this message encoded as a sub carrier wave," said Bowman. "Given the skills your crew has already demonstrated, I'm sure they've already decoded the message."

The captain turned his eyes toward Roberts, who gave a curt nod.

"I'll give you an hour to load the merchandise into our launch and be at the appointed place." Bowman's gaze turned icy. "Don't be late."

"Suki, don't do it. I'm not worth it!"

Bowman cuffed Sumika, causing her head to snap forward. "I can tell she is worth it to at least one member of your crew." Bowman smiled again. He retrieved a pocket comp. "The timer starts now. Bring me your collection of paintings and you can have Dr. Mori." With that, the image in the holographic tank faded, and was replaced by a view of the planet below.

Suki swallowed, then gazed at the captain. "So what are we waiting for?"

Instead of answering the question, Firebrandt extracted himself from Suki's grip and walked over to Roberts' station. "Awfully convenient of him to be standing around with Suki's mom in some hidden warehouse, just waiting for us to show up. What are the odds we've been played by an automated AI message?"

Roberts pursed his lips and shook his head. "I've been looking at that with Computer's help."

Computer turned to face the captain. "I've been checking the standard signatures for AI encoding and image manipulation. I calculate ninety-three percent probability that we participated in a genuine person-to-person exchange."

The captain retrieved his pipe and tamped in some tobacco while he considered. "That means there's a seven percent chance it really was an AI after all." He nodded. "Display the schedule of those ships actually registered to Chris Bowman's freight company in the holographic viewer." The captain turned to face Kheir el-Din. "In the meantime, keep us up in a high orbit."

Suki looked from Firebrandt to Roberts to el-Din. "Won't a high orbit delay the time it takes to get to the surface?" Fear made her voice unnaturally loud.

Nicole Lowry approached and put her arm around Suki's shoulder. "Let's give the captain a few minutes to put a plan together."

Suki opened her mouth to protest, but seemed to notice Lowry's earnest gaze. She swallowed and allowed Lowry to lead her to a chair. Firebrandt lifted the pipe to his mouth and lit it. This was not the time to voice his own fears about the fate of Suki's mother. Even if the image in the holoviewer was not a simulation, Firebrandt suspected Bowman had no good reason to keep Sumika Mori alive if they followed through with an exchange. She'd be a witness to his criminal activity. What's more Bowman had enough men in his employ that a launch full of pirates could simply be ambushed, killed and their cargo taken.

No, following through with Bowman's demands was not an option.

The list of cargo flights appeared in the holographic viewer. Firebrandt looked at the arrival times and positions of jump points. He pointed to one of the lines in the list. It glowed a brighter yellow than the others. "Yes, I think that will do nicely."

Roberts stepped up beside the captain. He glanced at the

list. "That ship is hauling stationary. Paper, pencils, erasers. That's not exactly going to hurt Chris Bowman or make us a big profit."

Firebrandt puffed on the pipe for a moment before answering. "If anything, that's exactly what I want. A ship no one feels is worth guarding." He pointed the pipe stem at the listing. "Also, it'll be coming out of jump nearby in about fifteen minutes." He turned back to Kheir el-Din. "That means you need to get underway, mister."

"Aye aye, sir." The helmsman made his course adjustment and activated thrusters. Lowry stood up from where she knelt beside Suki and went to the gunner's rigs to activate the weapons.

Suki shook her head. "I don't understand. Taking a ship now is going to make us miss the deadline." Her voice caught on the last word.

Firebrandt walked over to Suki and sat down beside her. He tried to find the right words. "The problem is, I see no way we can get your mother out of there."

Suki's mouth fell open. She shook her head, refusing to believe it.

The captain removed the pipe from his mouth and set it on the console behind him. He reached out and took her hands. "That doesn't mean we can't win. I know a person who can get her out of there, but we have to give him a good reason to come here and raid Bowman's operation. It's dangerous and it's not guaranteed to work, but I think it's our best shot."

"Is there anything I can do?"

"Get the intrasystem jump engine online and ready."

"For the raid you have in mind?"

Firebrandt shook his head. "It's the next step after the raid."

"We're in position by the jump point where that cargo ship will emerge," announced el-Din.

"Weapons are charged and ready," reported Lowry.

Suki turned around and set to work activating the intrasystem jump engine.

"Chronoton emissions from jump point," called Computer.

"Stand by on forward guns," called Firebrandt. "Take out their main thrusters as soon as they appear."

In the holographic viewer, the jump point glowed blue for a moment and the ship slid into three-dimensional space. Without waiting for an order, Lowry fired. The captain just had time to put his hand up to block the blinding flash. She fired more shots. The first rounds glowed red as they impacted the hull. She adjusted her aim and took out one maneuvering thruster pack followed by a second. A swivel turret on the ship turned to them, but she destroyed it before it managed a shot.

"She's locked on course to the planet," reported Computer.

"I've broken into her systems and taken control," said Roberts. "I'm swinging her into a wide orbit parallel to the one we were in."

"Outstanding," said the captain. "Bring us alongside." He tamped out the pipe and put it in his pocket. "Round up a few men just in case we need them, then have Sanaa Golan meet me at the airlock."

Firebrandt didn't wait for Roberts' acknowledgement before turning to leave the command deck. The first mate issued orders through the ship's intercom system as he climbed down the ladder to the deck below. He stopped off in his quarters and retrieved his hepler and sword. He hoped he wouldn't have to use them for anything more than to intimidate the freighter's crew.

Weapons in hand, he strode forward to the airlock. He found Roberts waiting with half a dozen crewmembers plus ship's chief mechanic, Sanaa Golan. A clang resounded through the walls and Firebrandt took a half-step to regain his balance. A moment later, the airlock opened. The freighter's captain faced them with his hands up.

"I don't know what you think you're doing, but we offer no resistance. We have standing orders not to resist pirates. Our cargo has little intrinsic value."

Firebrandt laughed. "It's not your cargo I'm after." He stepped forward and struck his fellow captain, sending him sprawling to the deck. He looked over his shoulder. "It's the ship's transponder."

Roberts and Golan looked at each other and grinned. They hurried forward to the captured ship's bridge.

While the first mate and chief mechanic set to work,

Firebrandt returned to the bridge. He sat down next to Suki. "Is the intrasystem jump engine online?"

She nodded, but chewed her lower lip. "I'm worried about my mother, though."

This time, the captain did put his arm around her shoulder. "I know and I wish we had a more direct way to help her." He took a deep breath. "I need you to write a report of what happened to you on Epsilon Indi. Leave out names, except Bowman's or his people. Describe what you were doing and why you think you were captured. Go ahead and mention that you got away, but you know Bowman has other people captive."

For the first time that afternoon, Suki's eyes brightened. She turned around and faced the console and set to work.

The captain walked over to the wheel console and glanced up at el-Din. "Do I remember correctly that the Earth Alliance has a small base on Epsilon Indi?"

"Yes sir," said el-Din.

"That also means they'll have a satellite in orbit to relay EQ signals back to Earth."

"It does indeed."

Firebrandt smiled and looked at Computer. "As soon as Miss Suki has finished her report, I want you to relay that report to Admiral Williams aboard the *Unification*. Make sure it's anonymous, and can't be traced back to us."

"Yes, sir." The captain thought he detected a note of interest in the frail man's monotone even as his eyes roved the deck uninterrupted.

Firebrandt turned to el-Din. "I want you to find that satellite."

The helmsman checked his display. A moment later, the satellite's position appeared on the main screen.

Roberts' voice came through the intercom. "We have the transponder."

"Get it wired into the *Legacy*'s systems."

"That's a violation of the Uniform Articles of War," piped in the chief mechanic.

"We're just stretching the truth a little," said the captain. He looked over at Suki. "Think we can jump over that satellite's position?"

"Piece of cake," she said.

He walked over to the gunner's rig. "Time's come for an unusual order…"

"As though any orders today have been usual…" Lowry's mouth ticked up in a wicked grin.

"I need you to be ready for some sloppy marksmanship."

☠

Admiral Luke Williams stood with his hands behind his back, staring at a screen reviewing fleet movements when his adjutant chimed. "What is it?"

"Admiral, we've just received a coded signal from our satellite at Epsilon Indi. Hackers hijacked it and sent us a report that a crime lord on the planet has been kidnapping people and torturing them as a perverse kind of game."

Williams looked at the ground and shook his head. "We've been hearing those rumors for years. I wish we had the manpower to help…"

"There's more," interrupted the adjutant. He paused for a moment, as though afraid of incurring his superior officer's wrath. "Right after this signal was sent, the satellite monitored use of an intrasystem jump engine. The ship blasted several holes in the satellite, then jumped again. The satellite was sufficiently damaged, it couldn't get a lock after the second jump."

"It was the *Legacy*, wasn't it?"

"No, sir," said the adjutant. "Transponder signal didn't match. The transponder belonged to a transport registered to Bowman Freightlines."

"Bowman? Are you sure?"

"No question," said the adjutant.

"And where was the *Legacy*?"

"Last transponder fix we had was Earth's asteroid belt. We just checked our scans and she's still in the solar system."

Williams swore under his breath. He'd been certain Ellison Firebrandt had somehow come in possession of the intrasystem jump engine. In fact, nothing about this latest report actually contradicted that conjecture, but it might affect the timeline. He didn't have details about the agents who transported the prototype engine. He'd assumed the *Legacy* had picked up the engine on the space station Xiūxí qū sān, but the agent could easily have been meeting contacts on Epsilon Indi. Both were discreet, out of the way places to make a transfer.

If a gangster like Chris Bowman had laid his hands on the intrasystem jump engine, he'd certainly be unscrupulous enough to use it for his own gain. He might even have sold a copy to Firebrandt. He had to determine the truth.

He had no authority to search for military hardware that didn't officially exist, but he did have authority to rescue hostages. His crews could search Bowman's records for locations of hostages and get them out. If they happened to learn about military hardware at the same time, so much the better.

He turned his attention back to the wall display. He had three cruisers in the vicinity of Epsilon Indi. It was time to pay Chris Bowman a visit.

☠

Ellison Firebrandt sat on the couch in his quarters with Suki cuddled up next to him as they scrolled through news feeds looking for updates from Epsilon Indi. They found reports of Earth cruisers raiding Chris Bowman's facilities and freeing captives who had protested his dabbling in government affairs. There was no word as to whether any of them were Sumika Mori, though generally the captives were described as "young."

A knock sounded at the door. Roberts entered upon hearing Firebrandt's invitation. The first mate walked directly to the captain's cupboard and retrieved a glass. He poured a glass of red wine, then sat down and faced the captain and Suki. "Computer and I have gone over and over that signal from Chris Bowman. My instincts tell me it's fake. I can't believe Chris Bowman just stood around in a warehouse waiting for us to signal. He may hate us, but he's a busy man. They must have obtained images of your mom from planetary imagery or public record and overlaid it over some other poor woman's image and programmed the whole thing into an AI." He took a gulp of the wine. "You didn't exactly feed it any hardball questions…"

"We've been watching the news. Earth forces have raided Bowman's establishments. They've freed a lot of people."

"I just hope one of them is my mom," said Suki.

A chime interrupted before Roberts could answer. "We're

receiving a call from Ceres," said Computer.

"Pipe it down here." Firebrandt and Suki joined Roberts at the table.

The image of Sumika Mori appeared over the table. "There you are, little one. Took me long enough to find you."

"Mom! You're all right! Where are you?"

"Back home, on Ceres," said Sumika.

"We heard about the warehouse explosions on Epsilon Indi," said Suki. "I knew you had gone to look for me and I thought it must be you. We went to search for you, but Bowman said he'd captured you. Showed us a hologram of you tied up."

Sumika snorted. "You might start by introducing me to your companions."

"Sorry, okaasan." Suki cleared her throat. "May I present Captain Ellison Firebrandt of the *Legacy* and his first mate, Carter Roberts." She gave an appropriate pause. "Gentlemen, this is my mother, Sumika Mori."

"Charmed," said Firebrandt.

"Pleased to meet you," echoed Roberts.

"I'm not so certain I'm pleased to find my daughter in the company of pirates." Sumika's frown deepened. "I'm even less pleased that their company has kept my daughter from calling home for six months. I only found out she was safe from my husband. *After* I had put my life in danger searching for her."

"But, okaasan, what happened?"

Sumika blew out a heavy sigh. "I discovered Bowman had captured you. He implied you'd been killed. I discovered that an old friend of mine who does mining in the asteroid belt had taken a load of ore to Epsilon Indi. I arranged transport home with him, so my departure wouldn't be noticed on the public records, then I blew up about half a dozen of Bowman's warehouses. I wanted to send that bastard a message that kidnapping people was not okay." She folded her hands, took a deep breath and composed herself. "On the way home, my friend mentioned he'd heard that the pirate Firebrandt had a new crewmember named Suki Mori—quite a troublemaker from what he'd heard. I thought that sounded like you, Suki-chan."

"Ma'am, I feel obliged to point out that I am a licensed

privateer for the Earth Alliance," said Firebrandt.

"You kill people and you steal things," countered Sumika. She turned to face her daughter. "If you are willing to leave this man's employ, you are welcome to come home, Suki-chan."

Suki gasped. Her mother's words brokered no misunderstanding. Sumika clearly implied that Suki would not be welcome as long as she remained in Firebrandt's employ. She sat silent for a time. The captain wondered what choice she would make. He couldn't blame her if she left, even if it would break his heart.

She reached out and took Firebrandt's hand. "I'm sorry I neglected to call you, okaasan. Much has occurred in the last few months. Before I knew the captain's heart, I feared for my life and did not feel free to request a call. Once I found a place on this ship, I saw the importance of the captain's work. My loyalty to him didn't allow me to call before the ship returned to Ceres on other business." She squeezed Firebrandt's hand, then let go and leaned forward. "I'm sorry you consider us criminals, but I believe we are doing important work for the Earth Alliance and I owe the captain a tremendous debt. I must remain."

"So be it, Suki-chan. I wish you well with your choice." With that, the image of Sumika Mori faded out.

Suki released a relieved sigh. "I'm glad she's safe."

Firebrandt shifted his chair closer and put his arm around Suki. "I'm sorry she forced you to make this kind of choice."

"She didn't force the choice. I've been making it over the last six months." She leaned forward and kissed the captain.

As the kiss lingered, Roberts cleared his throat. "Well, since we now know that Bowman's message was an elaborate AI hoax, I'll go mind the bridge."

Neither Suki nor Firebrandt looked up to acknowledge the first mate as he left the cabin.

Chapter Twelve
Calamari Rodeo

"Fish eggs."

"What? You mean like caviar?" asked the captain.

"No, I mean fish eggs in cryogenic containers," reported Nicole Lowry over the comm link. "I think this freighter was bound for a hatchery or something."

Ellison Firebrandt paced the bridge of the captured star ship, a wary eye on the merchant crew bound to their seats. After giving the matter some thought, he spoke into his headset. "Take the eggs. I have an idea where we can sell them."

"Very good, sir." With that, Lowry signed off.

Firebrandt's first mate, Roberts, looked up from pilot's console. "I've powered down their main engines."

"What?" The merchant captain struggled against the plastic zip tie holding his hands together behind the chair's back. "Without the engines we have no life support! We'll be dead in a few hours."

"That few hours gives you a fighting chance to live." Firebrandt shrugged. "I'm sure you can break those restraints and restart your engines with plenty of time to spare."

"You don't know that!" Sweat beaded on the merchant captain's forehead.

"True enough." Firebrandt took two steps away, then whirled around, drawing a sword from a scabbard at his belt and pressing it against the merchant captain's chest. "The alternative is that I could run you through right now. It would be quite messy and very painful, but it would assure your ... cooperation ... and, I'm sure would convince your crew to be well behaved without further bloodshed." Firebrandt looked up at the others tied to their chairs. "Am I right?" There were fast nods all around. The merchant captain fell silent, but he scowled and a faint twitch of his right cheek indicated his anger at the crew's disloyalty.

Firebrandt sheathed the sword and strode from the bridge,

a flicker of a smile on his lips. Any crew he spared meant points in his favor should he be captured and tried. Any dissent he fomented among those crews meant confused and obfuscated testimony—the perfect recipe for casting a reasonable doubt in a jury's mind.

Firebrandt's crew gathered the merchant crew's side arms and followed him out into the corridor. Once there, Roberts pulled the hatchway closed, then drew his hepler pistol and fired three times, spot welding the door to its frame. The pirates might not want to kill the crew outright, but they didn't want a quick pursuit either.

The captain turned around and directed his crew to help Lowry and her team carry the fish eggs aboard the *Legacy*, whose bow was clamped to the merchant ship's flank.

Roberts stepped up beside the captain. "So, you know someone who'll buy fish eggs?"

"Not off the top of my head, but I have a good idea about an Alliance colony where buyers should be plentiful and we can make a little additional money on the side."

Roberts narrowed his gaze. "What do you have in mind?"

"Have you ever been to the planet Los Mares?"

"No, but I think I see where you're going. Lots of ocean farming there, as I understand."

Firebrandt nodded slowly. "If I'm not mistaken, it's rodeo season."

Roberts stopped in his tracks and shook his head. "How do you have rodeo season on a water planet?"

"It's water rodeo, obviously," said the captain with a shrug. He leaned in close. "How well do you think marine animals would respond to a brain implant like Computer has?"

Roberts shook his head. "It depends on the animal, but surgery's easy to spot. Too risky if you want to rig a game."

"The animal's a squid."

"They have rodeos with squid?"

"They're big squid."

"How big?"

"Something in the ballpark of ten meters."

Roberts's eyes widened. "Ten meters?"

"They really like the oceans on Los Mares," said the captain.

"I should think so." Roberts cocked an eyebrow.

They fell silent as they continued on through the airlock and aboard their own vessel.

"How much do you need to influence this squid?"

Firebrandt pursed his lips. "Shouldn't need much, just something to keep it from veering too far left or right, or diving too low. Maybe have it lurch one direction or the other just when we want it to."

"A simple nano-cocktail designed to target the brain's motor control regions should do the trick. Nano-chemicals can be injected and they're virtually undetectable. They can remain dormant until they receive an activation signal and then break down on command. With the right mix, Computer should be able to tap into the squid's vision centers and steer it from aboard the ship."

"Steer a squid?" Suki stood before them with her hands on her hips. "What are you up to now?"

"Just planning a little seaside getaway." The captain flashed a charming smile.

He detected suspicion in the narrowing of her eyes. The fierce pirate's stomach fluttered at the notion of someone he trusted—perhaps even loved—questioning his motives, even in silence.

☠

Half an hour later, Lowry called the *Legacy's* bridge and informed them her team had stowed the cryogenic containers containing the fish eggs. "We were able to jury-rig a power supply, so they should be good as long as you need."

"Excellent." The captain retrieved a pipe from his trousers' pocket and lit it. "Set course for Los Mares, Mr. el-Din."

"Yes, sir!" called the tall helmsman, who stood at the upright wheel console in the center of the bridge.

Legacy's grappling claws squealed and scraped as they disengaged from the merchant ship's flank. Thrusters fired and the ship turned. The captain contemplated the data in the holographic tank at the front of the command deck. "How long until we reach the jump point for Los Mares?"

"One hour, twelve minutes present speed," reported Computer from his station at the side of the bridge. The pale man sat at a console but stared forward, oblivious to all around him.

"Any sign of pursuit from the freighter?"

"Negative," reported Roberts as he sat back in his seat and smiled. "So tell me more about this rodeo."

Firebrandt took a puff from his pipe as he considered where to begin. "Los Mares was colonized a few hundred years ago by South Americans. One of the sports they brought with them was Chilean rodeo. They adapted the sport to the animals they had. In Chile, they used cows. On Los Mares, it's squid. Search the nets, I'm sure you can find a holo."

Roberts searched the galactic network. A moment later, a hologram of a tube-like aquarium replaced the star field at the front of the bridge. Outside the aquarium's glass walls, eerily silent crowds cheered, waved, and held up banners. Near one end of the tube, two people wearing scuba gear, straddled sleek sea scooters. A round door opened in the wall and out shot a twelve-meter long squid, tentacles flailing behind. The two people in scuba gear shot after it, and forced it to follow the tube's outer wall.

Firebrandt removed the pipe from his mouth. "Each of the scooters is called a Nautilus," he said. "The squid must follow the outer wall until the end of the course, otherwise they get no points." Low-powered lasers glimmered through the water indicating boundary lines.

Suki stood up from her station near the back of the command deck and approached Firebrandt.

He continued his explanation. "They have to drive the squid through a ring at the end of the course. Their goal is to get the squid to touch the ring with some part of its body. If the squid shoots through without touching, they get no points because they didn't control it. They want the squid to touch the ring as far back on its body as possible. If just the tip of its longest tentacle touches, that's the highest score."

Roberts sat back and rubbed the top of his bald head. "That's why you want to control the squid. You want Computer to keep it against the wall and jerk at the last possible moment so you can get a high score."

"So, can you do it?" asked the captain.

Roberts looked to Computer. The pale man's eyes darted

back and forth. "Yes, the creatures have a suitably simple nervous system. I can compute a mixture of nano-chemicals which will allow me to control the creature's movements."

The captain felt Suki's hand grasp his shoulder. He looked up. In the hologram, the men had lost control of the squid. It stopped, reared back and knocked one of the men from his scooter. Then it darted forward and caught the other in its tentacles, whipping him from side to side. The hologram cut out as the creature brought the hapless diver to its beak-like mouth.

"I'd also like to keep that from happening," said the captain.

"You're crazy," breathed Suki. "Sell the fish eggs and leave the rodeo to the professional wranglers."

"There are two riders," interjected Roberts. "Who'll join you?"

The captain glanced over his shoulder at the helmsman. Kheir el-Din looked from side to side, then tugged on the beads woven into his long beard. "Begging your pardon, captain, but I don't know how to swim."

"You don't need to know how to swim." Firebrandt spoke around the pipe stem. "You just need to know how to pilot a scooter, and you're the best pilot I know."

"What about Mr. Roberts?" asked el-Din.

"We need him to sneak in and feed the squid his nano-cocktail." The captain turned his attention to Roberts. "When's the next rodeo?"

The first mate checked the computer. "Looks like there's an event in five days outside the city of La Serena." His eyes scrolled down the display, then he whistled. "The prize is a million in gold."

Firebrandt looked back at el-Din. "I'll cut you in for a double share if you help."

The helmsman looked dubious, but finally gave a slow nod. "I am a pretty good pilot," he said at last.

"All you have to do is help me corral ten meters of mutated, mean-ass mollusk." The captain grinned around the pipe stem. "Shouldn't be worse than our typical raid."

"I think you're both certifiable lunatics." Suki turned around and stormed off the bridge.

✠

Suki went to the galley and ordered a soothing cup of tea. As she sipped, Nicole Lowry ambled in, retrieved a cup of coffee and dropped down across from her. "You look worried, Miss Suki."

"Have you ever known the captain to engage in risky behavior?"

Lowry smiled. "What? You mean like liberating cargo from crews who don't want their cargo liberated?"

Suki sighed and shook her head. "That's his job. He knows the variables involved, the income he'll get for the resources and effort expended."

Lowry nodded. "So what exactly is bothering you?"

"Ellison wants to ride in some undersea rodeo on Los Mares."

"Los Mares…" Lowry blew on her coffee, then took a sip. "Good place to fence the fish eggs…"

"About the rodeo," snapped Suki.

Lowry laughed, then set her coffee cup aside and leaned forward. "You're absolutely right. The captain knows the variables and thinks about his crew with every raid. He does everything he can to minimize the odds of failure. Has it ever occurred to you that he might just need to try something he's a little less certain of?"

"He is trying to rig the game…"

Lowry laughed and sat back. "That's the captain for you!" She took another sip of coffee, then leaned forward again. "Maybe the captain just wants a chance to play? Perhaps he just wants to try something that doesn't put his crew's life on the line. Things have been intense the last few months."

"Those squid looked awfully dangerous." Suki folded her arms and looked down at the table.

"No doubt that's why the captain's planning to cheat."

✠

First mate Carter Roberts didn't entirely understand the relationship between Suki and the captain. The captain had rescued her from a drug cartel on the planet Epsilon Indi 2, but she clearly didn't see the crew of the *Legacy* as much of an improvement. Nevertheless, she cared about the captain, which led to her frustration when he took risks she considered needless.

The rest of the voyage to Los Mares went smoothly. One of the captain's contacts identified a potential buyer for the fish eggs. Firebrandt negotiated a favorable, though not remarkable deal, and left the details of delivering the eggs and collecting payment to Nicole Lowry.

In the meantime, Roberts piloted one of the *Legacy's* launch boats to the surface of Los Mares. Kheir el-Din watched monitors from the co-pilot's chair. Firebrandt and Suki sat in the back, in stony silence. Juan de Largo, the ship's cook and sometime-doctor, also accompanied them. His medical skills were dubious at best, but he knew his way around a spray hypodermic. Juan recited a limerick he made up on the fly about a squid from Nantucket and the miraculous feats it could perform with its tentacles. Roberts laughed in spite of himself, but the rest of the crew remained mute.

The aquamarine oceans covering the surface of Los Mares calmed Roberts. Most water worlds had no landmasses at all. However, Los Mares had a few small islands around the size of Japan. This proved a boon to human settlers who could use the landmasses for the colony and provided an exciting case study for planetary scientists. He radioed ahead and received clearance to land at La Serena.

The city stood at one end of a long, string-bean like island. As he followed the landing beacon down, the first mate began to suspect he had the wrong coordinates. Grass sprouted through cracks in old concrete. A set of benches sat nearby, shaded by an overhang. Vines crawled up a distant building. The only thing giving Roberts hope was a line of extravagant space yachts at one end of the tarmac.

Roberts landed the boat, then parked it next to the other space vessels. A port official met them, collected their fees and directed them to the marina where the rodeo would be held.

"This rodeo's a pretty big event, isn't it?" asked Roberts, by way of small talk.

The port official eyed them suspiciously. "It's the planetary sport of Los Mares. I worry about outsiders taking too much of an interest in it, though."

"Why's that?" asked Juan.

"I dunno." The official shuffled his feet for a moment, then looked back at the nearby yachts. "Gambling has always been part of the rodeo. I've placed a few bets myself, but I worry about the money going off world."

Kheir el-Din gave the man a consolatory pat, then the group followed the directions to the marina. As they walked, el-Din rifled through the man's wallet. He removed a couple of credit chips and some of the local script. "This should be worth something at least."

"You didn't just rob that man." Suki put her hands on her hips, incensed.

"What can I say?" said el-Din. "We are pirates, after all."

"Legally licensed privateers." Firebrandt held out his hands and el-Din handed him the money. "If you steal on an Alliance world, don't get caught." He folded the money and placed it in his pocket.

Soon, they reached a set of buildings which hugged the coast. The low tide revealed a set of tube-like passageways leading to the underwater stadium some distance from the shore. They soon came to an entryway. Just inside, a sign pointed upstairs to an office. A larger sign indicated the aquarium. It pointed down the hall to a wide set of stairs leading below ground level. Making note of that, the privateers walked upstairs and knocked on the first door they came to.

A woman inside smiled as they entered. "How may I help you?"

"We'd like to sign up as riders in the rodeo," declared the captain.

Roberts thought the woman's smile took on a decidedly shark-like edge. "There are some forms you have to fill out. Do you have your own equipment, or do you need to rent some?"

"We'll need to rent," said Firebrandt.

Roberts pointed to himself and de Largo. "We were wondering if we could see the squid used in the competition ahead of time."

The woman flashed a brief frown then pointed downward. "Follow the signs to the aquarium. Once there, you'll see more signs directing you to the squid tanks."

Roberts thanked her and turned to leave with Juan de Largo. He hoped the mixed emotions hadn't played across his face. On one hand, he was pleased that the squid were in public tanks. That meant they'd be easy to find and no one would question their presence. On the other hand, it meant getting to the squid and injecting them without being seen might prove a challenge.

Roberts and de Largo walked down the stairs and followed the signs to the aquarium. They pointed to the tubes they'd seen from the surface. People-mover walkways ran along the empty tunnel. Although signs indicated it was prohibited, Roberts and de Largo opted to stroll along the moving walkway to speed their progress.

Soon they reached the aquarium and they followed the signs directing them to the squid tanks. "Dios Mio!" exclaimed de Largo when he saw the tank.

On the way to Los Mares, Roberts read that a typical rodeo involved about half a dozen squid. He and Computer manufactured sufficient nano-chemicals to control about a dozen, just to be safe. What the first mate and cook saw was an enormous tank swarming with large squid, small squid, and every size in between.

"These can't be the squid they use in competition." Roberts tried to imagine corralling the largest of the squid into the rodeo chutes.

"Maybe they keep them in pens around back." The cook pointed to a nearby door.

Roberts shook his head. "Let's go back to the main walkway. I think our best bet is to find the stadium and see where the chutes are."

Ignoring him, the cook walked back and tried the door, which set off an alarm. The first mate swore and ran from the room before a gate fell. He walked quickly away from the tank, but a door opened ahead of him and out stepped two security guards. "Did you come from the squid tanks?"

"Uh, yeah," said Roberts, "but I left because some kids were throwing a ruckus."

The guards stood their ground, not falling for the lie. "Please come with us for questioning."

Roberts sighed and put up his hands. As he did, Juan de Largo emerged from the door behind the security guards. Apparently there had been some kind of internal passageway.

Ellison Firebrandt sat astride a powerful, shiny undersea scooter next to a large, round door. He held a long pole. The tip would deliver a minor electrical jolt to anything it was applied to. Renting the gear proved more expensive than Firebrandt had hoped, but if they won, it would be a worthwhile investment.

On the other side of the tube, Kheir el-Din waited. Firebrandt couldn't read his face because of the scuba gear but his body was rigid, tense. Arrhythmic bubbles rose, indicating the pilot breathed hard already. He moved his pole from hand-to-hand, getting the feel of its weight. Occasionally he cast glances around, trying to get the feel of the space they were in. That was just like el-Din—always alert, always attentive. Kheir el-Din had been the helmsman of *Ganj-i-Sawai*, the ship Firebrandt served aboard as first officer while he saved funds to buy the *Legacy*. The helmsman didn't follow Firebrandt immediately. Instead, he waited until the *Ganj-i-Sawai* retired from service. *Legacy* was the first ship el-Din sought employment aboard, citing Firebrandt's successes. The captain knew el-Din had been watching, making sure the untested captain would prove himself before moving forward. That was just what Firebrandt appreciated about him, no false moves—a pilot who could evaluate a situation carefully, then take the right action.

Firebrandt followed el-Din's gaze. The arena was a large, round tube that traced out an angled, three-dimensional U. The arm ahead traveled more-or-less straight, then turned a corner and dove toward the scoring ring. The pirates simply had to push the squid over against the right-hand wall and keep it there, then push part of its body—hopefully one of the tentacles—into the scoring ring.

Outside the tube, spectators sat in stands, watching through the glass walls. Suki was there somewhere. Her anger baffled him. He hadn't asked her to participate in the sport and the chances he'd die were minimal. She could return to the *Legacy*, or she could make a good life on Los Mares if that's what she chose.

A strange, high-pitched keening resonated through the water. It took Firebrandt a moment to realize it was the sound of a bell. The boundary lasers activated and the door opened. Out shot a nine-meter long squid. Firebrandt rotated the throttle on his scooter and bolted after it. A moment later, el-Din followed. The squid remained maddeningly in the center of the tank near but not crossing the shimmering, red boundary line. Firebrandt caught up and applied the wand to the animal's head.

It ejected a cloud of ink and shot forward even faster, though it was now closer to the wall. Blinded by the ink, el-Din collided with the wall and ricocheted out of control. The captain couldn't worry about that now. He rotated the throttle and prodded the squid again, this time, further up its fleshy body, closer to one of the diaphanous, feather-like fins. The squid darted ahead and batted at the pirate captain with a pair of its tentacles.

The turbulent wake threatened to topple Firebrandt. As he struggled to regain control, he saw they'd reached the bend and the course began to descend. Below him, el-Din had regained control and shot ahead of the squid. The helmsman applied his wand near the mollusk's pointed mantle. It cooperated and went right against the wall.

Firebrandt dove and followed the squid and el-Din. Although he couldn't hear anything besides the rush of the water around him, he caught sight of people in the seats standing and cheering. He pushed ahead and shoved his wand forward, but he missed the tender flesh he aimed for. The squid slowed and bit the end of his wand, nearly pulling Firebrandt off the scooter. At the last moment, the pirate captain finally let go.

Firebrandt and el-Din followed the squid down. The helmsman did his best to keep pace, but the squid rolled and circled to the bottom of the tank perilously close to the glowing boundary line. Firebrandt dove under el-Din and gave the animal a shove with the scooter's nose. The mollusk cooperated and moved back up to the side, but not without batting at the pirate captain. He lost his balance and tumbled off the scooter, landing on the bottom of the tank and forcing the mouthpiece out in an eruption of bubbles. The scooter continued a short distance forward without him, then began to drift. He recovered the mouthpiece and swam after the scooter.

Almost at the ring, el-Din reached out and gave the squid one last shock. It reacted and contacted the scoring ring with the middle of its body. They scored a total of five points. A good score, though not as good as Firebrandt had hoped. He wondered how hard this would have been if Computer had not been controlling the squid.

Firebrandt caught the scooter and rode through the ring where he could meet el-Din and get dry land under his feet again.

☠

Suki cringed and watched most of the spectacle through her fingers. She trembled with both relief and anger as Firebrandt and el-Din climbed out of the tank and took their place next to the other competitors.

"Ah, there you are."

Suki looked up to see Nicole Lowry. The pirate sat down next to her.

"How's it going?" asked Lowry. "Has the captain raced yet?"

"Just finished," said Suki. "There's a new team about to go. They call themselves the Diabolical Duo."

"I hear they're good," said Lowry.

In the raceway, two men in red wet suits with horns on their diving caps straddled sleek water scooters. The bell rang and out shot the squid. The men raced after it, almost instantly pinning the monstrous mollusk against the wall and holding it there for the entire course. They only let up when the squid reached the scoring ring. At which point, the bigger of the duo slammed into a tentacle right at the last moment causing it to hit the ring as it passed through. They scored a perfect ten and a thunderous ovation from the crowd.

"Good thing I bet on them," said Lowry.

"You didn't bet on the captain?" Suki narrowed her gaze.

"Hell no." Lowry smiled and let out a chuckle. "The fish egg negotiations went very smoothly. I even talked the buyers into a little extra money to cover the cost of powering the cryogenic containers during the voyage. When they asked about the captain, I told them he came to watch the rodeo. That's when they told me the Diabolical Duo always wins."

"So, what about the nano-chemicals? Didn't that give the captain and el-Din an advantage?"

Lowry shook her head. "When I got back to the ship, Computer told me that Roberts and de Largo had been compromised. Thanks to some fast thinking on de Largo's part, they managed to inject the chemicals into the guards who captured them. Computer helped them get away, but they figured they better return to the ship. That's why I'm here. I'm your ride. Since I had a little extra money, I went ahead and bet on the sure thing. It's not a lot of money, but it might pay for the captain's equipment rentals."

Suki folded her arms, determined. "I'm going to throttle that man when we get back to the ship."

Lowry laughed and shook her head. "Cool your jets, sweetheart. Let him have this moment."

"What do you mean?" Suki scowled at Lowry.

"Look, it's like we talked about a few days ago. He has to worry about the crew all the time. He has to worry what happens if we get captured. This was a chance for him to play." She pointed to the scoreboard. Firebrandt and el-Din were in third place. "That's not bad for a couple of rank amateurs up against an undoctored monster. He'll get a trophy and have some stories to tell."

Suki took a deep breath and let it out slowly. "I suppose you're right." She shook her head. "I still don't like him taking chances like that."

"Truth be told," said Lowry, "I'm not fond of it either."

Suki looked up and blinked.

"If the squid had eaten the captain, Roberts would have been in command. Idiot couldn't even dope a stupid squid without getting caught."

Suki laughed outright at that.

"That's what I like to see," said Lowry. "Let me buy you a drink and we'll raise a toast to the captain's valiant race."

"Shouldn't we wait for him to join us?"

"Why?" Lowry leaned in close. "It's my money. Let the captain buy his own damned rum!"

Chapter Thirteen
The Enemy's Tentacles

Captain Ellison Firebrandt half-dozed on the couch in his cabin. Suki snuggled against him while a news holo played over his desk. The engines purred in the background. The visit to Earth and subsequent side trip to Los Mares relieved many of the captain's tensions. Chris Bowman had gone quiet. Firebrandt's father now received quality care and Suki affirmed her loyalty to him. Their level of intimacy slowly simmered. He had hopes it would soon reach the boiling point.

"This just in, President Alexandra Sokolov has just announced a sweeping range of tariffs on products from Earth Alliance Worlds. These include Erdonium from Mercury along with numerous trade goods manufactured in the Asteroid Belt."

Firebrandt opened one eye and grunted. "I have a feeling we'll be called on to make life difficult for the Alpha Comans soon."

"Why's that?" Suki twirled a lock of the captain's long red hair.

"It's what we do." He gave her shoulders a squeeze, stood up and walked toward his pipe rack.

Suki scowled at him. "Must you smoke one of those things every time we have a discussion?"

The captain shrugged. "The nicotine helps me think better…"

"Nicotine replaces the neurotransmitters in your brain with more efficient ones, true." She stood up and poked him in the nose. "But the ones you've got naturally are just fine."

"I like the way it smells." In spite of her objection, he reached for the jar of tobacco and packed the pipe.

"I'll give you that," she said. "At least initially. After you've finished, it just smells stale and close in here."

Firebrandt frowned. "It doesn't do anyone any harm … not since the introduction of Dairtox."

She took the pipe from him and set it back on the rack.

"I've had my shots. I like to breathe when I visit Earth. It doesn't mean you should contaminate the ship's air." She led him back to the couch. "You've wanted our romance to go up to a new level? It would help if I didn't feel like I was kissing your ashtray."

The captain blinked and thought of a couple of rejoinders, but decided this wasn't the time. He let her unbutton his shirt. Her kisses started at his mouth but worked their way down his neck to his chest. The captain's hand roved down Suki's back. In their position, he couldn't quite reach the pleasant swell of her bottom. His breath caught as she nibbled on a nipple.

He reached up with his free hand and took Suki's shoulder, sat her back and considered her pullover top. He leaned in for a kiss and embraced her. He met no resistance and no distraction as he began to lift the shirt.

The intercom chimed.

The captain ignored it as he lifted the shirt over Suki's head.

The intercom chimed again.

"Perhaps you'd better answer it," said Suki. "It could be urgent ship's business."

"I'm sure it is, but Roberts can handle it." Firebrandt took a moment to admire the view before him. He leaned in and kissed her neck, then following her lead, he allowed his kisses to go lower as he worked on her bra clasp. *Nearly a thousand years of design,* he thought, and *these things are still a bloody pain.*

The intercom chimed a third time. Firebrandt sighed. He looked up into Suki's eyes and she gave him a reassuring smile. He stood and walked over to the intercom. "This is the captain. What is it?"

"Sorry to interrupt," said Roberts. "We're getting a message from our contact on Draper's Refuge. Would you like me to relay it down there?"

"Can you record it and I'll be up in a little bit?"

"I think you'll want to hear this now."

"All right go ahead."

"This is Hank," came the voice from the intercom. "We've just learned that Alpha Coma has struck a trade agreement with Alpha Centauri."

The captain swore under his breath.

The intercom continued. "We have intelligence that the Alpha Centaurans will deliver a shipment of Erdonium and Quinnium to Alpha Coma within the next three days. We're sending you coordinates of a jump point they're known to favor. I have it on good authority that Earth would like to see this shipment interfered with and I have buyers ready to purchase the items. Will you take the job?"

The captain nodded. "Roberts, let Hank know we're in and get the details. I'll be up in a while to discuss strategy."

"Yes, sir."

Firebrandt silenced the intercom, but stood there, staring off into space.

"You seem bothered," said Suki.

"Never raided an Alpha Centauran ship before."

"Why not?"

Firebrandt shrugged. "The various races of the galaxy just don't intermingle that much. Sure, back when we got into space, we traded a bit with the Rd'dyggians. The Titans gave us some guidance, but for the most part, each species just has their own set of interests that rarely intersect."

"Aren't we all part of the Confederation of Homeworlds?"

Firebrandt glanced at the pipe rack, but stayed put. "The Confederation has always been more like the United Nations on Earth. It's not really a government. It just facilitates communication between species and provides coordination among defense forces when needed." He shook his head. "It also exists to assure that more advanced members don't exploit more primitive members."

"Is that what's bothering you? You're afraid the Confederation may step in if you attack Alpha Centauran ships?"

He shrugged and turned around. His breath caught. Suki had removed her bra. She flashed the captain a nervous smile as though afraid his mind had moved on to other things. "The Alpha Centaurans are more advanced than us, so I don't think the Homeworlds will intervene." He pulled off his own shirt and tossed it on the floor, then sat down on the couch next to Suki. "Be that as it may, I don't think the Alpha Centaurans are my most important concern at the moment."

☠

Admiral Luke Williams stepped from his launch craft onto the tarmac at the Earth Alliance Fleet Headquarters in Houston. An amber sky hung overhead with swirls of gray cloud—or was it smoke? The admiral coughed into his arm, then pulled out his handcomp to check the date of his last Dairtox inoculation.

He deliberately turned his thoughts to his favorite Korean restaurant. They had a source of natural, Earth-raised meat and made Galbi both tender and delicious. His stomach rumbled anticipating a good meal. It was one of the few things that would lure him off of his ship to Houston.

A hover car set down nearby. An enlisted man sprang from the driver's seat and opened the rear door for the admiral, then delivered a crisp salute. Williams strode over, returned the salute and slid into the hover car. He thought about reviewing his notes, but he knew the report he'd sent inside and out. Instead, he looked out over the Houston skyline. Like most coastal cities on Earth, it had moved inland and onto higher ground as sea levels rose. Sometimes he wondered why humanity clung so tenaciously to the mother planet. There were much nicer worlds out in the galaxy.

The hover car landed and the driver hopped out and opened the door again. Williams strode past him into the main admiralty headquarters. He paused to check in at the front desk. The clerk checked a screen, then cleared him to proceed to Admiral Mukombe's office.

Luke Williams crossed the Chief of Staff's threshold and delivered a salute as crisp as the driver's. Admiral Ayanda Mukombe stood from her desk and returned the salute. The short woman in her early 70s made Williams think of a bear trap's tightly wound steel spring. He had no illusion she was just as dangerous as one of those antique devices.

She held out her hand and Williams sat.

"It seems you were led on a merry chase, Luke." Mukombe's eyes remained fixed on Williams as she took her seat.

"Chris Bowman's operation on Epsilon Indi won't be missed. What he was doing ... he deserved what he got." Williams decided any attempt to justify his assault on the businessman's compound by reiterating the false leads he'd been given would only invite trouble.

Mukombe nodded. "Oh he deserved it all right and that's the one thing that saves us in the public eye. We can spin your attack on him as a way of helping overwhelmed civil authorities and finally putting an end to Bowman's criminal operation." She leaned forward. "The problem is we *have* to spin it. Even if you'd found the intrasystem jump engine, we couldn't admit it. You should have handed what you had to me and let me coordinate with civil authorities."

"If the engine had been on Epsilon Indi, do you think the civil authorities could have retrieved it from Bowman?"

Mukombe pursed her lips, but didn't reply to that. "According to your reports, you suspect Ellison Firebrandt has the engine."

"I need to get more evidence before I can search his ship."

"More evidence than you had for Bowman?" Mukombe's eyes widened as she sat back and held out her hands.

"I'm in charge of Earth's privateers. If I search with too little evidence, I risk alienating all their trust."

"Then turn it over to another commander." Her gaze narrowed.

Williams shook his head. "I can't do that either. I have the trust of the privateers because I stand between them and the military."

"That's become less important, Luke." She took a deep breath, then leaned forward, her hands folded in front of her. "Congress wants to disband the privateers. There have been too many bad incidents. Privateers raiding ships they shouldn't ... attacking some of Earth's own companies..."

"And I take care of those rogues."

Mukombe held up her hand. "You do a good job of it, too, but I see the writing on the wall. Support for the privateers is dwindling in Congress. What's more, the intrasystem jump engine is too important. We have to get it back."

Williams heaved a sigh. "Can you tell me more about the history of this thing? I've been operating under the assumption that it was built at one of our secret labs and we were transporting it to Earth using privateers to keep it under wraps."

The Chief of Staff sat back and tapped the desk in front of

her as though weighing how much she could reveal. "Even I haven't been told much about this thing. However, it appears that it was actually designed by aliens."

"Aliens?" Williams' voice resounded from the walls. "Do we know who?"

Mukombe shook her head. "They used Earth Alliance contractors for the components. Apparently we're good at making the cheap stuff. The Alliance contractors figured out what they were working on and back-engineered the device. They were going to sell it to the highest bidder when our agents discovered what they had. Agents captured the device in a raid and were bringing it back here for study. If the aliens who build this thing figure out how we developed the technology..."

"It could be bad."

"That's an understatement." Mukombe smiled for the first time since the meeting began. "Get on this immediately." She stood and Williams knew the meeting had ended.

"Right after dinner," he said.

She shook her head. "Immediately means now. I had to bring you here because I couldn't relay any of this over open channel, but I can't afford any delay fixing this mess."

"Yes, ma'am." Williams saluted and spun on his heel, his stomach rumbling for Korean ribs he wouldn't eat until the mission concluded.

The *Legacy* held position near the jump point where they expected the Alpha Centauran freighter to appear. Nearby, an elliptical, spotted star pulsated, and Earth ships rarely attacked aliens. Firebrandt hoped they would be mistaken for a science vessel studying the star. He also hoped the strong magnetic field in the system would make sensor readings of their precise position difficult, masking any minor course corrections they made as they prepared to strike.

"One of many problems with attacking an alien vessel is that I can't easily load a virus into their systems and shut them down." Roberts stood next to Firebrandt on the command deck, his arms folded.

The captain nodded. "We're going to have to take them the old-fashioned way. We'll take out their main engine, any guns, latch onto their main airlock and blow our way in."

"The more we discuss this, the less I like it." Roberts stared at the deck and shook his head. "Isn't there anything we can use as a special advantage to minimize casualties?" He looked over his shoulder to Computer. "Are they at least susceptible to any gasses or chemicals we could pipe in before charging headlong through the airlock?"

"Checking..." Computer's eyes began to track back and forth as he checked the ship's databases.

"I've heard Alpha Centauran blood is flammable," suggested Kheir el-Din from the steering console.

"So we can set them on fire—on a ship hauling dangerously explosive Quinnium?" Roberts lifted his eyebrows.

Firebrandt held his hand up. "Don't dismiss anything." He gave a nod to el-Din. "I'm happy for any advantages we can come up with."

"How is it even possible for them to have flammable blood?" Roberts muttered the question to himself. "They're from a phase-locked planet orbiting close to their star. You'd think they'd evaporate or something..."

Computer's eyes locked on the captain. "Alpha Centauran cell structure makes them particularly vulnerable to liquid nitrogen. Whereas humans will suffer severe frostbite, Alpha Centaurans will quickly freeze."

Roberts slowly looked up and his grin widened into a broad smile making him look especially skull-like. "That's the kind of advantage I like."

Firebrandt strode over to his first mate's station and activated the intercom. "Ms. Golan, can you bleed off three or four dewars worth of liquid nitrogen from the engine coolant stores. Give me hoses so I can direct the spray."

"No problem, Captain. How big do you want the dewars to be. I have ten and twenty-five-liter containers down here for maintenance."

"Ten-liter will do the trick," said the captain. "I don't want something too big for men to carry."

"Okay, I'll get that done. Golan out."

"Better tell her to step on it," interjected Nicole Lowry. "We have chronoton emissions from the jump point."

"Action stations," called Roberts as he sprinted back to his station.

Firebrandt strode back to the handrail in front of the main holographic viewer. He reached into his pocket for a pipe, looked over his shoulder at Suki and had second thoughts. Soon, the Alpha Centauran freighter emerged. She reminded the captain of Earth freighters—a large black cylinder. The physics of jumping into the beyond limited variations in ship geometry. The display plotted the freighter's projected course. It should pass near the *Legacy*.

"Hold us steady," said the captain. "Let her come to us."

"I'm not reading any guns on her hull," said Lowry.

"Are you sure?" The captain glanced back at her. "Their guns might not read like ours."

"I've been reading up on Alpha Centauran armaments. Nothing on that ship looks like a gun."

The captain nodded slowly. "Let's hope that's good news."

The freighter continued on its course. Either they didn't detect *Legacy*, or they didn't care just as the captain hoped.

"Target is at closest approach." Kheir el-Din made his report in a near whisper, even though there was no way for the Alpha Centaurans to hear.

The captain nodded and patted the air. "Steady on. Let them pass. We're just harmless tourists watching the system's strange star."

"Range increasing," said el Din.

"Now!" The captain pointed at the freighter's holographic image. "Swing about, take out their engine."

Kheir el-Din turned the ship while Nicole Lowry calculated a targeting solution. Moments later, Lowry fired off a few rounds from the main pulse cannon. A moment later, text in the holographic display indicated the ship's engines no longer functioned.

"Bring us up to their docking port." The captain pointed to Roberts. "Have Ms. Golan get that liquid nitrogen to the airlock."

"Right away, sir."

"Chronoton emissions from the jump point," interjected Computer.

"What?" Firebrandt whirled on his computer officer. "Who are they?"

A moment later, four Alpha Centauran warships appeared on the display.

"That's why she's unarmed," said Lowry. "She has an escort."

Firebrandt swore to himself as he considered possibilities. Fighting the Alpha Centaurans presented too many unknowns. He considered using the intrasystem jump engine to get to the freighter, but rejected the idea. While the warships probably wouldn't attack with *Legacy* clamped onto the freighter, they'd just have to wait for the privateer to disengage. He turned to Suki. "Jump us across the system to another jump point. We're running away."

Suki swallowed and scanned the area. "Calculations are in and we're ready to go."

"Jump," called the captain, making sure to grab the handrail.

Firebrandt remembered games as a child where he'd wear a blindfold while his friends turned him around until he didn't know what direction he faced. This jump was similar except it felt like he'd been tumbled head over feet. When his vision cleared he fought to focus on the holographic display.

"What the hell?"

The warships vanished. A moment later, they surrounded the *Legacy*.

"We're being ordered to stand down and surrender to search parties," said Computer.

Roberts stood up from his station and strode over to the captain. "So they have intrasystem jump engines, too."

Firebrandt nodded. He turned to Suki. "Go to engineering. Remove all the components from our engine you weren't able to replicate. Go hide them in the secret room."

Suki gave him a curt nod then jumped to her feet and ran to the ship's stern.

The captain turned to el-Din. "Shut down our engines and hold position." He then turned to Computer. "Tell the Alpha Centaurans they may board and search." He shook his head. Roberts put his hand on the captain's shoulder. Firebrandt looked up and smiled at his friend. "Shall we go down and greet our guests?"

☠

Suki ran back to the engine room. There, Sanaa Golan worked with two techs to secure tools and hide equipment they didn't want the Alpha Centaurans to capture as contraband, whether it was or not. "Ellison ... the captain has asked me to take some parts from the intrasystem drive engine."

Golan nodded. "Good idea. Do you need help?"

"Tools to open the main compartment and an extra hand wouldn't hurt."

Golan grabbed two magnawrenches. She handed one to Suki and kept one for herself. They soon lifted one panel. Suki scanned the internal electronics. She grabbed three chips and pulled one control board. "I think if I had these, I could build another."

The chief mechanic tossed her a shoulder bag. "Now you're beginning to think like a pirate, Miss Suki."

Just then, the decks and walls shuddered. Suki imagined the Alpha Centaurans must have docked. "Can you close this up?"

"You get going. You've got the important job."

With that, Suki ran to the main ladder. As she passed the second deck, Firebrandt raised his voice at someone. A strange, ethereal yet commanding voice responded. Footsteps clanked on the deck, heading her direction. She continued down. On deck three, she passed through the cargo hold into a room containing pipes and conduit. At the end stood a nondescript door that resembled a service hatch. She tapped in a code and entered. Lights popped on revealing the captain's most valued treasures. Her stomach knotted once again to think these were kept on a pirate ship and not in a museum where people could enjoy them.

Nevertheless, she wasted no time. She stashed the shoulder bag containing the chips and control board behind the Mona Lisa. She dragged a tarp over and covered them. If someone used a handcomp to scan for the correct materials, they'd find the chips immediately. Nothing to be done for it. She turned off the lights, left the room and closed the door.

She whirled to leave, but gasped. Firebrandt strode into the cargo bay followed by the strangest looking creature she'd ever seen. When Suki heard Alpha Centaurans had tentacles, she imagined some kind of space octopus or squid like the animals on Los Mares. This being was over six-feet tall, translucent and stood on four tentacles. Two tentacles writhed from each of its two shoulders. Black eyes bulged on its head over thick lips that both repulsed and enticed Suki.

"I assure you, your scanner records are mistaken," said Firebrandt.

The creature held a handcomp in one tentacle. It spoke in a deep sonorous voice. The handcomp translated. "I clearly scanned Quinnium making its way through the ship to this location." The Alpha Centauran pointed to the door Suki had just come through. "What's in there?"

"Nothing of consequence." Firebrandt shrugged.

"Open it," said the Alpha Centauran.

The captain strode forward. Suki tried to get his attention but he ignored her. He punched in a code. Suki narrowed her gaze. She didn't recognize the code he used. A moment later, the door opened. Suki's heart skipped a beat. Inside was not the secret room. Instead, she faced a room containing a handful of controls and conduit. The false alcove must slide up from belowdecks.

"You may search to your heart's content."

If not for the Alpha Centauran's purple garment, she might actually see the being's heart through his translucent skin. A mass in its head was no doubt the brain. The creature ambled forward on its tentacles and scanned the small room. If it had been human, Suki felt certain its brow would have furrowed. "I'm not sensing anything other than normal ship's equipment."

"Just as I told you," said Firebrandt with forced exasperation. "Ms. Mori was down here doing routine maintenance when you waylaid us."

The Alpha Centauran's handcomp beeped. The creature flicked a control on the device. It spoke with another Alpha Centauran. This time their words were not translated. When the conversation finished, the first creature touched a control then looked at Firebrandt. "My associate has found contraband in your engine room. We will confiscate it. You will not stand in our way."

The captain shook his head. "Of course not."

The Alpha Centauran strode past Firebrandt. Suki had numerous questions but sensed this wasn't the time to ask. They passed through the cargo hold and the alien proved extremely nimble as it climbed up the ladder with its tentacles. The captain followed. On the upper deck, they met a second Alpha Centauran who cradled the intrasystem jump engine in its tentacles. Again, the two aliens spoke to each other in their own language.

"Captain Firebrandt, how did you acquire this field generator?"

"A man whose identity we didn't know hired us to transport it to Earth. Enemy agents killed the man. We didn't know who the device belonged to and so we kept it."

Suki smiled, thinking the explanation was remarkably close to the truth.

"You have been most cooperative," said the Alpha Centauran. "We will take this unit and pursue the matter no further." The two aliens carried the device down one deck toward the airlock. The captain followed. Suki watched them for a moment then decided to return to the command deck.

There she found Roberts, Nicole, and Kheir speaking in hushed tones.

"Any problems?" asked Roberts.

Suki shook her head. "They've got the drive but I..."

Roberts held up his hand and Nicole shook her head. Suki understood. Not knowing details of Alpha Centauran technology, it was possible the aliens could listen in to their conversations while docked.

"Captain has closed the airlock," reported Computer.

A moment later, a shudder rolled through the ship

"Alpha Centaurans have disengaged."

With that, Roberts went to his station. Kheir and Nicole followed suit. Not knowing what else to do, Suki took her usual seat at the engineering console. A few minutes later Firebrandt strolled onto the command deck. Suki admired the confidence he exuded, even in the wake of this setback.

When she first met the captain, she saw him as an outlaw and a renegade. As she got to know him, she understood that he honestly believed he fought on the side of justice. As she traveled with this crew, she came to realize they all believed they served Earth and they would die for their home planet.

"Course setting, Captain?" asked Roberts.

Firebrandt opened his mouth to respond when Computer interrupted. "Sir, we've received a message from Admiral Williams. He expects us to meet him at Draper's Refuge at the earliest opportunity."

The captain turned and faced Computer, brow creased as though he wanted to question the orders. His shoulders slumped and he nodded and pointed to Kheir. "You heard the man. We're heading for Draper's Refuge."

Kheir el-Din nodded and laid in the course.

Soon after the *Legacy* jumped into the HD 115404 system, home of Draper's Refuge, the *Unification* sent a tactical shuttle. The shuttle docked with *Legacy* and soon after a contingent of Earth marines boarded and searched the ship from stem to stern. They entered every cabin and checked every shipping container in the cargo bay. A computer officer went to the command deck and copied numerous log files.

Once the marines completed their search, their leader, a sergeant with a buzz cut and a permanent sneer approached Firebrandt. "Captain, Admiral Williams orders you to report."

Firebrandt considered and rejected several retorts. He didn't like being ordered anywhere, but knew he had little choice. He followed the sergeant to the tactical shuttle.

They crossed from the *Legacy* to the *Unification*. A few minutes later, the captain found himself in Admiral Williams's office. The admiral made a pretense of scanning the log files copied by the marines.

"There are rumors you have been using some kind of intra-system jump engine," said the admiral at last.

"Really?" The captain widened his eyes, feigning surprise. "I'm sure you've seen from our logs that we have no such capability." Firebrandt trusted Roberts to have erased any evidence of the jump engine's records from their logs.

"And yet, the Alpha Centaurans have lodged a complaint with Earth central. They say one of their prototype engines was aboard your ship." Williams leaned forward. "What's more, they say you sabotaged it and it no longer functions."

"Let's say for the sake of argument that I did have such a device…" Firebrandt stroked his beard. "An intrasystem jump engine you say. You mean it would let us make jumps within a star system? Would we need gravitational nodal points?"

The admiral snarled. "Don't play coy with me, Firebrandt. You were going to say something."

"If I had such a device, you would have found it. If I'd hidden a device at some safe port, you'd still see evidence in my ship's logs, now wouldn't you. The Alpha Centaurans have more resources to fake a report than I do. So, who are you going to believe?"

Williams narrowed his gaze. "You have a point, but you can bet that I'm going to have my experts go over these logs very carefully. Until that time, I'm suspending your letter of marque."

"What? You can't be serious!"

The admiral folded his hands. "I'm serious as a rash on your nether region, Mister. If you had the engine and hid it from me, you deserve to be shot as a traitor. If the Alpha Centaurans are making up lies, we still need to appear to take some kind of action to show our good faith until we clear this up."

"So you're throwing me to the dogs?"

"Go find an honest job for a while and let's hope it's the Alpha Centaurans who are lying to me."

Suki spent the day questioned by marines. Why had she been captured by Chris Bowman? Why had she joined the crew of the *Legacy* after the captain rescued her from the gangster? Did she have any knowledge of Bowman's business dealings outside of Epsilon Indi?

Once the marines left the ship, a feeling of dread hung over the crew. Their contact at Draper's Refuge, "Hank," had called the ship asking where the Quinnium and Erdonium were. Roberts told him he'd need to speak to the captain.

The command crew kept their stations well past the beginning of the evening watch's duty cycle. At last, the marines returned Ellison Firebrandt. He trudged onto the command deck. His long hair hung loose about his shoulders. The skin under his eyes had turned puffy and dark.

As far as Suki could tell, no one had done the captain physical harm, but he'd been harmed nonetheless.

"Hank's been calling." Roberts spoke in a quiet voice.

"Tell Hank to get stuffed," said the captain. He turned to el-Din. "Get us away from here. I don't care where. Just someplace quiet where I can think."

Kheir el-Din nodded, then laid in a set of coordinates. The *Legacy* turned and moved toward a jump point. The captain himself turned and trudged off the command deck without even looking at Suki.

She rose from her station and followed. Before she reached the door, Nicole intercepted her. "Love, this might not be the best time."

Suki frowned as she watched Firebrandt's back retreat down the corridor. She shook her head. "We have love because of times like this." With that, Suki pushed past Nicole.

She reached the captain's cabin just a moment later. From within, she heard a yell of rage. Something hit the wall. Glass shattered. Without hitting the chime, Suki entered.

Firebrandt sat on the couch face in his hands. On the floor near the door lay the letter of marque—the captain's privateer's license—in a crumpled heap among glass shards and a broken frame. Suki could guess what had happened aboard the admiral's ship.

She folded her hands in front of her. "Do you want to talk?"

Firebrandt shook his head.

"My parents show their love for each other not through the physical act but through the emotional bond they share," said Suki. "If you demand I go, I will. I'll go—for good. Otherwise I'm staying until you're ready to talk."

Captain Ellison Firebrandt remained silent.

Suki walked over to the couch, sat down beside him and put her arm around his shoulders.

Chapter Fourteen
Good Deeds, Well Punished

The *Legacy's* corridor's seemed unnaturally quiet as Suki walked from her cabin to the captain's. The walls hummed, punctuated by the susurration of fluids moving through the overhead pipes. The sound reminded Suki of a cat who couldn't decide whether to be content or to lash out.

The ship had fallen into a new routine since Admiral Williams had revoked the captain's letter of marque. They hopped from system to system hauling cargo and even the occasional passenger. *Legacy* had just rendezvoused with a salvage ship. The captain used some of his savings to buy their haul. They now traveled to Hamal c where Firebrandt knew a junk dealer. She had to admit, she enjoyed this new, legal lifestyle.

Still, she couldn't shake the feeling that she heard whispers behind her back and the odd grumbling. As she passed an open doorway, she thought she caught the phrase "leave the ship at the next port and look for a better job."

She knew better than to look back and see who had spoken.

Suki continued on to the captain's cabin, knocked, and then entered without awaiting a response.

Ellison and Roberts examined a holographic display hovering over the captain's desk. From the back, Suki thought it looked like the ledger of accounts. Ellison smiled at her but Roberts gasped, like a lover caught in a guilty act.

"Did I come at a bad time?" Suki took a half-step back, indicating her willingness to leave.

Roberts opened his mouth to speak, but the captain cut him off. "Do come in. This concerns you as much as Roberts."

"You know as well as I do that we can't sustain this ship and the crew on the odd jobs we've been doing." Roberts spoke the words in a tense half-whisper.

Firebrandt nodded, then looked at Suki and explained. "I'm thinking about selling the ship and releasing the crew.

There's no reason they should be punished for my actions."

The first mate's brow furrowed. "What would you do?"

Suki edged around to the couch and sat down.

"I would buy a new ship—a smaller ship better suited to the work we're doing." He turned his compelling gray eyes toward Suki. "You'd be welcome to accompany me."

She frowned at the phrasing. While she appreciated that he didn't assume she'd join him, it kind of stung as well. The duality of the feeling confused her, then she thought about cats that both purred and lashed out. She took a deep breath and listened further.

Roberts glanced from the captain to Suki. She tried to read the emotion behind expression. Not exactly hatred. Almost jealousy.

The captain appeared to notice as he laid his hand atop Roberts. "Of course, you'd be welcome to join us as well."

Roberts yanked his hand away from the captain's and stormed to the wall opposite the couch. He frowned and folded his arms, looking down at the deck. "Running off to be freight haulers is not what I signed on for." He looked up at the captain. This time, Suki thought she read hurt in the first mate's intense gaze. I owe you ... but I have other ... objectives..."

Not for the first time, Suki wondered about the history between these two men. She'd asked Ellison, but all he would say was that he and Roberts had served together since both of them shipped out on their first privateer and that they had moved up through the ranks together until Firebrandt bought his own ship.

Sexuality still baffled Suki, though over the last few months, the captain had helped her develop a certain appreciation for how nice it could be. She also knew sexuality manifested as a complex spectrum. She looked from Roberts to Firebrandt and wondered if there had once been something more to their relationship.

The captain held up his hands. "All right, Mr. Roberts, do you have a better idea?"

Roberts closed his eyes and faced the deck again. When he finally looked up, he seemed more composed—more the Roberts she had come to know over the last few months. He walked over to the display. He swiped the ledger aside and brought up a schematic of a ship that resembled a pod with a big engine. From the size of the hatch on the side, it seemed small. Perhaps Roberts had a specific ship in mind for them all to fly off in together.

"That's an Alpha Coman drone pod." Firebrandt narrowed his gaze.

Roberts nodded. "I've been thinking ... if we were able to catch a few of these, we could make some good money from the plunder. Alpha Coma's a rich system. They're unmanned, so we wouldn't be fighting. What's more, they plan for a few losses. That's why they send these in swarms."

The captain shook his head and sat back. "It's crazy. Those things are near impossible to catch."

"Not if we had a new intrasystem jump engine," said Roberts.

They both looked up at Suki.

"I don't understand." Suki shook her head. "What's an Alpha Coman drone pod?"

Firebrandt expanded the display and turned it so she could see better. The single ship shrunk and became one member of a whole swarm of identical ships. "They're tiny unmanned freighter ships used by the Alpha Comans. Because they're unmanned, they can be sent on courses that keep them in the beyond for longer periods of time than manned ships. They only have to return to normal space for short periods of time. They are a bit limited. They can only transport non-perishable items that can deal with gravitational shocks, but there's a lot of valuable stuff that falls in that category." He shook his head, then looked up at Roberts with a glance she thought was reserved for her. "Audacious but I like it." He turned to her with the same look. "Can you do it?"

Suki chewed on her lower lip. "We still have the plans and we have the extra parts we salvaged from our previous jump engine." She paced toward the door and back again. "If I can get the rest of the parts, I think I can build a working engine."

"We'll want to build it discreetly so Williams won't know what we're doing," mused the captain.

"We *are* heading for a junk dealer," said Roberts.

The captain looked at his first mate again, this time with suspicion. "Sometimes I wonder if you do these things on purpose."

Suki's stomach churned. "Let me have a look at the dealer's inventory and I'll see what I can do."

☠

Nicole Lowry piloted the launch heavy-laden with salvage bound for Hamal c. Suki sat next to her in the co-pilot's chair. The planet below looked like Mars as visualized in Victorian times—a red, dusty world crisscrossed with canals. In this case, the canals didn't draw water from the polar caps, but carried water from aquafers to farm fields around the world.

Nicole's brow furrowed. "I can't imagine we're going to get much for the scrap we're hauling, especially on a backwater like this."

Her grumbling echoed many complaints Suki had heard over the last week. Much as she liked the idea of being alone on a ship with the captain, she knew these people relied on Firebrandt. Likewise, the captain felt responsible for them. He wouldn't cut them loose unless he had no other option.

"Ellison and Roberts are working on something." Suki tried to sound non-committal.

"I hope it's a good something," growled Nicole. "A hungry crew is a dangerous crew."

Suki sucked in a breath. "You mean they might mutiny?"

Nicole continued facing forward. "Mutiny assumes a military chain of command. On a privateer, the crew may convene and vote on a new captain."

"What could a new captain do that Ellison couldn't?"

"At a minimum, they could apply to have our letter of marque reinstated." Nicole cast a sidelong glance at Suki, as though weighing how much to tell her. "A new captain might not be afraid to do whatever it takes to feed the crew."

In other words, a new captain might turn to full-on piracy, without relying on the niceties of a letter of marque. Suki's stomach lurched despite the planet's gravity. "Would you stand with the captain or against him?"

Nicole chewed her lower lip and stared out the window several minutes before answering. "The *Legacy* is my boat—my girl. I stand with whomever keeps her flying. I don't know anyone else among the crew who would make a better captain than Firebrandt."

Suki nodded. Lowry's answer was pragmatic as she expected. "The captain's plan is a gamble, but I think it's a good one."

Nicole grunted as she brought the launch in for a landing. A few minutes later, she opened the door at the back of the launch and the wind blew in like a blast furnace. Suki unbuckled her harness and followed Nicole out the back into a bright, red-lit world. The star, Hamal, hung bloated and heavy in the sky. Nearby, a rusty, tilted sign declared "Ram's Head Salvage."

A man emerged from a Quonset Hut wearing a dirty t-shirt, denim pants, and a tattered straw hat with a wide brim. Several days' worth of stubble dotted his chin and he smoked a cigar. He looked from Suki to Nicole. "You from the *Legacy*?"

Nicole gave him a curt nod.

"I'm Victor. Got your message. I'll take your cargo for 100,000 Allies." He referred to the Earth Alliance's currency.

Before Nicole could answer, Suki stepped forward with a handcomp. "I've been going through your online inventory. We have a few parts we'd like to buy."

He grabbed the handcomp, looked down the list, then whistled. "I have it, but by the time we do the swap, you'll owe me 10,000."

Nicole lifted her hepler and pointed it to the junk dealer's head. "I think you can do better than that."

Sweat rolled off Victor's brow. "I can't go lower than 7,500."

Nicole didn't lower the gun. Suki gritted her teeth. They had to be discrete getting these parts, otherwise Victor might take a closer look at the inventory. If he talked, Luke Williams—or someone even more dangerous—might figure out what they were building. Suki stepped forward and put her hand on top of the hepler. "7,500 is fine," she said. She looked at Nicole. "I think you'll like what we've got planned."

Nicole lowered the gun, but kept her gaze fixed on Victor. "Don't expect help unloading this crap."

Suki loaded the parts acquired from the junk dealer onto an anti-grav sled and brought them to the engine room's main workshop. She brought up a three-dimensional schematic of the intrasystem jump engine, then laid out the new parts. As she worked, Sanaa Golan looked in and nodded, but didn't offer to help. Suki did her best to put aside thoughts of potential mutiny—tried not to think about who would side with whom. Instead, she buried herself in her work.

Once she'd checked all the newest parts and confirmed they all worked, she sent a list of the parts she still needed to the captain. That chore done, she set about assembling the parts she had in hand. In some ways, the new drive proved more of a challenge than the original counterfeit. She didn't have a working engine to compare it to, and the first hadn't needed to work. At the same time, this new engine didn't need to look identical to a counterpart, so she could move things around and make it easier to see some of the internal electronics.

Suki worked late the first night. When finished, she yawned and stretched. She thought about going to the captain's cabin, but decided to return to her cabin instead. Inside, she dropped into her bunk and fell into a sound sleep.

The next day, Golan came in and helped. She spoke little, just made the occasional bad joke as they worked. Sometimes Suki wondered if the woman thought about anything other than engines and how to make space vessels fly. She enjoyed learning that Golan had an interest in historical dramas. Suki considered asking her what happened during mutinies on seagoing pirate vessels, but decided she didn't really want to know.

That night, she finished early and went to Firebrandt's quarters. She found him stretched out on the couch still dressed, only his boots off. She kissed him on the forehead and retrieved a blanket from the bed and covered him. She turned off the light. As she left, she turned around and looked at him, realizing she really wanted to please him.

The next day, Roberts helped, but seemed distracted. When crewmembers walked by, he stopped work and crept to the door. He craned his neck as though trying to hear what people said. Aside from that distraction, Suki found the work relaxing. It allowed her time to focus on something other than the confusing emotions surrounding Captain Firebrandt.

Part of her wanted to run away before her relationship with the captain became more intense, but she didn't know where she would run to. Home didn't seem to be an option anymore. Even if Chris Bowman's operation on Epsilon Indi had been shut down, she suspected he still had allies. Returning there would not be safe. She could always find another planet, or even return Earth, but then she would be alone ... and she did enjoy spending time with the captain.

It took five cargo runs for *Legacy* to acquire all the parts Suki needed. Two of the runs turned a tidy profit, which settled the crew's mood. Both Firebrandt and Roberts relaxed.

Nicole Lowry showed up in the lab as the engine neared completion.

"Hey stranger," she said.

Suki blinked at her. "Hey back."

"Sorry I haven't been around. Things have been busy ... and a bit tense."

"So I noticed."

"Will this thing work?"

Suki gave an enthusiastic nod. "It's the second one I built. I feel pretty confident."

"The last one you built..." Nicole ran her finger in a circle on the counter in front of the engine. "We don't know what happened to it. You said it wouldn't work."

"That's because we were missing critical parts. We have those from the first engine." Suki projected more confidence than she felt.

If Nicole noticed, she gave no indication. "I believe in you." Her smile heartened Suki.

The next day, Suki went down to the secret room, entered the code and retrieved the parts she'd taken from the working engine. She returned to the lab, installed the chips and boards, then stood back and examined her work, hands on hips. The original had been shiny and silver. This one had rust spots, swaths of mismatched paint, and strange protrusions where parts didn't fit neatly into the makeshift housing she used. She plugged in a handcomp, which took the place of the onboard screen and activated the engine. It produced a nice, clean chronoton field.

She went to the captain's cabin. "I think we have a working intrasystem jump engine," she said.

Firebrandt looked up from his computer display. He still looked pale, but better than he had been. He stood and pulled her into his arms. She listened to his heart beat. "You've done me proud. Thank you."

"It's been a good challenge." She looked up into his eyes.

He followed that with a strained kiss.

"What's the matter?"

He shook his head. "Just the stress of the last few weeks." He released her and dropped onto the couch, then pulled on his boots. "We should test the drive."

"I'll get it hooked into the main engine." She reached out and squeezed his hand, feeling renewed strength before she left the captain's side.

An hour later, Suki entered the command deck. The captain asked a question with his gaze and she nodded. He beckoned her close and pointed to an asteroid in the display. "Think you can get us alongside."

Suki swallowed, but nodded. "Let's give it a try."

"Very good," said the captain

Suki said a silent prayer as she walked over to the engineering console. She sat down and made her calculations. "Ready to go."

"Jump," said the captain.

The world tumbled and swirled as it always did when they went into a jump, but she blew out a deep breath when Roberts grinned in the way that always made her nervous, and announced that they were right alongside the asteroid.

Firebrandt grinned the way Suki loved and her stomach fluttered as he gave the command to proceed to the jump point where they expected to intercept the Alpha Coma drone swarm.

Later that day, *Legacy* reached its objective. Roberts projected the swarm's expected position on the holographic display and sent the coordinates to Suki's console. She made the calculations.

Soon afterward, a countdown timer started.

The captain watched the holographic display carefully.

"Chronotons from the jump point."

Firebrandt pointed to Suki right as the countdown reached zero. She activated the jump.

By this point, Suki had been through enough jumps to get a sense of their disorienting effects, but this one was different. In a normal jump, senses often became confused. She often smelled light and felt the squeal and rumble of the ship as it moved into dimensions perpendicular to those normally sensed by humans. This time, something shuddered through all of her senses as though an enormous wave crashed into the ship. The command deck expanded, then contracted. Time stopped, ran backwards for a moment, and then resumed. Then reality hit, leaving her breathless.

Kheir el-Din who always seemed unfazed by jumps had dropped to his hands and knees, retching. Firebrandt held his head, moaning. A moment later, he looked up and blinked at the holographic display.

"Where are they?" He took a step closer to the display. "Where the hell are the drones?"

Roberts shook his head. "They already jumped."

"What?!"

"And we're off target," said Roberts, brow furrowed. "We jumped 500 kilometers too far."

Firebrandt whirled around on Suki.

Her mouth went dry and she turned to face her display, trying to find out what went wrong.

"There has been a catastrophic gravitational shift," reported Computer in his usual monotone. His eyes roved back and forth. "A supernova is reported in sector 1065."

The captain pounded the wall. "Damn the bad luck!"

Suki swallowed and took a deep breath. The new intra-system jump engine hadn't failed after all. They just had the bad luck of trying to catch the drones right as a nearby star exploded.

"Receiving a distress call from the starliner *Princess Andromeda*," said Computer as he plotted the position on the holographic display. "They're in this system, off course and dangerously close to the star."

The captain pulled out his pipe and studied the display. As he did, Kheir el-Din pulled himself to his feet. He still

trembled and his skin had taken on an unnatural pallor. Fortunately, he hadn't actually vomited onto the deck grating,
which would have run down and into the electronics below.
Suki had smelled that once before. The memory made her
nose twitch.

Firebrandt lit the pipe, then pointed at the display with the
stem. "Set course for the starliner. We should help them out."
He shrugged. "Who knows? Maybe there will be a reward."

Strained laughter sounded from around the command
deck as el-Din laid in the course.

Roberts analyzed the starliner's course. He plotted jump points
near the liner's location and checked their course, then concluded they must have had the bad luck of jumping into the
system soon after the gravitational waves from the supernova
shifted the system's jump points. They came out of jump unex-
pectedly close to the star.

He scanned the liner as it struggled against the star's gravity. It had enough forward momentum from the jump that they
had entered an orbit. The problem was that the orbit spiraled
into the star itself. Roberts analyzed their thruster activity. They
only used about half of their lateral thrusters. He shook his
head. "Their thrusters are damaged, but even if they all functioned they wouldn't have power to get into a hyperbolic orbit
away from the star."

Firebrandt grunted as he examined the image in the holographic tank. Pipe smoke formed a diaphanous cloud around
his mane of red hair. At last he removed the pipe. "Can we give
them a nudge and help them out?"

Roberts's memory twinged. He remembered a time when
he'd been on a starliner with his mother and Alpha Centauran raiders had captured it. He closed his eye on the memory
of screams and pain while focusing on the one bright spot—a
young man with a mane of red hair who made the pain stop.
Roberts would do anything that man asked. He brought up his
own holographic display and plotted *Legacy's* course and the
starliner's orbit. There were only so many ways those paths
could intersect.

He devised one scenario where they entered a lower, but

increasing orbit around the star. He sent the plan to Computer who analyzed it, and sent back numerous red-flagged parameters. By the time they intercepted the freighter, both ships would be dangerously close to the star.

He came up with another idea and ran that one by Computer as well. The officer's eyes moved back and forth twice then locked onto Roberts. "That plan has a ninety percent chance of success."

The captain glanced their way. "You have something for me, gentlemen?"

Roberts projected his plan into the main holographic tank, then strode over to the captain. "We continue at full speed to this point." Roberts indicated a green arc indicating their position in the tank. "Once there, we use the intrasystem jump engine to jump to here." He pointed to a position near a red arc that showed the starliner's position. "We fire full thrusters and come about. We can latch onto their main gangway hatch and push. That should give them the impulse they need to break orbit." The first mate thought for a moment before proceeding. "We could board and help them with their lateral thrusters."

Firebrandt turned and faced Suki. "Can we do it?"

Suki checked calculations on her own panel and nodded. "No problem. I can have the intrasystem engine ready for a jump in three minutes." Without waiting for the captain's orders, she started preparations.

Roberts pondered her for a moment. She owed the captain her life, just like he did. Firebrandt brought her into the world of privateers just as he had Roberts. When she first came aboard, he hadn't trusted her. When she attempted to hijack the ship from them, he felt justified in his lack of trust, but since then … she had become one of their best crewmembers and the most loyal to the captain save himself.

And the captain seemed to genuinely love her. Roberts liked that his captain had found some peace and some happiness, but it left him with a hollow feeling in his stomach and a pang of something like regret. Roberts chewed his lower lip as he returned to his station.

"Intrasystem jump is ready," reported Suki.

"Are we sure we want to do this?" interjected Lowry. "It

does reveal we have the engine to the starliner's crew."

Roberts narrowed his gaze at the gunner. Lowry's concern was well founded, but he didn't like her questioning the captain's authority with tensions running high.

"I think they'll be busy enough they won't have time to notice," said the captain, brushing her concern aside. "Sound the jump warning."

Roberts sounded the klaxon, then buckled in. He looked at Firebrandt, grabbing the nearby handrail. He wished his captain wouldn't put on bravado and just stand there, but he had done so through so many jumps. He seemed to enjoy riding through the beyond like a surfer riding a wave.

"Jumping," announced Kheir el-Din.

The *Legacy* slipped from familiar three-dimensional reality into the disorienting beyond. The jump lasted just a moment. When the ship emerged, Roberts thought gravity had reversed and he hung from his harnesses. It took him a moment to realize that, in fact, Computer had already fired the dorsal thrusters and the ship's graviton generators had not yet compensated for the sense of acceleration.

The first mate brought up his display and watched as Computer adjusted the thruster pattern. Meanwhile, the graviton generators came on, gradually compensating for the acceleration. *Legacy* swung into position.

Before Roberts could ready himself, a shudder rumbled through *Legacy's* hull. The first mate reached down and activated the docking clamps.

"Fire rear thrusters," called the captain. "Full power."

Kheir el-Din activated the thruster controls on his console and the ship shuddered even more. In the main holographic viewer, the green arc of *Legacy* now pushed the red arc of the *Princess Andromeda* into a higher orbit.

Roberts looked over at Computer. "Can you establish communication with them?"

The officer's eyes roved back and forth a moment, then looked at Roberts. A chill shuddered down the first mate's spine. "No, sir," he said in his reedy voice. "Their communications appear to be down."

The first mate blew out a sigh and turned to the captain.

"It's going to be hard to let them know our intentions are friendly if we try to board."

"Understood," said the captain. "Have Golan meet us at the docking bay. Might be good to have Juan de Largo as well."

Roberts snorted. "I'm guessing they have a better doctor than our medic."

"Probably true, but with communications out, we don't know their doctor's status."

The first mate issued the orders as el-Din throttled back the thrusters. Roberts then followed the captain off the command deck. Suki and Nicole also followed, but without invitation. He almost turned around and ordered them to resume their stations but Firebrandt cut him off.

"No swords, no guns. We want to make sure they know we're friendly when we board." With that, the captain descended the ladder to the deck below. He turned and strode forward. Golan and de Largo were already there. The cook had his ratty canvas bag of medical supplies. The mechanic held a tool kit.

"Are we ready?" asked the captain. All nodded and the captain pointed to Roberts. "Do the honors, please."

Roberts deployed the forcefield-protected gangway between the two Earth ships. Then, he opened *Legacy*'s outer airlock door and added atmosphere to the walkway. He then swallowed and opened the inner door.

The captain strode across and activated the starliner's airlock door. He stepped back as the door raised. Once the airlock was halfway open, a hepler pulse lanced through the captain's shoulder. He collapsed to the deck. Both Suki and Lowry rushed to his side while Roberts, de Largo, and Golan pressed themselves against the walls. Lowry retrieved a weapon concealed who-knows-where and tried to aim into the starliner's darkened corridor.

Firebrandt reached up with his good hand and pushed Lowry's hepler down. "Let them know ... we're here to help..."

Suki beckoned de Largo who leapt down beside them and helped them pull the captain out of the fireline.

"We're here to help," called Roberts.

"You're the *Legacy*," said a voice from the shadows. "We know you to be a privateer vessel. What did you do? Set off a gravity mine so we would fall into the star?"

"It was a supernova," said Roberts. "It moved the jump point. You came out in the wrong place." Suki and de Largo had moved Firebrandt out of sight. Roberts tried to think what the captain would do, what the captain would want. He swallowed, then stepped away from the wall, his hands in the air. "We're unarmed. We've been stripped of our privateer's license."

"She was armed." Roberts knew the voice referred to Lowry.

"Against the captain's orders." Roberts waited a moment. "We have experts over here. Let us help you get your ship fixed up so we can both be on our way. It may take mapping vessels a few days to figure out the new jump routes after that supernova."

Whispers sounded from the other side. "You'll be wanting a reward, I suppose."

Roberts snorted. He looked around at Nicole, then looked up. "We won't turn one down, but we won't demand one, either."

A moment later, red emergency lighting came on across the way in the starliner. A man with a gray beard wearing a captain's uniform faced them. He lowered his hepler. "All right. We can use some help, but your people will have an armed escort."

"That's fair enough." He nodded to Golan. "Come with me." He turned back to Nicole. "Check on the captain and let me know how he's doing."

Lowry lifted her chin at the starliner. "Do you have a doctor aboard?"

"They're pretty busy at the moment with our injured."

Roberts looked from Lowry to the starliner's captain. "Can you spare someone to look at our captain?"

The starliner's captain frowned and his eyebrows came together. He looked suddenly guilty. "Yes, we may not be able to give you a reward, but we owe you that … as long as this isn't a trick."

Roberts nodded. "No trick." He pointed to Lowry. "Wait here for their doctor and take him to the captain."

She nodded. "Yes sir."

With that Roberts and Golan walked across to the starliner.

Once out of the fire line, Suki knelt beside the captain and de Largo called for a stretcher. While they waited, Suki listened to Roberts plead his case that they were only there to help. She could understand the starliner captain's distrust. Not even a year ago, if she'd seen pirates force their way aboard, the first thing she would think would be that the pirates were about to take everything that wasn't bolted down.

She looked down at the captain. He gritted his teeth against the pain and looked around. When his eyes locked on Suki's he held up his good hand. She reached out and took it. In this moment of Firebrandt's vulnerability, the simple connection was almost more intimate than anything else she'd shared with him. He wanted comforting in a moment of pain. Did she read fear in his eyes?

Soon, two crewmembers ran up with an antigrav stretcher. She helped de Largo heft the captain onto the stretcher and they walked to the *Legacy's* small medbay. The space was not the nice orderly medical facility one might find on a starliner or a military ship. Juan de Largo rifled through haphazardly stocked cabinets. He found a jet hypo and injected the captain.

Firebrandt grimaced and groaned as his face contorted, but a moment later he relaxed. "Just a little something for the pain," explained de Largo.

He gently pulled the cloth of the captain's shirt from the wound. Even with the painkiller in his system, the captain winced anew. Again, Suki took his good hand. He squeezed tight enough to hurt Suki, but she tried not to let it show.

"The wound's mostly cauterized," said de Largo. "It's just seeping a little. I'll treat the burn and he should be mostly okay."

Suki looked at the wound's location and shook her head. "Will he be able to use his arm again?"

The cook turned around and grabbed some more supplies. "That's beyond my pay grade," he admitted. "I'll do what I can for him. As for the rest, time will tell."

Chapter Fifteen
O Captain! My Captain!

Pirate. Privateer. The words conjured images of desperate criminals on the high seas doing whatever they needed to make a living. Suki stared down into Ellison Firebrandt's face relaxed, now that painkillers had taken hold. Juan de Largo had cleaned and dressed the wound, then left the two alone. The captain's eyes fluttered closed and his face settled into a gentle smile, almost as though he'd escaped into a pleasant dream. Like the pirates of old, Ellison Firebrandt lived on the fringes of society. She didn't always approve of what he would do to see a job through, but she had learned he was a good man with a moral compass.

When she came aboard, she feared the crew and took desperate action to get away. A pirate captain of old probably would have killed her, but Firebrandt and Roberts gave her another chance. She knew the captain desired her. Despite that desire, he took his time expressing it, let her understand the joy and comfort of close contact. Now, she wasn't sure what she would do if she lost that contact.

Nicole Lowry knocked on the medical bay's door frame. "I have someone who might be able to help," she said.

A woman with salt-and-pepper hair and a green lab coat walked past Lowry. She wore a name badge that declared she was Dr. Bogart of the *Princess Andromeda*. She approached, raised a handcomp, and pushed a wand to the captain's shoulder. She frowned. "That's not good. There's massive joint damage. It'll fuse in place if left alone."

"Isn't there anything you can do?" asked Suki.

"I can use nanotherapy to rebuild the bone and tissue, but it'll be expensive." She changed screens on the handcomp. "We're looking at about 250,000 Allies."

Suki sucked in her breath, but nodded. That was a large fraction of her share from selling the salvaged Rd'dyggian ship in the home system. She looked at the captain, then glanced back at Lowry. If Firebrandt's right arm were damaged permanently, he would no longer be able to lead raids. He might even have a hard time running a ship as a legitimate businessman. True, he could always buy a cybernetic exoskeleton for a fraction of that, but it would always be subject to breakdown if stressed too hard. "I'll pay it."

Lowry stepped forward and put her hand on Suki's shoulder. "Miss Suki, do you even have that kind of money?"

Suki looked into Lowry's eyes. She saw the concern of the person she'd grown to think of as a big sister. Pay had been short and tensions high. She didn't want to ramp up those tensions any further by asking the crew to help with this. "I can pull it together," said Suki at last.

"I can chip in some," said Lowry. "I'm sure I can persuade others to chip in as well."

Suki's mouth dropped open. She quickly recovered and narrowed her gaze. She led Nicole out into the hall while she tried to figure out how to ask a diplomatic question. "Just a few days ago, you were talking about the discontent on the ship…"

"Yeah." Nicole sighed. "It's true people have been worried about how we were going to make a living without a letter of marque, but the captain and Roberts are doing their best. The new jump engine works. The crew will see that Ellison Firebrandt's the best man for the job of *Legacy's* captain."

Juan de Largo staggered up the corridor, looking as though he'd been dipping into the kitchen's rum supply. "What did I miss?"

Lowry smacked him in the shoulder. "Chip in for the captain's recovery … or else!"

The cook held up his hands. "You got it!"

Lowry winked at Suki. "See, no trouble at all."

Admiral Luke Williams entered the *Unification's* bridge. Officers sat at their stations and monitored ship's systems, keeping the vessel in a state of readiness. The captain occupied the command center, flanked by his first and second mates. They huddled in a discussion of ship's business as the security officer at the doorway announced "Admiral on the bridge."

The bridge crew hopped to their feet and saluted the admiral. He waved them to their chairs. "As you were. I'm just out stretching my legs." Like most ships, the *Unification* was stranded until mapping vessels made their way to their part of the galaxy, updating jump points in the wake of the recent supernova blast. He walked over to Captain Liu. "How are we doing?"

"Latest update says the *Sanson* should be in this sector within 24 hours. We should be able to get underway once they upload their data to the net."

"That's good news."

"Admiral, we have an incoming message for you," said the officer at the information technology station. She had a crisp uniform and precisely coiffed hair, even though she had the usual vacant expression of IT officers. Not for the first time, Williams wondered if Captain Liu assigned an officer just to make sure his communications officer appeared presentable.

"Who is the message from?" asked Williams.

"Dr. Laura Bogart of the *Princess Andromeda*," replied the IT officer.

"You may take it in my ready room," said the captain.

"With thanks." The admiral stuck out his chin and strode toward the captain's ready room, just off the bridge. The small room held a desk and a handful of chairs where the captain could work or hold private meetings. Williams sat down behind the desk and activated the computer.

A moment later, a hologram of Dr. Bogart appeared above the dais. "You've put on weight, Luke. Looks like I made a mistake leaving the service. I don't think your doctor's taking good care of you."

"Problem isn't my doctor, it's my cook," said Williams, patting his girth. "He does his job too well." The admiral leaned forward. "I presume you're not sending an EQ message just to check up my health."

"No. I've been working as ship's doctor aboard a luxury liner, the *Princess Andromeda*. It's a good gig and I'll put our cook up against yours any day."

Williams laughed. "You're on. Did the supernova give your ship much trouble?"

She sat forward and steepled her fingers. "That's why I called. When the jump points shifted, we came out too near a star. We were lucky, though. A vessel called the *Legacy* came along and helped us out. I seem to remember you had a vessel by that name under your thumb."

Williams narrowed his gaze and nodded. "Go on."

"They got to us awful fast. Captain Fitzgerald said they were actually above us in the gravitational well, then suddenly appeared below us. It was like they jumped from one position to another." The doctor snorted a laugh. "Normally I'd dismiss that kind of story as a sensor malfunction or a sailor's over-active imagination, but there have been rumors of a privateer with just that kind of tech. I figured if this *Legacy* had it, you'd want to know." She laid her finger by her nose. "Unless you know already."

"Let's just say, I've had Captain Firebrandt in my sights for some time."

"Well, so did Captain Fitzgerald. Shot him in the arm when he tried to board before he figured out the *Legacy* was there to help us out."

Williams nodded slowly. He thought about the intrasystem jump engine the Alpha Centaurans had taken from the *Legacy*. Had there been more than one engine? It wouldn't surprise him if Firebrandt had scanned the plans, but to actually have someone who could build it. Laura cleared her throat bringing him back to the present. "I definitely owe you one, Doctor. Remember if we're ever in the same system, there's always a seat for you at the poker table."

"You can bet I'll be there. I know your tells."

"I'll work on my poker face." Williams terminated the connection. He returned to the bridge and approached the captain. "Let me know as soon as we can jump. Monitor the nets for the *Legacy*. I need to have a word with Captain Firebrandt."

"Yes, sir," said Captain Liu.

☠

Legacy held position near the jump point where they expected the Alpha Coma drones to appear. Captain Firebrandt stood by the holographic viewer smoking his pipe and working the kinks out of his right arm, newly repaired thanks to Suki. He looked back in her direction and smiled. Once she returned the smile, he turned his attention back to the hologram.

A blue orb indicated the jump point they watched. A clock hanging in space counted down the time until the drones were expected to make their appearance. They had just over five minutes.

The captain awoke in the medical bay just a few hours after they had rescued the *Princess Andromeda*. The pain in his arm had mostly vanished. A doctor from the starliner watched a display. He remembered Suki leaning down and kissing him on the forehead, a sweet concerned smile on her face. She explained how the crew had taken a collection to pay for the nanotherapy needed to repair his injured arm.

The doctor had given the captain a physical therapy routine to follow once she'd purged the nanobots from his system. He concentrated on the physical therapy while waiting for mapping vessels to come through the system. Meanwhile, Roberts had scoured the Alpha Coma network for updates on the drone flight paths. Internal communiques from their sector of the galaxy indicated only small changes to jump points and routes.

Roberts also checked to see if their previous attempt on the drones had been detected. Fortunately, he found no sign. After all, the *Legacy* had not jumped in close enough to the drones to be a threat. They may not even have long range sensors given their brief appearances in particular stellar systems.

The countdown timer in the holographic viewer had reached the two minute mark. The captain turned and pointed to Suki, el-Din, and Lowry in turn. "Stand by."

"Ready to jump," reported Suki.

Kheir el-Din nodded.

"Weapons on standby," said Lowry.

The counter reached zero. The jump point marker in the hologram glowed a brighter blue indicating increased chronoton emissions. "Jump!"

A moment later, the *Legacy* was behind a swarm of Alpha Coma drone ships. The captain smiled. Without waiting for an order, Lowry opened fire. She cleanly took out one ship's engine. She turned her attention to a second one. This time, her aim proved too good and she blew the small ship out of the sky. She missed a third, but took out the engine on a fourth. At that point, the remaining ships in the swarm jumped away.

"All right, let's go see what we got," said the captain. "Take us to the first drone."

Lowry stood, her hands in front of her, looking down at her feet. "I'm sorry I destroyed one of the ships."

Firebrandt tried not to laugh. She looked so much like an abashed school girl. "It's all right." He turned to Computer. "Scan the wreckage, anything we can salvage."

Computer's eyes roved from side to side for a moment. "It appears the destroyed ship hauled Erdonium. I estimate we will be able to salvage eighty-two point six five percent of the cargo."

"Very nice." The captain looked at his pipe, realized it had gone out. He tamped down the spent tobacco.

"Docking with the first drone," reported el-Din.

The tiny ship was so small, *Legacy* barely shuddered as they clamped on. He ordered teams to go aboard. The captain paced the command deck while he waited for the report.

"We measure two tons of Erdonium over here, Captain," came the report.

"Outstanding. Let's get it aboard."

The day proved one of the easiest hauls the captain had ever made. The second intact drone proved to have a load of industrial grade gemstones. They finished the day sending the launch vessels out to salvage the Erdonium from the destroyed drone.

That night, Firebrandt treated Suki to a comforting meal of fried chicken and mashed potatoes.

"Why do you cook your own meals?" asked Suki as she wiped her mouth with a napkin. "You have a cook aboard."

"Have you tasted Juan de Largo's cooking?" The captain made a face.

Suki wadded up her napkin and threw it at Firebrandt. "It's not that bad!"

Firebrandt laughed. "No, it's not bad at all, but I like cooking for you."

"You do it very well," admitted Suki. "How did you learn

to be such a good cook?"

"My mother left when I was very young and my dad was busy in the mines." The captain shrugged. "I didn't want to eat bad food, so I learned to cook well."

The captain gathered the dishes and put them in the washer, then he walked over to the couch where Suki joined him. He gathered her close with his newly repaired arm. "I could get used to days like this. We should make enough from this haul to pay the crew for several weeks."

"The Alpha Comans will catch on." Suki pursed her lips.

"No doubt." Firebrandt couldn't resist. He leaned in and kissed Suki's pursed lips then sat back. "Hopefully we can get a few more raids in at different locations before they catch on. That'll buy us time to build up business from other means." A pang of regret made him sigh.

Suki narrowed her gaze at the captain as though reading his mind. "You enjoy being a privateer. You'll miss it."

He squeezed her shoulders. "I won't miss hurting people. I won't miss endangering my crew … my friends. What I will miss is having a purpose that goes beyond commerce."

Suki considered that as she reached up and stroked the captain's long, red hair. "Maybe if you capture a few more of these drones, it'll buy you time to find a new purpose beyond commerce that doesn't involve all the risks."

Firebrandt considered that. He had to admit, he kind of liked the adrenaline rush that came with the risks. Still, he decided this wasn't the time to admit it. He turned his mind to other exciting activities, but before he could voice his thoughts, the intercom chimed.

The captain stood and pressed the button. "Go ahead."

"Sir, an Alliance heavy cruiser has just jumped into the system," said Roberts. "It's the *Unification*."

"Any chance we can jump out of this system before they spot us?"

"Too late," interjected Computer's voice. "They are calling. They order us to hold position. Admiral Williams will be coming over in a launch within the hour."

"Damn it," growled the captain. "All right, do as they say. We'll be ready." He turned off the intercom.

"Are we in trouble for attacking the drones?" asked Suki.

Firebrandt shook his head. "I don't see how we could be. They just jumped into the system, so they couldn't have seen the attack. Even if they did, the worst they'd do is slap me on the wrist. It's not like taking cargo from drone ships would be more than frowned upon."

He stepped into the lavatory and cleaned up. Once satisfied, he stepped out and donned his dress coat and trousers, then strode forward to the command deck. A look at the holographic viewer confirmed that *Unification* had already launched a boat in their direction. The captain glanced to the side and noted Roberts also wore a dress uniform.

"Shall we go meet the admiral?"

"Lead the way, sir," said Roberts.

They strode down to the launch bay. Computer's voice sounded over the intercom, announcing the arrival of Williams' boat. A drop of perspiration slid down the captain's side as he waited for the airlock to cycle. When it did, he and Roberts stood at attention as Luke Williams boarded the *Legacy* followed by his aide de camp.

"This is a rare honor," said the captain.

Williams snorted. "You've been holding out on me, Firebrandt. Take me to your engine room."

Firebrandt swallowed. He wished he'd had the foresight to send Suki to hide the intrasystem jump engine. They strode to the vessel's stern. As they reached the engine room, they found Suki and Golan disconnecting the drive. The captain smiled in spite of himself. He loved that she had anticipated what might happen, even if they were too late.

Williams walked around the makeshift intrasystem jump engine. "This is quite a marvel of engineering. I'm impressed."

"Thank you, sir." Suki's voice held a slight tremor.

"Shall we continue to disconnect the engine?" Golan stood straight, her hands behind her back. From his vantage, Firebrandt could see her hands trembled. "I presume you'll be confiscating it."

"Who says I'm confiscating it?" Williams kept his eyes on the engine. "You've clearly learned a lot about this if you're able to build your own."

"Some parts aren't readily accessible," admitted Suki.

Williams nodded to his aide de camp. "Hopefully they never will be, but I presume your scans will tell us what we need."

Firebrandt cleared his throat. "Begging the admiral's pardon, what exactly do you want?"

"I'd like your plans for this engine plus all scans you have of the previous one." Williams turned and looked the captain in the eye. "You've learned a lot about this and it will help us understand the one that got away. In return, I'm willing to reinstate your letter of marque."

The captain's heart skipped a beat. Suki's downcast expression muted his enthusiasm and Firebrandt took a deep breath. "May I ask how you knew we still had an intrasystem jump engine?"

"An old friend was aboard the *Princess Andromeda*," said Williams. "Your actions convinced me you can do good for Earth with this engine. Maybe, just maybe, this can be a win-win situation."

Firebrandt looked to Suki. "How soon can you get the plans to the admiral?"

"I can send them to the *Unification* right now," she said.

The captain nodded and Suki sat down at a nearby console and set to work. Williams nodded at his aide de camp who produced a new letter of marque. The captain took it and looked at it, hardly believing it was real. A lump formed in his throat despite his best efforts to appear calm, cool and collected. He looked up into the admiral's stern face. "How did you know where to find us?"

"I guessed you must be up to something in this system, otherwise you wouldn't have been in position to help the *Princess Andromeda*. I took a gamble the supernova interrupted your plans and you'd still be here."

Firebrandt opened his mouth to speak, but the admiral cut him off. "I don't want to know. At best, I probably don't care. At worst, the letter of marque is retroactive, so whatever you did is now legal."

"Thank you, sir."

"The scans and schematics are sent," said Suki.

Williams grunted. "Very good. Now, if you'll excuse me, I

have a poker game to return to with Captain Liu." With that, the admiral strode out of the engine room followed by the aide de camp. Roberts followed to assure they found their way back to the launch bay. Firebrandt noticed the admiral did not invite him to join in the game. He looked over at Suki, grateful for the omission.

☠

The *Legacy* orbited Prospero. The planet held many pleasures, for those who could pay. After selling their load of erdonium and industrial gemstones, the crew had money to spend. Firebrandt let them burn off steam.

He and Suki rode a gondola through the canals of New Venice. He held her in his arms while they admired five-centuries old architecture on one of the first major worlds colonized by humans. They planned on dinner followed by a play.

As the gondolier pulled up to the pier, Firebrandt's stomach sank. Roberts leaned against a wooden post. The first mate held out his hand and helped the captain onto the pier. "What are you doing here? If there's an issue, you could have called me."

"I've been trying," grumbled Roberts.

Firebrandt patted his jacket and trousers. Suki giggled. "I guess I left my handcomp at the hotel."

Roberts grunted. "Never mind that. I was able to pick up some Alpha Centauran translation algorithms here. I've been scanning their nets and I found the freighter that lured us into a trap."

Suki paid the gondolier and the three walked closer to the nearest building. "This is what you do on your day off?" she asked.

Roberts ignored her. "They're on their own and they have a fat load of Erdonium. I'd like to inform them of our displeasure—and we can make a tidy profit in the process." He checked his handcomp. "We can intercept them near the Orion star forming complex if we leave by tomorrow mid-day."

Firebrandt nodded. "Very good. Let the crew know not to drink too much tonight. No hangovers tomorrow."

"Yes, sir!" Roberts grinned like a death's head. "It's good to be back in business." With that, he turned on his heel and strode away.

Suki looked down at the ground. Firebrandt reached out and took her hand. "The view's better if you look up and see what the city has to offer."

"Is this what our life has come to?" Suki sighed. "Revenge?"

The captain shook his head. "I could care less about revenge. I do see an easy mark and I see a chance to learn more about the people who built the intrasystem jump engine. I suspect Admiral Williams will be glad for the information."

"Be careful, you're starting to sound more like a patriot than a pirate."

Firebrandt thought about men like Sir Francis Drake, Henry Morgan, and Jean Lafitte. "Some pirates were patriots. It all depended on what side of the gun you were on." He leaned down and kissed her.

"O Captain! my Captain!" she said, "rise up and hear the bells!"

The captain laughed. "Let's hope that's not the end of this story and if you're going to quote Whitman, I prefer, ' That the powerful play goes on, and you may contribute a verse.'"

About the Author

David Lee Summers lives in Southern New Mexico at the cusp of the western and final frontiers. He's written novels about space pirates, vampire mercenaries, mad scientists in the old west, and astronomer ghosts. He's edited thrilling anthologies of space adventure that imagine what worlds discovered by NASA's Kepler mission might be like. When he's not writing or editing, David explores the universe for real at Kitt Peak National Observatory. To learn more about David or his books visit his website at http://www.davidleesummers.com

www.ingramcontent.com/pod-product-compliance
Lightning Source LLC
Chambersburg PA
CBHW020110180626
46812CB00006B/2548